Burnt Sea

A Seabound Prequel

Jordan Rivet

Staunton Street Press
HONG KONG

For the Kornhill crew.
Thanks for sticking with me
since the beginning.

Table of Contents

About, about, in reel and rout
The death-fires danced at night;
The water, like a witch's oils,
Burnt green and blue and white.

–SAMUEL TAYLOR COLERIDGE

1. Earthquake

SIMON RAN HIS FINGERS through the dirt. Sand and soil broke apart at his touch, releasing the silty smell of coastal earth. He had discarded his gardening gloves to get a better grip on a particularly tough weed. The soil was warm, matching the early-morning California sun on the back of his neck.

Sweat dripped onto the dirt as Simon twisted the weed, working it out of the ground. He grumbled genially, but he was grateful for the way this small, green problem took his mind off the woman in the house.

The earth rumbled. It was a gentle shaking, no more violent than driving his coughing, elderly

Mazda over potholes. Simon put his palms flat against the ground until the earthquake subsided.

He looked up at the house, a 1960s bungalow. It was a squat, unassuming old home, and when he'd moved to San Diego a few years ago, an untenured history professor with a wife and two young daughters, it was all he could afford. It was sturdy, though, all the windows still intact after the quake.

The screen door squeaked open, then closed with a bang.

"Daddy! Mom says to come in now. You need to take me to school."

Simon's younger daughter, Esther, had her dark hair tugged into messy pigtails. Since turning six a few months ago, she'd been wearing a Thomas the Tank Engine T-shirt she got for her birthday almost every day. His wife had bought an identical Thomas shirt to keep Esther happy when the other one needed to be washed. And it needed to be washed nearly every day. Esther was forever digging, climbing, and spilling. Simon suspected she was messier than all the boys in the first grade combined. But she wasn't fooled by the replacement shirt. "It smells different, Daddy," she'd say.

Simon resumed his work on the weed. "I'm not taking you to school today, button. It's Mommy's turn."

"She's taking Namie to the dentist," Esther said.

Simon felt a twinge of irritation. "I have a meeting at eight thirty. Tell your mother . . ." Simon stopped abruptly. They may be going through a rough patch in their marriage, but he and Nina had sworn never to argue through their children. He brushed the earth off his hands and followed Esther inside.

"Did you feel the earthquake, button?" he asked as the screen door banged behind them.

"Yeah! Mommy said I still have to go to school, though. It's not fair. Namie doesn't have to go."

"But you like school."

"It's okay, I guess," Esther said, winding a finger around one of her pigtails.

"Did something happen? Are those girls picking on you again?"

A brief frown wrinkled Esther's forehead. "I hafta find my shoes!"

She darted away down the hallway to the room she shared with her eight-year-old sister, Naomi, whom Esther still called Namie. Simon figured he'd have to give up his study eventually so the two girls could have their own rooms. He hoped that was still a few years away. He liked having a little space for solitude. It was getting hard to find peace in the rest of the house.

Nina was slamming spoons into the dishwasher. She glanced up when Simon walked into the kitchen, then clattered Naomi's yellow cereal bowl into the top rack. Her usual collection of bracelets clicked as they slid along her wrists. The radio crackled on the counter. Simon wished for the quiet of his garden.

"I have an eight thirty with Morty today," he said. "I can't take Esther to school."

Nina stared daggers at the kitchen sink. "I have to take Naomi to the dentist this morning. I told you last week."

"Can't you drop Esther on the way?"

"It's the specialist across town. We'll be cutting it close as is."

Simon leaned against the cool tile counter. The radio anchor was talking about the earthquake. Not much damage. More aftershocks than usual. Something about Wyoming. Simon turned down the volume.

"Can you reschedule?"

"They're booked for months."

"But Mort—"

"Just tell him no," Nina snapped. "You can't keep hopping to his schedule, Simon."

"He's the department chair," Simon said. He felt the jolt of anxiety that always accompanied any mention of his boss lately. "If I'm ever going to get tenure—"

"I know." She cut him off. "Please, I don't have time to listen to the saga of Morty and his choke hold on the history faculty. Make *him* reschedule for once." Nina dried her long, thin hands on a periwinkle towel.

It's not that simple, Simon thought. *I can't miss out on tenure. Not again.* Money was only getting tighter as the kids got older.

"Did you hear back from insurance about that dental specialist?" he asked. "This isn't the best month for this. The car—"

"Don't start. I'll take an extra shift on Saturday." Nina tossed the towel onto the counter.

"No, don't do that," Simon said. Nina had been taking extra shifts at the hospital too often lately. He hated that she had to compensate by working harder as his career stalled worse than the Mazda. Nothing made him feel more like a failure. Some of the heat went out of Simon's voice. "Doesn't Esther have a birthday party at the Sambergs' this weekend that you were planning to help chaperone? You haven't been able to hang out with Valerie much lately."

Nina swept a hand through her dark hair, her bracelets clattering. "I was looking forward to seeing her. But Simon, we need to do something about the car, and the specialist can't wait. We need the money."

"I'll try to fix the car myself. That YouTube tutorial worked well enough last time."

"Get Esther to help you," Nina said. "That will make her happy."

Simon laughed. "Pretty soon she'll be fixing the car by herself. She could be making her own video tutorials in a few years."

Nina smiled. The morning sun touched the side of her face. "I'm sorry for snapping, babe. I've been so frazzled lately."

Simon drew close to her. "Hey, it's okay. I've been kind of a grump too. This stuff with Mort . . ." He put his arms around Nina's waist and smelled her apple blossom perfume. It reminded him of when they'd sit beneath the apple trees by the university greenhouse and study together. God, she was cute. "Morty can wait. I'll take Esther to school—like I said I would. You have a good time with Valerie on Saturday, and on Sunday let's go out. We'll get a sitter to watch the kids."

She sighed and leaned into him. "Chinese food?"

"Yes, ma'am." They swayed in the kitchen, pretending for a moment that the pressures of their too-busy lives didn't exist.

The voice on the radio was a hum, barely distinguishable from the buzz of a car driving past the kitchen window.

JUDITH

Judith turned off the alarm at exactly 7:42 a.m. She rolled out of bed and strode to the desk, four steps away. She tapped her laptop sharply to wake it. As the screen lit up, she heard her roommate, Sonya, open the front door of the apartment, home from the night shift at the twenty-four-hour bagel café at their university. Judith and Sonya rarely saw each other, which suited Judith just fine. She avoided distractions whenever possible.

She brought up her email and opened the folder labeled "Alumni Contacts." She read the email again, probably for the hundredth time. She'd had it memorized by the fifth read, of course.

Dear Judith,

We are pleased to invite you to interview for the Junior Analyst position at Gilbertson & Cob. The VPs were impressed with your résumé. It'd be nice to have a fellow alum on the team. Please find the interview details below.

Kind regards,

Donald Herz

Judith smiled. This was it. She was on track to graduate summa cum laude in just over a month—and if the interview went well today, her dream job would be waiting.

A news alert blinked on her laptop dashboard, but Judith ignored it. No distractions. Today she would focus. She'd already planned out her answers to hundreds of possible interview questions. She was president of three different extracurricular clubs, including Future MBAs and the Honors Society. Last summer she'd aced an internship at a prestigious Silicon Valley tech company, walking away with her best recommendation letter yet. Gilbertson & Cob would be stupid not to hire her.

She stood and smoothed the iron-gray suit hanging from a hook on her bedroom door and picked a tiny piece of lint off the sleeve. The earth rumbled. The floor shuddered beneath her and the suit swung back and forth, making the hook creak against the door frame. Judith gripped the doorknob, her other hand steadying the suit until the shaking stopped.

"You okay in there, Judith?" Sonya called.

"Fine. It was a small one."

Judith went to the dingy kitchen to make her morning protein smoothie. Sonya stood by the counter wiping up milk that had slopped over the side of her cereal bowl. She smelled of espresso beans and sour cream.

"Bad omen, don't you think?" Sonya said.

"What?"

"The earthquake. Don't you have an interview today?"

"Eleven thirty."

Judith pulled her bag of flaxseed down from the tacky yellow cupboard. She couldn't wait to move into a sleek starter apartment, probably uptown somewhere. She let Sonya's voice wash over her.

"I was listening to Silas B's night show at work. Apparently there've been way more earthquakes than usual all over California for the last two weeks—mostly small ones, but still."

Sonya carried her cereal bowl to their folding card table and pushed aside her dinner plate from the night before. Judith's side of the table was clean.

"Well then, it probably doesn't have anything to do with my interview," she said.

"None of the major media outlets are talking about it, though," Sonya said. "That's why we haven't heard about it more." She pushed a spoonful of cereal into her mouth.

"Is that right?" Judith said. *Should I wear the black pumps or the gray ones to the interview? The black ones have a more stable heel, but the gray ones are the perfect shade.*

Sonya kept chattering while Judith assembled her smoothie. "Silas B thinks the government's covering something up. Like maybe the Big One's coming, and they don't want people to panic."

"Mmm." Judith turned on the blender. If Sonya said anything more, her voice was drowned out by the noise. No distractions.

At exactly 8:13, Judith closed the apartment door. She stretched on the doorstep, limbering up her slim runner's legs. The sun was mellow, drifting slowly higher above the pastel San Diego buildings. Judith tightened her ponytail and jogged briskly out of the apartment complex. As she turned into her normal route, she noticed that traffic seemed a bit slower than usual. She'd factor that in to her departure time later.

Judith went over her interview answers as she jogged. She had to be perfect. She'd never really doubted that she'd be successful, but she had to make sure her future colleagues recognized her potential too. She would make the most of the two, maybe three years she'd work there before going on to get her MBA. She would be the ideal candidate of course. She was confident that everything would go according to plan. She'd worked too hard to accept anything less.

The traffic hummed as Judith jogged along the sidewalk. It was already warm. The smell of the sea mixed with exhaust and warm concrete. Other runners passed her, but she kept her pace slow and easy until exactly 8:28. When she reached North Harbor Drive, she started to run.

SIMON

It was late and the car wouldn't start. Simon gripped the wheel and leaned his forehead against it. The clock on the dash was the only thing in the car that still worked reliably. 8:13 a.m. He would definitely miss his meeting with Morty, and now Esther was going to be late for school too. He tried the key in the ignition one more time and got only a choking, sputtering death rattle.

"I can fix it, Daddy," Esther chirped from the backseat. "I helped last time."

"Yes, you did, button. I don't think we have time to do it before school, though. I'll have to explain what happened to Mrs. Malhotra."

Nina and Naomi had already left in Nina's little Honda, the same car she'd been driving since college. He'd managed to steal a kiss before she dashed out the door, but he knew their problems were far from over.

It hadn't been so bad when they'd first had kids. They were constantly exhausted, but they had marveled together at their daughters: tiny noses, tiny fingers, tiny dresses—at least until Esther got old enough to choose her own clothes. It had only been in the last year or two that they started having problems communicating. The stresses in their lives had piled up exponentially.

Simon had failed his first attempt to get tenure when they lived back East. That's when their troubles really started. It had been such a blow, a betrayal, and it had sent him spiraling into a six-month depression. Nina thought moving to California would be the breath of fresh air they needed, and in some ways she was right. With the change of scenery and pace, he'd managed to pull out of the nosedive. He enjoyed his new job. He liked being able to walk down to the San Diego harbor from their little house. He'd even planted a garden.

But he'd be up for tenure again soon. It was an exhausting, emotional process, and he was terrified he would fail again. Nina would have to take up the slack for him—living in California was expensive after all. He hated the feeling of impotence that came while he waited for academic review after review, not sure that he'd come out the other end with a stable job and better salary. Somehow he felt further from his goal after every publication. The very real possibility that he'd have to start all over again loomed. It didn't help that the history department chairman had his own brand of review and liked to test exactly how far he could push tenure candidates before they'd snap.

"Daddy?" Esther said, tapping Simon on the shoulder.

"I'm sorry, button. What did you say?"

"If we're not going to drive, can I get another Pop-Tart?"

Simon glanced at his daughter's wide brown eyes. She had a smudge on her forehead like an extra quirked eyebrow. Why couldn't he just enjoy moments like this? He missed the days when the girls were younger, when they would dance on the carpet in socks with Nina and then sneak up behind him and shock him with the static. All he had to do was gasp theatrically to send them shrieking and laughing around the house. Why couldn't he make everyone happy so easily? He needed a shock now. He needed to break away from this endless treadmill of worry and inadequacy.

"I have a better idea," he said. "Let's go for a walk by the harbor. I'll buy you an apple pastry." They were going to be late anyway. And Nina was right: he shouldn't have to hop whenever Morty said rabbit. Simon reached into his pocket and turned off his cell phone.

A few minutes later they were strolling toward North Harbor Drive. Gulls sang in the air. Car horns squawked in unison. Morning rush hour was in full swing. Simon and Esther waited for the traffic light and then crossed the street to the harbor front. He bought apple pastries from their favorite stand on the corner. Dockworkers and tourists lined up together for the steaming, sweet pockets. The smell of cinnamon hung in the salt breeze.

"You heard what I heard about the earthquakes, Ed?" The pastry man chatted with a regular as he scooped the pastries into paper wrappers and sprinkled cinnamon sugar on top.

"Aftershocks?" said the man leaning against the cart, licking syrup off his fingers.

"Naw, more than that," the pastry man said. "I ain't felt any aftershocks. 'Parently there's something going on up in Wyoming."

"Nothing goes on in Wyoming." Ed chortled. He had on a faded Mariners cap, and there was grease under his fingernails.

"I mean at Yellowstone. The geysers up there are acting strange. Old Faithful himself ain't keepin' the faith like he used to. Guy on the radio says it's all connected."

"That right?"

"Only tellin' you what the radio says. Here you go, little one. Extra cinnamon for you."

"Thanks!" Esther wrapped her small hands around the crinkly paper. Simon handed the pastry man a few bills. He was still telling Ed about what the radio host had said as Simon and Esther walked off toward the waterfront promenade.

The breeze picked up, sifting the sounds of the busy harbor in to land. Sunlight bounced off steel and sea. The glassy harbor sparkled, tossing reflections like confetti. Flat-gray navy ships stalked past sleek white yachts. Lumbering fishing boats cut momentary tracks through the water as they returned from their early-morning work. A San Diego Bay tour boat disgorged passengers in their path.

Simon breathed deeply. He pushed Morty and tenure and expensive dental work out of his head. He wished he and Esther could play hooky from school every day. This was why they had moved to California. The sea. The sunshine. The way you could stroll along the harbor even at rush hour on a Tuesday morning and not feel out of place.

Esther swallowed a huge bite of her pastry. She wore a fuzzy mustache of cinnamon on her lip. She chattered to Simon about the birthday party she would be going to at the Sambergs' that weekend.

"Joey says we can win candy in the games. And there will be a real popcorn machine. In their back-yard!"

"That sounds fun," Simon said. "Is everyone from your class going?"

Esther's nose twitched. "I guess so." She took another bite of pastry, looking pensive.

A thin blond girl, probably around college age, jogged past them. Her ponytail flipped back and forth like a pendulum.

Esther looked up at Simon, dark eyes solemn. "Daddy, do you think I look like a boy?"

Simon laughed and patted her right on top of the head. "Of course not. You always look like Esther. Why?"

"It's nothing." Esther kicked the toe of her sneakers against a piece of gum ground into the pavement. There was a trail of crumbs on her Thomas the Tank Engine T-shirt.

"Tell me. Did someone say you look like a boy?" Simon pressed.

"Just a girl in my class. She talked about it with her friends. Joey heard them in art."

Simon sighed. Kids could be cruel, but he didn't know they started so early.

"Don't listen to them, button."

"Namie says I should wear a dress to the party 'stead of shorts. She says then no one will call me a boy."

"You could do that," Simon said slowly, wishing he knew how to teach Esther to stand up for herself when he couldn't even reschedule a meeting with Morty without anxiety clutching at his stomach. "Do you want to wear a dress?"

"No way! I can't do the three-legged race in a dress!" Esther licked the apple syrup off her fingers.

Simon laughed again. "Okay then. You should wear shorts. Show those girls from school that you're the best three-legged racer ever."

Esther nodded solemnly. "Daddy?"

"Yes?"

"Why aren't you going to work today? Did someone say something mean about you?"

"No . . . I'm just a little worried sometimes. I'm afraid I won't be good at my job."

The direction of the wind shifted, carrying an odd smell, like rotting eggs mixed with burning rubber. Someone must be having car trouble.

"Well, you should show them you're the best professor-er ever."

"Thanks, button. I'll try."

The wind blew harder. Gulls swooped over their heads, screeching as they flew toward the sea. There seemed to be more than usual, all heading in the same direction. Strange.

Across the harbor promenade a woman screamed.

JUDITH

Judith worked up a satisfying sweat as she ran along the waterfront. She started near the south end of North Harbor Drive. She watched the ships as she ran, noting which ones had also been there the previous few days. She always took the same route. Fewer distractions that way.

On the opposite side of the harbor, Coronado Island rested between them and the sea. Judith hadn't been out there in ages. Maybe she'd have some time after graduation, depending on when her new job started. She *would* get the job. She'd accept nothing less of herself.

She passed a dock, where a cruise ship waited like a beached whale. A couple of passengers lined up at the gangway, suitcases in tow. One woman wore a flowing peasant skirt and a floppy purple hat. She had long lavender hair. Another held a mousy little boy tightly by the hand. She handed a piece of paper to a skinny ticket agent. Two security guards lounged nearby, giving the suitcases a cursory check before gesturing to the belt of the hulking luggage scanner.

The promenade was busy for this time of morning. Judith ran briskly around strolling elderly couples and dockworkers carrying tools and lunch pails. She passed a man with curly, graying hair and a child in pigtails and a blue T-shirt. Judith wondered why the girl wasn't in school.

Judith ran on, breathing rhythmically. She had to wait as the crowd from a sightseeing tour boat milled around the promenade. She pinched her lips, irritated at the delay. She bounced up and down to keep her heart rate up until the crowd cleared.

A strong breeze blew a loose strand of Judith's hair across her face. Gulls cried as they sped overhead toward the water. The little crowd in her way slowed to stare up at the birds.

Tourists. Just as she was about to push through them, someone screamed.

2. The Cloud

SIMON

SIMON LOOKED AROUND FOR whoever had screamed. A man cursed loudly from the deck of a fishing boat just beyond the promenade rail. Someone leaned on a car horn, releasing a long, loud blast. The strange smell in the air was stronger, like a fire started with too much lighter fluid.

Across the promenade, faces turned toward the city. Simon whirled toward the midsize skyscrapers occupying the waterfront, his senses heightened and alert. Something was very wrong here.

The sky above the city boiled. White, gray, blue, black, even purple. The clouds expanded outward, oozing above the buildings and coalescing into one mass. At its heart the cloud grew darker by the second. But it wasn't the darkness of a thunderstorm.

This cloud was somehow denser, grainier than if it had been composed of mere water vapor.

"What's going on?" someone yelled.

"Are we getting bombed?"

"Oh God, is it a nuke?"

"What do we do?"

The cloud began to swallow the tops of the buildings, rolling toward them like a breaking wave. Sirens wailed across the city. Ash fell from the cloud like snow. Panicked cries rang out across the harbor front as the cloud sank lower over the buildings. A man far up the street fell to his knees, gasping as the ash enveloped him.

"Esther, we need to go right now," Simon said, grabbing her hand.

The cloud stretched as far as he could see. There was no way to get back into the city, nowhere to go. Behind them the sea waited.

Esther pointed a sticky finger. Simon looked where she was pointing, then picked her up and ran.

JUDITH

An avalanche of clouds tipped over the nearest buildings, engulfing them one by one. Judith felt like she'd been extracted from her own body, like there was some other runner on the boardwalk watching a dark cloud of smoke hurtling toward her. This couldn't be real.

The horns from North Harbor Drive became frantic. Tires screeched, and there was a bang as an SUV tried to force its way through the gridlock. People jumped out of their cars and ran along the street. A man in a Mariners cap bumped into her, then ran past. He reached the railing at the edge of the promenade and jumped straight into the harbor. Others simply stood and stared at the approaching cloud. Ash fell among them and they began to choke.

Suddenly Judith felt herself snapping back into her body. Her heart raced, and fear wrapped a fist around her stomach.

People jostled Judith as they ran in both directions, some of them screaming. A few feet away the man with the little girl scooped his daughter into his arms. Others stood, as Judith did, and looked about wildly for somewhere to go. The ground shook then, like a building was being demolished nearby.

The man started to run, carrying the little girl. He moved with more purpose than many of the others. Not sure what else to do, Judith followed him. He seemed calmer than some, and he'd be trying to get his daughter to safety. They bolted along the promenade, back in the direction she'd come from. Should she return to her apartment? It must already be under the cloud. She wanted someone official to tell her where to go, like a police officer or a soldier. The little girl's pigtails bobbed in front of her. Judith followed them like a beacon.

They reached the gateway to the cruise ship dock. It still sat there, a white floating hotel. The security guards and gate agents had disappeared. The man with the little girl ran toward the ship. Judith followed, along with a dozen others. The smell of ash grew stronger in the air.

SIMON

A rumbling sound indicated that someone had fired up the engines of the cruise ship. Simon glimpsed the name *Catalina* emblazoned on its hull as he took the gangway at a leap. When he reached the deck of the ship, he looked back. The sky was the gray of pencil lead now, the cloud completely obscuring the skyscrapers. The city was being swallowed. Sirens screamed.

Others ran across the gangway after him, a panicked throng trying to get as far away from the cloud as possible. A blond girl in running shoes darted on board, eyes wide in her angular face. A plump woman wearing a cross necklace dragged three sobbing young boys after her onto the ship.

People on the promenade were falling, clutching at their throats, choking. The cloud would reach the ship soon.

"Esther, listen to me," Simon said. He set her down and knelt to see her face. "You need to go inside and find some stairs. Go as far down into the bottom of the ship as you can. Try to close the door wherever you are."

"But Daddy—"

"Everything will be fine, button. You have to go now."

The ash—Simon was sure that's what it was— crept closer. He hated letting Esther out of his sight, but he had to get her away from the poisonous air. And they needed to move.

"I want Mommy."

Simon squeezed his eyes shut for a split second. "I'll call her right now. Go on. Remember to close the door."

Esther nodded and darted into the ship around a tall black man wearing a crew uniform. Simon mashed the power button on his cell phone. Each second it took to fire up felt like the jab of a switchblade in his stomach.

"Come on, people," the crewman said. He had a deep smoker's voice, but he looked young. "We're casting off. Hurry." A middle-aged couple, both wearing suits and gripping each other's hands like lifelines, were some of the last to run on to the ship. The sailor started to crank up the gangway.

"Wait!" A panicked voice reached them. "Please wait!" A heavily pregnant woman jogged toward them, both hands wrapped around her belly. She was tall, with bright-red hair and terror in her eyes. She stumbled.

Simon looked back at the door where Esther had disappeared. He wanted to follow her into the protected depths of the ship, but she was as safe as she could be right now.

The pregnant woman was sobbing.

"I'll get her. Wait for us," Simon said to the sailor.

He ran back onto the dock. The woman had fallen to one knee, her arms wrapped around her stomach like she was holding a football. Simon grabbed her arm and helped her stand.

"We need to move," he said. The woman stared at him wildly, unseeing. They had to be fast. The ship was going to pull away, and his daughter was inside. "Let's go!"

"I'll help."

The blond jogger appeared by his side. She took the pregnant woman's other arm and helped Simon guide her to the gangway. Still winded from running to the ship, Simon tried not to breathe too much as the ash cloud neared.

"Hurry! We're moving. I can't stop it," the sailor shouted, but he didn't raise the gangway.

The ship started to creep away from the dock. The gangway scraped along the pavement, getting closer to the edge. In seconds it would pull away from the dock completely. Their chance to escape was slipping away.

The trio wasn't walking fast enough. Simon made eye contact with the jogger. It was now or never. They lifted the pregnant woman between them, almost dragging her across the pavement.

Almost there. A gap appeared between the gang-way and the dock. They were too late! The gap widened. His daughter was on that ship!

"Jump!" Simon gasped.

The jogger didn't hesitate. They jumped, hoist-ing the pregnant woman between them. The gang-way shuddered under their weight as they landed, but it held. Simon caught a glimpse of the water beneath them, dark in the shadow of the ship. It was at least forty feet down. That would be like fal-ling on concrete.

They scrambled toward the ship, pulling the pregnant woman forward. The young sailor reached out both hands and lifted her onto the deck. Simon and the jogger followed. The gap between the ship and the dock widened.

People further back on the dock screamed for the ship to stop, but it was too far away now. There was no turning back.

JUDITH

As Judith darted from the gangway to the deck, there was a crash. The ship shuddered violently, tossing her off balance. The man grabbed her arm to keep her from falling. She started to thank him, but he was already helping a tall black sailor lower the pregnant woman onto the deck.

The sailor swore liberally. "Something hit us. I need to check the hull."

A plump woman wearing a cat angel shirt and a cross necklace rushed forward. She had been huddling just inside the ship with three towheaded boys.

"Let me help. Honey, just breathe. How far along are you?"

The man nodded gratefully and pulled a cell phone out of his pocket. He pressed it to his ear like he was staunching a wound and turned to stare at the clouds consuming the city behind them.

"Eight months," the pregnant woman said, her eyes the size of dinner plates. "What's happening?"

"Never mind that now. Breathe in. Breathe out. The Lord'll watch over us."

An older woman with lavender hair and a floppy hat joined the plump lady, trying to calm the pregnant woman. She brushed the sweaty hair off the woman's forehead with tiny hands.

Judith stood frozen beside them, not sure what to do. They were on the promenade deck right beside the ship's entrance. A gleaming rail ran along the edge of the ship, with a gap for the gangway. A doorway led inside, where there was some sort of check-in area. Dozens of people crowded in the entryway, sobbing, calling out names, and tapping cell phones. A few stared at nothing, in shock. No one seemed to be in charge.

The ship shuddered. They were moving faster. The pregnant woman whimpered and gasped.

"There, there," said the woman with the lavender hair. "You're safe here, sweetheart. Just breathe."

The lady with the cross necklace had both hands pressed against the woman's stomach, feeling it carefully. She seemed to have things under control, so Judith hurried along the railing toward the bow. There was a wider deck there with an unobstructed view of San Diego. She had to see.

The gray cloud stretched across the sky for miles, bearing down on the city with the weight of Mount Everest. It had become noticeably darker. The cloud ate up the sun, the buildings. They were close enough to the dock to hear people screaming and choking. Some jumped into the harbor to swim.

Boats sprang into motion around them, some sailing erratically, others speeding north. Their ship was heading north too, groaning forward, picking up speed. They sailed parallel to the shore, the ash cloud growing ever closer.

Judith ran to the other side of the ship, across the narrow bow. She realized why they weren't heading straight out to sea. The harbor curved inward along the coast of San Diego like a crooked finger. Coronado Island separated them from the open sea on the left. They were sailing directly toward Point Loma at the mouth of the harbor, but they had to stay close to the shore. Too close.

Up ahead boats clogged the harbor mouth, trying to escape. Ships crashed into each other as they tried to force through the bottleneck. Metal squealed, and shouts and curses filled the air. A few smaller vessels managed to break free and speed out to sea. But this cruise ship was the biggest one around. They'd never make it through.

The wall of cloud neared. Wind whipped across the deck, carrying shouts, a sulfurous stench, and the first grains of ash.

SIMON

Tears blinded Simon's eyes as he hit Redial on his phone again. For the tenth time he heard a blank high note, neither a dial tone nor a busy signal, as if the cell phone network was screaming under the weight of the cloud.

Oh God, Nina. He had to get through.

Simon gripped the railing as the ship crawled along the harbor. A fishing trawler floundered behind them. It had hit the *Catalina* moments ago, causing that shuddering jolt, and now it was sinking. The fisherman stood on the roof of his cabin, staring up at the shore.

Half the sky was black now. People ran wildly across the harbor front. As the cloud rolled further across the boardwalk, people fell, choking, sobbing, unable to breathe the ash-filled air. The city seemed to shake under the weight of the cloud. Simon watched the ash crawl closer, praying that Esther had found the very deepest corner of the ship.

Naomi. Nina. If they were under that mass . . . He punched the buttons on his phone again.

The wind picked up. It wasn't the natural landward breeze of a San Diego morning. It was as if the ash rode on a diabolical wave, pushing the clean air before it, gobbling up everything in its path. Simon tasted ash, felt the stinging, glassy grains. He pulled his shirt over his nose and mouth. Around him others did the same.

The phone wailed a dirge into Simon's ear.

A group of women now surrounded the pregnant lady. She had calmed down a bit, but she was deathly pale.

"Get her inside quickly," he said. "Try not to breathe until you're inside the ship. Shut all the doors and windows you can find."

"We've got her," said the woman with the cross necklace, "but a few people went to the front of the ship. You'd better get them before we close the door."

"I'll be right back," Simon said.

The women carefully lifted the pregnant lady to her feet and guided her indoors. Bloody water gushed down her leg.

Simon pulled his shirt back up to his nose and ran to the fore. A few people stood at the rails, staring between the city and the harbor mouth. The logjam was worse. They weren't going to make it out of the harbor.

JUDITH

Judith bent forward over the railing, as if she could force the ships to clear away by staring hard enough at them. The ash scratched her throat. She should get inside, but she couldn't look away.

A pair of yachts tangled with a huge sailboat in front of them. Metal screeched and groaned as the boats tried to find some way to maneuver around each other. Judith could just hear the curses of the people on board. The cruise ship bore down on the tangle. They weren't going to stop.

At the last second the cruise ship swung to the left and made a slow, lumbering arc around the struggling ships, narrowly avoiding the tangle. As they eased around, the boom of the sailboat scraped along their hull, making a shrieking sound worse than fingernails on a chalkboard. Judith felt like making that sound herself.

The harbor mouth was a solid mass of flashing steel and flailing sails. She could barely distinguish one ship from another. There was no way they were going to dodge that. Behind them, what had once been a billowing cloud was now a massive wall bearing down on them like a fog bank.

A few others on the deck stared out at the devastation, pale faced, shaking. The man from the promenade had joined them. He stared at the city, phone still pressed to his ear. Tears filled the corners of his eyes but didn't fall. Judith looked back at the harbor mouth, her own eyes dry. They were almost there, but it wouldn't matter. They weren't going to get through.

Suddenly, a steely mass appeared on Judith's left. That was the port side, wasn't it? A warship cut through the water beside the cruise ship, sitting low in the water. Navy sailors wearing gas masks moved purposefully across the deck about ten feet below Judith. A single sailor manned a crow's nest that was level with the deck of the cruise ship.

As it came even with them, Judith locked eyes with the sailor standing there. Thick eyebrows above a gas mask. A strong, high forehead. A crisp uniform. Then the warship passed her, carrying the sailor with it.

Ahead, the jam of ships pulsed like a tangle of sea snakes in the harbor mouth. The wind whipped violently around them, seeming to come from all directions at once. The warship didn't slow as it approached the jam.

It must be there to help, right? It's the US Navy!

A heavy whump sound burst forth. A shell exploded from the warship into the gaggle of civilian boats in the harbor mouth, blowing a yacht into the sky. Chunks of fiberglass rained down with the ash. Seconds later the warship fired another shell into the mass of ships. A wider gap opened. Screams rent the air. A third shell exploded, and then the warship barreled into the civilian boats, its prow cutting through them like butter. Boats fled from the warship as quickly as they could, but some were already sinking. A gap widened like wake behind the warship.

Whoever was steering the cruise ship must have seen the gap too, because they sailed in behind the navy vessel, keeping close as it plowed through the smaller boats.

Judith's fingers wrapped so tightly around the railing they hurt. The warship was wide and low, but she didn't think the path it cleared would be big enough for them. Nevertheless the cruise ship squeezed into the space after it. Every second Judith expected to feel the bone-rattling jolt of a collision.

But the other boats were fleeing the navy vessel, and the cruise ship slid through too.

For a moment the clear blue of an empty sky burst above a pure crystal sea. Then the ash rolled over Judith's head.

SIMON

Simon felt numb as the navy ship shoved struggling, sinking civilian vessels out of its way. Their occupants leapt into the water or hung on to scraps of fiberglass. Bodies floated, some in pieces. People were dying not forty feet away. He'd never known with absolute certainty that people near him were dying. But it was happening now, on the boats, in the water, in the city behind him.

Nina. Naomi. Their names roiled in his mind. Was there any way they could have survived the onslaught of that cloud?

Miraculously, their cruise ship was able to follow in the path of the navy vessel. Whoever was steering knew what they were doing. They cleared the mouth of the harbor and swung perpendicular to the shore. Then they headed straight out to sea.

The water beyond the harbor mouth was clear as glass for a moment. Sparse sunlight rippled on the sea, more like twilight than morning sunshine. The sky was the blue of sapphires.

Boats fleeing to sea shattered the illusion. The ash rolled above them. The bomb—or whatever it was—must be enormous. As far as Simon could see down the coastline, billowing ash spilled over the land in a solid mass. The thin shirt over his mouth and nose wouldn't protect him for long.

Simon waved to the others on the deck, gesturing toward the interior of the ship. They needed to get inside if they had any hope of surviving this. But many ignored him, staring numbly at the whirl of destruction that was once their city.

Simon edged along the railing and tapped the blond girl in running shoes on the shoulder. He gestured to his nose covering and pointed to the ship. She nodded and helped him round up the others, dragging a man in a suit firmly by the arm when he didn't respond to her right away. Simon's eyes stung. He closed them to slits, and white powder accumulated on his eyelashes like snowflakes.

As they reached the nearest door and pounded on it to be let inside, something changed in the wind. At first it was subtle, but as the door slid open and the young crewman helped people inside, Simon became more sure. They had sailed into some sort of slipstream, a current that blew parallel to the coast. It was sweeping the ash in one direction, but they were sailing away from it. As Simon stepped into the ship, he looked back. The shoreline, once San Diego, cowered under its noxious cloud, but the ash went no further than the wind current that was already dusting them off for their journey out to sea.

3. The Ship

SHELL-SHOCKED PEOPLE FILLED THE entryway of the ship. Some sat on the floor, huddling against each other like families in a hospital waiting room. Others stared vacantly, disconnected from reality. A handful of people had sustained injuries on their run to the ship: scraped knees, twisted ankles, spreading bruises. Confused passengers asked overloud questions, unable to figure out how their cruise ship had turned into a bomb shelter. Some had been inside their staterooms when it happened. They hadn't even seen the cloud.

The tall sailor closed the double doors behind Simon and the other stragglers, sealing them off from the ash, and then darted away to check the other doors. There was no sign of any other cruise employees. Where were the officials? The hospitality folks? Where was the captain?

The survivors reeled, looking for someone to tell them what to do. Panic rose. An old man began shouting, and his wife hissed at him to be quiet. A child wailed. Simon was too numb to feel terrified, but his hands shook.

The group around the pregnant woman was the quietest. The women were clearly distressed, but they had something tangible to do. Their charge lay on a couch, breathing too fast and sobbing as the woman with the cross necklace spoke to her in a soft Southern accent. Her three boys stood back, clutching each other, and kept their eyes fixed on their mother. She was the calmest person around as she coaxed the pregnant woman to breathe more slowly. The others in the group hung on her every word, and it helped. Someone needed to do the same for everyone else.

"Excuse me. Can I have your attention please?" Simon said.

No one looked at him. The panic was reaching a feverish pitch. Children and adults alike cried in corners, clutching at each other. The pregnant woman screamed, her breathing becoming more urgent. The sharp smell of blood tinged the air.

Voices rattled around the entryway, growing in intensity, bordering on hysteria.

"We've been nuked!"

"None of the phones work."

"It's the terrorists!"

"WE'RE GOING TO DIE!"

This wasn't helping. Simon waved his arms, trying to get people's attention. "Everyone, we need to calm down and—" No one was listening.

"I think a power plant exploded."

"No way. Had to be the Russians."

"Or the Chinese!"

"I want to go home!"

Suddenly the blond jogger, who'd stayed close to Simon when they entered the ship, climbed onto the empty reception desk. She had a glass cup in her hand that she must have found in the lobby somewhere. She hurled it to the floor behind the desk with a smash and shouted, "Shut up and listen, people!"

In the sudden silence following the crash, she turned to Simon expectantly. Red-rimmed, frightened eyes followed her gaze. He nodded at her and cleared his throat.

"Okay. Sorry to yell," Simon said. "I think we need to stay calm and figure out what's going on."

"Stay calm!" The suited man roused from his stupor. "Did you see that cloud?"

"We've been nuked I tell you!" shouted a voice from the back. "It's already too late!" A few heads nodded in agreement.

"We're poisoned!" said a middle-aged woman wearing a wide hat with sunglasses swinging from the neck of her polo shirt. She clutched at her throat.

"I was just outside." Simon spoke slowly, as if he were soothing a frightened horse. "I saw the cloud. But the wind currents are keeping the ash close to land. As long as the ship keeps moving out to sea, we should be okay." He had no idea if that was true or not. *How long does radiation take to kick in if you aren't in the initial blast?* It had to be almost immediate at this range, and his skin was still firmly attached to his body.

"What happened out there?" asked the elderly woman who had shushed her husband. She appeared to be one of the passengers.

"Are we at war?" asked an old man with a thick accent.

"Was it the terrorists?"

"I don't know what happened," Simon said, "but panicking won't help right now." He stayed still, fighting to use his best, authoritative teacher voice, the one he used to calm students the day before a big final. "I think we need to focus on helping this lady and getting the kids calmed down. We should also find the captain."

One by one the adults—and some of the teenagers—nodded. They looked at him anxiously, waiting for him to tell them what to do.

"Uhhh, okay. Let's try to arrange care for any injuries. Does anyone here have medical training?"

Nobody volunteered. The ship had to have a doctor or a nurse. Someone else should be taking control by now, telling them where to go. All Simon wanted to do was search for Esther, but the crowd was still watching him. They huddled together, strangers pressed against strangers, many whimpering.

"Maybe we should move further into the ship," Simon said finally. "It's pretty crowded here. Is there a central meeting area or dining hall or something?"

"We can go to the plaza," said one of the passengers. "It has space for hundreds."

"Good. Let's try to get everyone together there. And let's find someone official from the cruise who can help us." He singled out the older couple. "Would you two please take all the children out of here so we can give the lady some space? And would you"—he turned to an Asian woman with an ID card on a lanyard around her neck—"please ask around for anyone with medical training?"

On cue the pregnant woman hollered again. Simon felt like throwing up. He went over to the group surrounding her as the people he had delegated leapt to their duties.

"Will you be able to move her?" he asked quietly. The blood smell was stronger.

"It's too late," said a tiny older woman with long lavender hair. "This child's coming any second."

"Okay, we'll get out of your way," Simon said.

"What can I do to help?" The blond jogger had climbed down off the desk.

"Can you find the bridge?" Simon said, turning toward her. She looked scared but determined, and she'd already proved she could keep a cool head. "See if you can find the captain or an officer to take over."

"No problem," she said. She gave a sharp nod, setting her ponytail swinging.

"Thanks. Sorry, what's your name?"

"Judith."

"I'm Simon."

Judith bared her teeth in what was probably meant to be a smile, but her face was grim. She turned and ran down a passageway.

"Okay, the rest of you, let's head to the plaza and settle everyone down," Simon said. The pregnant woman screamed. "And see if we can find a doctor!"

JUDITH

Judith jogged down the dim passageway. She was heading for the front of the ship, but beyond that she had no idea where the captain should be. Doors lined the passageway, ornate numbers set in plates beside each of them. A pile of suitcases had been abandoned on the carpet. She leapt over them and ran on. If she kept running, kept her heart rate up, maybe she could avoid the terror that threatened to overwhelm her. *How can this be happening?*

At the end of the passageway she found two elevators. She pushed the buttons, but the panel where the numbers should appear remained blank. No elevators then. There was a service door nearby with a porthole-like window in it. She was reaching for the handle when a face appeared in the window, right at eye level.

Judith gasped and jumped back. The face disappeared, then the door cracked open. A young man with a mop of black hair above a round, dark face emerged. He wasn't much older than Judith, and he was very short. He wore a white uniform with a sailor's collar and a blue embroidered logo that said, "Catalina: Your Island at Sea."

"Excuse me," Judith said. "I'm looking for the bridge. Can you help me?"

"Bridge?" The young man's eyes were the size of headlights. He had a cut above one eye and blood dripped into his eyebrow.

"I need to find the captain."

"I'm not allowed on the bridge," the young man said softly.

"It's an emergency," Judith said.

He looked around the passageway, still halfway behind the door, like a rabbit peeking out of a hole.

"What's happening?" His voice sounded like a child's.

For a moment Judith wanted to cry. "I don't know."

They stared at each other, lost, fearful.

Get a grip, Judith, she thought. *You're both adults.* She adopted a confident voice, the one she'd practiced to use in her interview to describe her accomplishments. *The interview!* It was too late for that now. She supposed she wouldn't need her sharp gray suit now, but she pictured herself dressed in it anyway, hair in a perfect chignon.

"Take me to the bridge," she commanded.

The young man nodded and beckoned her into the stairwell. As they climbed, he chattered like a frightened bird.

"I am Manny. I am from the Philippines. I am only working here for three months. I heard the screaming, and some of the crew ran away. I am thinking the ship is safer than the land."

"You're probably right."

"What's your name?" Manny asked.

"Judith Stone."

"You are a guest?"

"What?"

"A ship guest," Manny said patiently. "We do not call them passengers here."

"Oh, no. I ran to the ship when the cloud started coming down. I'm from San Diego."

"I am sorry for your family."

Judith stopped short. Her final step echoed through the cold stairwell. She stared at Manny without really seeing him. Her family was in San Francisco. Her father ran a busy tech company and rarely had time to see her. Her mother and stepfather were preoccupied with their second family—a spoiled four-year-old boy and a colicky baby. Judith had barely thought of them. They were in *San Francisco*. They would be far enough away from the bomb or chemical attack or whatever was going on out there. *Wouldn't they?*

"They're fine," she said. They had to be.

"As I say, I am sorry," Manny said. He seemed to take comfort in having something to do. He walked quickly through the ship, urging her to watch her head when they stepped through a low doorway. He pointed out the passageway leading to the galley, the service elevator, now silent, and the back entrance to the captain's clubhouse. "For the vip guests."

"The what?"

"You know, the extra-special people. The vip guests."

"VIPs?"

"Yes. I am thinking this is the first time you are on a cruise ship."

"I don't really like the ocean."

"But you are living in San Diego?"

"I go to college there. They have a good acceptance rate for Stanford Biz." She'd had her eye on

Stanford since junior high. Her father was an alum, of course, and she'd peppered him with questions. *Not now, Judy. I'm busy.* That's how it always was. He often forgot that she had only gone by Judith since her tenth birthday. Judy was a kid's name. But she *was* going to Stanford Business School. Someone would clear up this mess. The military. The cavalry. An image of the navy ship blasting through the jammed civilian boats in the harbor flitted before her, but she pushed it down.

"This is the bridge," Manny said.

They arrived at a plain white door at the end of a long corridor lined with identical doors. She'd expected something grander, perhaps with a voice-recognition panel or fingerprint scanner or something. Manny hesitated. She waved at him, indicating that he should hurry. Manny pushed open the door and stepped back to allow her through.

The bridge was full of ash. Judith breathed in before she could stop herself. No, not ash. Cigarette smoke. There were only three people inside. She had thought there would be more. She had imagined rows of headset-wearing experts at computer consoles, like Houston in space travel movies. Computer consoles stretched the width of the bridge in two rows, with a short aisle in the middle, but sailors in smart uniforms occupied only two. One, a woman, was young and stocky, and the other was a middle-aged man, flabby and a bit green in the face.

At the front, incongruously, she had expected a big, old-fashioned pirate ship wheel. Instead, there was just a silver-haired man, one clawed hand wrapped around a phone, the other keeping a death grip on a cigarette.

Beyond him windows filled the space above the computers. The sea stretched before them, endless, open. A scattering of other ships sped toward the horizon, interrupting the expanse. The sky was darker than it should have been. It was still morning, long before she should have been leaving for the uptown offices of Gilbertson & Cob, but the sky was twilight darkened, with no stars.

"Excuse me. Captain?" Judith said, her confident interview voice forgotten.

The silver-haired man whirled around. He had deep grooves in his dark-olive skin and a prominent Roman nose.

"I told you. You will not be getting a refund on your cruise from *me*, if you get one at all. Out!"

"Sir, I'm not here for a refund," Judith said. "I—"

"I also don't have a working phone connection," he said. He had a faint accent that Judith couldn't place. Maybe Italian?

"I don't want the phone," she said. "I—"

"Chances are ninety-nine point one in a hundred that I can't do whatever it is you want me to do, including turn this ship around."

"No, sir. You've already saved us by getting us away from the shore. I saw how you steered after that battleship."

The captain relaxed, but only by a hair. "Yes, well, I did what I had to. My pilot abandoned ship at the first report of the disaster, so I did it with my own hands too." The captain flicked a crumb of ash off the end of his cigarette.

"There were warnings?" Judith asked. She recalled Sonya's words over breakfast. Something about a cover-up and the earthquakes. Where was Sonya now?

"Mere minutes in advance. It's a goddamn travesty." The captain took a long drag on the cigarette.

"I was jogging on the harbor front this morning," Judith said. "Everything seemed normal. I didn't see emergency bulletins or anything!"

If there had been some warning, she might have been able to get out of the city. *I could have cancelled my interview at least.* She knew it was a stupid thought, but she couldn't process the idea that the life she had run out of this morning might no longer exist.

"The harbor front?" the captain said.

"Yeah, the San Diego boardwalk. I'm not a passenger, er, guest."

The captain stared at her and puffed on his cigarette, uncomprehending.

"Um, a bunch of people ran onto the ship at the last minute," Judith explained. "The guards and ticket people were gone, and there was nowhere else to go."

The captain blew a smoke ring. It joined the haze hovering near the light fixtures, reminding Judith uncomfortably of the cloud over San Diego.

"Well, that complicates things."

"I mean, I guess we can pay you eventually if—"

"I'm not worried about your cruise fare." The captain turned to the stocky young woman manning the computer console. She wore her brown hair in a pixie cut, emphasizing her heart-shaped face. "We'll have to recalculate, Ren."

"Already on it, Captain Martinelli." Her fingers tripped across the keyboard.

"What are you calculating?" Judith asked.

"Exactly how long we can survive with the supplies we have on board," Ren said.

"More people, more complications," the captain said, taking another drag on his cigarette. Judith eyed it, and he held it up to her, eyebrow raised.

"No, thanks," she said. "Isn't smoking on a ship against the law?"

"I believe we may have witnessed the end of law this morning."

"What do you mean?"

"This disaster has not affected San Diego alone. Whatever is going on, it's not an isolated incident."

"More cities were bombed?" Judith felt the tight pinch of fear. *Not San Francisco. Please, not San Francisco.*

"If we were bombed." The captain chewed the edge of his cigarette, nearly at the butt. "Young man, you might as well stop peeking around the door like a goddamn whack-a-mole."

Manny came into the room, face a dark red. "Yes, Captain, sir."

"You don't think it was a bomb?" Judith asked.

"I have a theory," the captain mused. "It's almost ridiculous to think about. A one in ten thousand chance. But it fits."

"Sir?"

"Perhaps. Perhaps there was a warning." The captain stared, unseeing, then seemed to remember she was there. He dropped the cigarette butt on the floor and ground it in with his heel. "In any case there will be time for theories later. Exactly how many people ran onto the ship with you this morning?"

"I don't know. They're gathering in the plaza. We're trying to make sure anyone who's injured gets help first. We should be able to get a head count."

Judith felt like the captain should really be the one telling her all this, not the other way around.

"Good. Good. Is Bennington still on duty down there?" the captain asked.

"Sir," Manny chimed in, "I saw him running away from the ship this morning, sir."

He was now half-hidden behind a computer console in the row behind the fleshy middle-aged man who hadn't spoken yet. The man's face had turned greenish gray. He stared limply at his computer screen. Ren was still typing feverishly.

"Son of a bitch." The captain didn't look surprised. "Well, he's not the first goddamn hotel manager I've chased away from this ship."

"There's a man taking charge down there," Judith said. "He ran on when I did. Simon. He sent me up to find you. Would you come down and speak to everyone? People are pretty scared."

"If Simon wants the job, he can have it," the captain muttered. "All right. Ren, you can handle things here for the moment. And make sure Vinny doesn't vomit on the equipment again. Maintain our present course."

The woman held up a hand to stop them. She had the other pressed to the ear of her headset.

"Wait, sir. There's a message coming in. I think you need to hear it."

4. The Plaza

SIMON

WHEN SIMON REACHED THE plaza, it had already begun to fill with people. It was an open atrium, with balconies rising three stories high. Shops lined each level, just like in a mall. Railed promenades fronted the shops on the second and third levels. A grand staircase dominated one end of the room, with a crystal chandelier hanging above the plush velvet steps. At the top of the plaza, a glass skylight revealed the darkened heavens.

Simon searched the growing crowds for his daughter. People gathered everywhere, leaning over the balconies, looking for answers. In addition to the survivors from the docks, passengers filed in from the stateroom corridors. They asked frantic questions, bewildered at the array of injuries displayed by the survivors. Dozens carried bright-orange life jackets with them.

There was no sign of Esther. Irrationally, Simon imagined that she had somehow gotten off the ship and returned to the city. He had told her to wait somewhere far from the poisonous air, but she may have followed the crowds to the plaza. He had to find her. He looked into the shops lining the atrium one by one in case she'd hidden inside.

The people from the docks—Simon had already begun to think of them as the runners—assembled in front of a huge gift shop on the bottom level of the plaza. Pewter models of the ship sat in the windows. Racks of T-shirts and sweaters marched back into the shop. Hats. Sunglasses. Picture frames. The storefront had the ship's slogan etched into the glass: "Catalina: Your Island at Sea."

Simon wanted to keep searching for Esther, but the pregnant woman they'd left back in the lobby needed help soon. There was a coffee bar across from the gift shop with tables grouped around it. The image of Judith standing on the reception desk and shattering the cup flitted before Simon's eyes. He crossed to one of the tables and climbed on top.

"Everyone," Simon called, "I think we're safe for the moment. Is there a doctor here?"

Immediately, questions thundered from all quarters.

"Can we turn around?"

"Do you work for the cruise line?"

"What's going on?"

Simon raised his voice. "I don't have any more answers than the rest of you. I'm just looking for a doctor."

"Does your phone work?"

"Are we gonna die?"

"All I know is that we need to stay calm and help each other," Simon said. "Does anyone else need medical attention? Is there a first aid station somewhere?"

"The ship, it has a clinic," a woman shouted from the top balcony in a rich Eastern European accent. "Deck Four. The doctor is going on shore leave this morning."

"Thank you," Simon called. He couldn't see the speaker. "All right. If anyone has any medical experience, even first aid training, would you head for Deck Four? Anyone with injuries or medical issues, head there too if you're able. We'll send a messenger down to you as soon as we know anything. We also need someone with medical training to go to the reception lobby to help a pregnant woman. I think she's in labor."

"I'll go. I'm a nurse," said a woman in a lurid floral sundress who was pushing her way through the people gathering on the grand staircase. She was obviously a passenger, and she had a glass with a stick of celery in her hand.

"Thank you," Simon said as she set the Bloody Mary on the table at his feet and swept out of the room.

More people began to shift around, making their way toward the end of the plaza. Some clutched at their chests or walked gingerly on twisted ankles. Arms slung around each other, they headed for the fourth deck, along with the assorted medical personnel. There were a few children among them, but still no Esther. Simon stayed atop the table, searching the growing crowd for her bright-blue T-shirt.

People shouted questions from all sides.

"What happened?"

"Are we at war?"

Simon deflected them with the same answers about waiting, staying calm, listening to the captain when he arrived. He didn't know any more than they did. But the questions continued.

"When can we go back to land?"

"Are we going to die?"

Simon kept waiting for someone from the cruise line to turn up and take charge so he could go look for his daughter, but everyone else was just as lost as he was.

"Is there anyone from the kitchens?" he asked finally. "Can we get these people some food?"

"I am head chef," said the same woman's voice from up on the balcony. "I give you answers. The deliveries, they are arriving this morning. We have lots of food."

"That's good. Will you come down here, ma'am?"

"I can see you better from up here," she said.

A few people chuckled.

"Fair enough," Simon said. "What's your name, Madame Chef?" He scanned the faces peering over the top of the third balcony. A woman with dark hair and severe maroon lipstick pushed forward.

"Ana Ivanovna," she said.

"Okay, Ana. Can you arrange food for everyone? And some water bottles?"

"I will take care of everything. Don't worry."

She barked orders to a group of people in kitchen uniforms gathering around her on the top floor.

More and more passengers emerged from the corridors, demanding to know what was going on. They flooded out of the passageways and tramped down the staircases, some looking like they had just woken up. Many were dressed in shorts, sundresses, even swimsuits. The sound of flip-flops slapped through the crowd.

"The captain will be here soon," Simon told them. "I'm sure he'll have news. In the meantime, let's stay organized, so families can find each other. If you ran onto the ship this morning, please stay here on the ground level. If you're a passenger on the *Catalina*, gather on the second level. Crew and hotel staff, please go to the third level. Tell the others as they come in."

People shouted for their family members, scanning the faces of those who had already gathered, a mixture of fear and hope in their eyes. But having a bit of order helped. As the groups organized themselves, more families reunited, hugging and clutching hands like they hadn't seen each other in years.

Simon searched for Esther in the throng. He still felt like he was in a strange, hazy dream. He knew pain waited somewhere beyond the haze. He just wanted to find his little girl.

There was a flash of movement in the big gift shop, a hint of blue. Simon climbed off the table and rushed over to the shop. The cash register had been abandoned. The shelves looked freshly stocked with kitschy cruise mementos and sundries. Simon made his way to the far corner. A tiny figure in a blue shirt huddled behind the final shelf.

It wasn't Esther. It was a little boy, only three or four years old, with a black bowl cut. Tears streaked his face.

"Are you okay, son?" Simon said.

"I want my mommy," the little boy whimpered.

Simon's heart constricted in his chest. He was finding it hard to breathe.

"What's your name?" Simon knelt beside the boy.

"Adi Kapur. My phone number is 5-5-5-8-0-9-2. Mommy said to say my number if I get lost."

"That's very good, but the phones aren't working right now," Simon said. "Are you on the cruise with your family?"

"Yes. We're going on the big boat to Mexico. Mommy said we'll see dolphins."

"I hope we will, Adi. Listen, right now you should go out to the second floor and stay right by the stairs, okay? Your mommy will find you there."

"She's there?"

"I hope so. I'll help you look for her if she's not, okay?"

"Okay." The little boy stood and headed for the door.

Simon stayed where he was on the floor of the gift shop. It was quiet, a needed reprieve from the commotion in the plaza. He took a second to listen to the quiet. He desperately wished to be home with his family. He thought of Naomi giving him a quick hug good-bye as she darted for the car, Nina giggling as he stole a kiss at the door. He closed his eyes. But when he opened them nothing had changed. He was still kneeling in the empty gift shop of a cruise ship, and the world had gone to hell.

He had to keep moving, to stay busy. They should collect the names of all the people on the ship to help families like Adi's find each other. He picked up a stack of notepads with glossy pictures of the *Catalina* on the front and a handful of souvenir pens. He held his breath before opening the door and rejoining the chaos in the plaza.

Simon handed off the notepads and pens to a handful of relatively calm people with instructions to get everyone to write their names and whether they were missing anyone who was supposed to be on the ship. They could post them somewhere central.

People continued to file in from all over the ship. They separated themselves out. First floor, runners; second floor, passengers; third floor, cruise staff. The third group was the smallest, and no one seemed to rank very highly, besides Ana Ivanovna. Cleaning ladies and porters conferred in tight knots, divided by native language. There weren't very many cruise employees. Maybe some were on shore leave. Simon hoped that wasn't also true of the engineering crew. Someone had to sail the ship.

Several hundred people had already squeezed into the plaza. Simon had hoped there wouldn't be so many—and immediately felt guilty for the thought. Every one of these people had survived. But as they packed the balcony, he realized this would not be a crowd of a hundred or so making their way to a safe harbor. There could be close to a thousand people on board.

Dividing into groups did help, though. A woman on the second-floor balcony shrieked and pushed her way through the crowd to sweep little Adi into her arms. A pair of runners found each other by the coffee bar, each wearing the same conference lanyard. Others asked around, describing features, clothing, anything to help them find their loved ones. But Simon didn't see Esther anywhere in the plaza. She must have gone deeper into the ship.

"Have you seen my son?"

A man approached Simon. He was in his midsixties, with a large gray mustache and a beer belly, making him look a bit like a walrus. "His name is Daniel. He's tall and he was wearing a green polo shirt."

"I'm sorry," Simon said. "I don't think I've seen him."

"He went into the city today," the man with the mustache said. "I stayed behind to nap. We're on vacation to celebrate my retirement from Boeing."

"I came from the city," Simon said quietly. He took a slow, steadying breath. "It didn't look good. My wife and daughter are there too."

He thought of the blank dial tone on his phone. He'd been tapping the call button periodically but still couldn't get through. He desperately wanted to hear Nina's voice. Was it possible that she and Naomi had survived whatever was happening in the city? He had no capacity to imagine his life without them. And Esther needed her mother.

The old man watched him, waiting.

"I'm sorry," Simon said again. "What's your name?"

"Frank Fordham."

"Frank, I'm Simon. We need to focus on the people who are here now, okay? Let's get through this and then we'll find our . . ." He took a deep breath. "We'll find them."

JUDITH

Judith and Manny waited anxiously as the captain listened through the headset. Ren hovered beside him, arms folded over her crisp uniform. Once, the captain snapped his fingers sharply, and Ren leapt to get him a scrap of paper and a pencil.

Outside the huge windows the sky grew darker still.

The other crewman, Vinny, whimpered softly. Judith stayed as far from him as possible in case he vomited again. She joined Manny in the second row of computer consoles. She'd only known him for about ten minutes, but she already felt like they were a team. She found a box of tissues by one of the computer consoles and helped him wipe the blood from the cut above his eye.

She thought about what the captain had said: it wasn't just San Diego. This incident, whatever had happened, was not isolated. She had assumed the rest of the world carried on as usual, watching the reports from San Diego with fascination. They would organize relief efforts, fund-raisers. One day she'd be able to look back on it and describe what it was like to be here.

But what if other cities really were affected? What if they were at war? Wars were something that happened in other countries, to people on the news. She was too young to experience one first-hand!

"Are you praying, Judith?" Manny whispered.

"What?" She had closed her eyes, her hand still holding the wad of tissues over Manny's brow.

"I am praying too," Manny said. His eyes were wide and scared. "Every minute since we are leaving the shore."

"No, I just . . . What happened to your head anyway?"

She didn't want to admit how terrified she felt. She tried to ignore the way the captain's jaw worked back and forth as he listened to the radio.

"I fell," Manny said simply. "It is nothing. We are hitting something, and I fell against the cart for the bags."

"You're a porter?" Judith asked.

Manny nodded. He seemed about to say more, but then the captain straightened from the computer console. His face was waxen, the life drained from it at what he had heard.

"Yes," he said. "It is as I feared."

SIMON

The plaza was packed now, and arguments began to break out. People were getting restless. Fear seeped through the crowd like the smell of rotting meat. The passengers teetered on the edge of hysteria. Simon felt it too.

Where were the officers? The emergency protocols? The ship must have standard procedures in place for accidents. Why weren't they being used?

Simon fought down panic and climbed back onto the café table. It wobbled a bit, but he wasn't too heavy. He had to keep everyone occupied. *Where is the captain?* He called for everyone's attention. The crowd took a long time to quiet down, but eventually silence descended. Wide-eyed faces turned toward him.

"The captain should be arriving any minute," Simon said. "And everyone will get some food soon. We need to find out what's going on out there. I don't like the look of that sky. Has anyone been able to get on the Internet or reach anyone on the phone?"

"I've been trying. Can't get through," said a man sitting on the plaza floor with a laptop open on his knees.

"Aren't we too far away from shore?" someone called from the balcony.

"We've been sailing for barely an hour."

"I can't even get a busy signal."

"It's no use!"

They grumbled and tapped at their phones, but no one had managed to get any sort of connection. Simon was so used to being able to call or text his wife at any moment. It was surreal to be completely cut off.

"The ship must have its own computers," Simon said. "Anyone know how to get into those? Someone from the crew?"

The tall sailor who helped them at the gangway had been sitting on the staircase. He stood.

"The cruise director and most of the reception crew ran for it when they saw the security guards go," he said, voice booming across the plaza. "They thought they'd be safer in the terminal building on the waterfront. They're the ones with access to the computers at reception. But if anyone's good with that stuff I'm sure they're not *that* secure."

"I can help." A young woman leaned over the second railing. Her hair was bright pink and spiky. Her face glinted with piercings. "As long as the computers are running, I can get into them. I'll try to get a connection."

"Thank you," Simon said. "Can you also figure out how many people are supposed to be on board?"

"You got it." The young computer expert saluted and disappeared from view.

"What next?" someone asked.

The crowd looked expectantly at Simon. He opened his mouth, but before he could answer, a voice spoke from the top of the grand staircase.

"Well, well."

The captain had arrived.

Murmurs pattered around the balconies like rain on a roof. The captain had silver hair and a craggy face, and his brass buttons shone. He looked every inch the hero. Simon breathed a sigh of relief and stepped off the table.

"Don't let me interrupt," the captain said. "You seem to have things well in hand."

"Thank you, sir. I'm glad you're here to take over now," Simon said. He noticed Judith, the blond jogger, standing behind the captain with a short, dark-haired man in a crew uniform, barely more than a boy.

"On the contrary," the captain said. He had a slight accent. "My sniveling hotelier seems to have run off, along with my pilot and half the bridge crew. How would you like to manage passenger affairs for the time being? I need to sail this ship, which is something I don't ordinarily do, incidentally."

"I was only getting things started," Simon said. It had been a long time since anyone had actually been eager to give Simon more responsibility over people. He just wanted to find his daughter, find answers about Nina and Naomi.

The questions started to hammer down again.

"Captain, what happened?"

"Where are we going?"

"Can we turn around?"

"Was it a terrorist attack?"

The captain held up a hand. That was all it took to get people to be quiet again. He lit a cigarette and blew smoke out of his nose. The tendrils curled into nothing above the stairs.

"Ladies and gentlemen, I am Captain Ignatius Martinelli. We are currently sailing directly to the Hawaiian Islands. The disaster is centered in the contiguous United States. We're gathering information via radio, but it's sporadic at the moment. The cell networks are down, as you have probably noticed. I have reason to believe San Diego is not the only city to have been destroyed. You will be able to disembark in Hawaii in four days, where we should learn more."

A firestorm of questions burst forth as Captain Martinelli paused to take another drag on his cigarette.

"Destroyed?"

"Four days?"

"What about our families?"

"Which other cities?"

"Are you sure San Diego is destroyed?"

"Four days!"

"We're supposed to be going to Mexico!"

"Are we at war?"

Captain Martinelli raised a hand. "Not war," he said quietly. "Yellowstone."

The word was a gong.

"You mean the volcano?"

Captain Martinelli inclined his head. For a heartbeat, the plaza was deathly silent.

"Ridiculous!" someone shouted.

More voices joined in, panic escalating again. It was like someone had let off a hundred fireworks.

"That's conspiracy theory stuff!"

"Was it really the volcano?"

"Why didn't we have any warning?"

"If we're not at war, why can't we go back to the city?"

"What do you mean, destroyed?!"

Captain Martinelli raised his hand again. It took longer for the crowd to calm down this time. Simon's numbness had begun to recede, replaced by bone-rattling shakes. The captain wasn't making him feel better.

"That cloud you saw rolling over the city was volcanic ash," Captain Martinelli said through another puff of smoke. "It contains glass and sulfur, among other things. It is dangerous to the lungs and very heavy when wet."

The captain spoke calmly, but his words set off another flurry of conversations around the plaza.

"Yellowstone is hundreds of miles from San Diego."

"He's lost it."

"I want to go home!"

Frank, the older man with the mustache, leaned over and spoke to Simon. "I was in Washington when St. Helens blew. I've seen this kind of ash before. He could be right."

Simon tried to recall everything he knew about the volcano deep beneath Yellowstone National Park. It was one of the world's only supervolcanoes. If it truly had erupted, the results would be catastrophic. Apocalyptic even.

Nina. Her name beat in his mind like a drum.

"Another few minutes in port," the captain continued, "and the ash would have clogged up our engines worse than a pound of sand in a gas tank. Over the next few days it will fall atop buildings and vehicles. Add a bit of rain, and it will get heavier and heavier, until they collapse under its weight. Everything close to the eruption will be as flat as Kansas soon."

"But we're in California!"

"I think he really has lost it."

"What do we do now?"

"Can we get a new captain?"

"You may do as you like," the captain said. He didn't seem to share the fear and panic that thundered around the plaza. He just sucked on his cigarette like it was his only source of air. "As I said, we are on course for Hawaii. Perhaps we'll reach it. Perhaps we won't. If that was the Yellowstone supereruption, we won't have long no matter what we do."

Tremors ran through the crowd. *Conspiracy. Fear mongering. Lost it. Impossible. Apocalypse.*

Could it be true? Simon remembered what the apple pastry man had said about the earthquakes. The image of the ash cloud rolling over the city was forever burned into his memory. The explanation fit, but if it was true—if the captain was right—God help them all.

Nina. If the Yellowstone volcano had erupted, was there any chance at all that she and Naomi had survived? Such an event could wipe out the entire continent.

He had to stop this spiral of thoughts. Simon climbed the steps to where the captain stood. Frank followed him.

"Sir," he said. "My name is Simon Harris."

The captain shook his hand. His palms were dry as dust.

Simon spoke quietly so the other people in the plaza couldn't hear him. "I'm not sure we should get everyone worried about Yellowstone until we know for certain. We've all seen the documentaries and . . . well . . . I can't see people staying calm for long. Has it been confirmed?"

Captain Martinelli looked him in the eye. Simon shivered. Emptiness. It was like there was nothing at all behind his irises.

"We've just been in touch with another ship via radio," the captain said. "Cell towers are down all along the West Coast. The ship was just off San Francisco. Or where San Francisco used to be. They saw it all."

Judith stirred nearby, but her severe face stayed still.

"Are you positive it was Yellowstone? Maybe Mount St. Helens . . ." Simon felt like he was grasping at straws, looking for anything that could pull him out of this spiral.

"The volcano blew," the captain said. "They're saying it was the big one. No one within a hundred-mile radius is talking. At all." The captain took a long drag on his cigarette. "The ash has spread across the West and as far away as Ohio."

"When did it happen?"

"This morning. 7:00 a.m. on the nose."

"Why weren't there warnings?" Judith interjected. "We could have done something."

Her face had gone deathly pale. She must have seen the documentaries too. The boy in the crew uniform beside her looked equally scared.

"Like what? Evacuate the entire North American continent? Send everyone running through Mexico? It was too late. I suppose the government knew they couldn't do enough. Perhaps we'll get to Hawaii and find the president holed up in a bunker."

"This can't be real," Simon said.

The captain shrugged. "We'd better hope Hawaii doesn't close the borders."

Simon looked out at all the people. He felt detached from his body, as if he were eyeballs and a racing, sputtering heart suspended above the steps. The plaza contracted before his eyes. This *couldn't* be real.

The captain's words infected the crowd like a virus. They were angry, scared. They didn't want to believe it, but the captain was the only one with access to news of the outside world. Simon saw the situation escalating. It could erupt at any moment. He found his lungs again. Breathed in.

"Hey! Everyone listen to me. We don't know if what the captain says is true. It's just too soon. I was in New York when the Twin Towers fell. Back then we thought every major city was under attack. We thought the world would end right alongside Manhattan. It didn't. Before we start crying apocalypse, let's focus on the trip to Hawaii. Let's all pitch in, folks. It'll be good for us." He turned away from the crowd. "Captain, will you help us get everyone settled? We need your authority."

The captain lit another cigarette. Simon wanted to throw his lighter across the room.

"Do whatever you want," Captain Martinelli said. "I intend to sail us to Maui and watch the world end from a white-sand beach."

He turned and walked back up the stairs.

5. *Catalina*

JUDITH

THE PLAZA BOILED LIKE a kettle. The captain disappeared down the corridor they had come from. He had delivered his news and abandoned his passengers to deal with the consequences.

People gathered in front of the shops, talking in tight groups, some weeping. Even the children had adopted their parents' somber attitudes. They clutched hands and hid behind legs as their mothers and fathers grappled with what was happening. There were quite a few children, Judith realized, many with orange life jackets securely fastened around their small bodies. She had always thought of cruises as the domain of retirees, but this one catered to families. Bright colors—cartoonlike and cheery—adorned the shops. One corner had a playground with low, soft things to climb on—all fish themed—like the play area of a shopping mall. In addition to the expected assortment of gifts and designer goods for sale, there was a game shop and an ice cream stand.

Judith heard a shuddering sob. A pale woman sitting on the floor near her spoke softly to her mousy son.

"Neal, sweetie, we'll go home as soon as we can. I know you're scared."

"I'm cold, Mommy." The boy's teary eyes were wide and luminous.

"I packed sweaters in our suitcases." The woman hugged the boy close. "We'll find them after we have some lunch."

Judith felt very alone. It couldn't be true about San Francisco. Her mom and the kids would be all right. She would see her father again. The captain had to be wrong. The whole country couldn't be wiped out, even if the volcano had erupted. She had too many things she wanted to do with her life, too many plans. There had to be some mistake.

She joined Simon and an old man with a large gray mustache.

"We need to keep people busy and avoid a panic," Simon was saying.

"You're right," the older man said. "That kind of fatalism never did anyone any good." He jerked his head in the direction the captain had gone.

"I agree with Simon," Judith interjected. "We should also figure out how much food and fresh water we have."

"I'm sure Ana Ivanovna can help us with that," Simon said. "First, we need to get everyone fed in an orderly fashion and organize some people to—"

"Excuse me." A voice broke into the conversation. "Why are you making the decisions now? You don't work for the cruise line." It was a middle-aged woman, Latina in appearance, wearing a polo shirt, with sunglasses on a cord around her neck. Several children surrounded her, including a sharp-eyed adolescent girl.

"I'm not deciding anything," Simon said. "I'm just trying to help."

"Why should you be in charge?"

"I'm not trying to be in charge."

Judith thought it was perfectly obvious that Simon should be calling the shots. He was remarkably calm considering the circumstances. And he wasn't as unsettling as Captain Martinelli, that was for sure.

"There's room for everyone to lend a hand," said the man with the mustache. "No reason we can't be civilized."

The woman eyed them. Something about her face made Judith think of a seagull. "I'll gather the passengers for the meal."

"Thank you," Simon said. "Everyone will feel better once we get some food in us. What's your name?"

"Rosa Cordova." The woman swept back up the steps, the children following her. Simon gave Judith a look that was probably meant to be a smile and then started down the stairs.

"I have to find my daughter," he said.

Judith shivered. She still wore her jogging gear. The plaza had grown darker, colder. Many of the lights were off. The skylight above them looked like dark sunglasses. Was that ash? What would they do if the sky never cleared?

She thought about her family, but she couldn't reconcile what the captain had said about San Francisco with reality. They would get to Hawaii in four days and discover it was all a terrible mistake. They just had to hold on until then. The first order of business was to get warm.

She went into one of the shops, smelling wood polish and cotton when she pushed open the door. No one manned the register. Her debit card was tucked into the pocket of her running shorts, but that wouldn't do her much good here. She hesitated, then put on a sweater with the *Catalina*'s logo screen-printed on the back. She found a pair of navy-blue yoga pants and pulled them on over her running shorts. The feeling of thick cotton against her skin was comforting, almost like a hug. She pulled off the tags and pocketed them. She'd find a way to pay later, when the world was back to normal.

She took a pile of sweaters from the rack and returned to the plaza. She gave one to the boy, Neal. His mother gripped Judith's hand wordlessly.

Judith went over to a group of people who looked like they had come from San Diego. They wore an assortment of office clothes, workout gear, and even a fast-food uniform, complete with a visor and a button that said, "How can I help you?"

"There are sweaters in the gift shop," she said. "Under the circumstances I think we can use them. Spread the word."

They thanked her and began to tell the others.

Judith clutched her pile of sweaters close and made her way back to the reception lobby, where they'd left the pregnant woman, unsure what she would find there.

SIMON

The tall sailor still sat on the plush carpet steps, running his hands over his shaved head. He kept shaking it, as if arguing with himself, denying something.

"Excuse me," Simon said. "I wanted to thank you for your help at the door. And on the gangway."

"Just doing my job." He stood and rolled his broad shoulders. "Name's Reggie."

"Simon. Did you see where my daughter went? I told her to find the deepest corner she could and shut the door."

"Try the laundry room and the bowling alley," Reggie said, "and the engine room if she's not afraid of big machines."

"She's definitely not afraid of machines," Simon said. "How do I get there?"

Reggie gave him instructions, and Simon set off into the bowels of the ship. He made his way down staircases and through corridors, occasionally passing bewildered-looking passengers and crew. He asked if they'd seen a little girl with pigtails and urged them to head to the plaza. No, he didn't know what was going on. No, he didn't think they were going back.

The ship was large, but it wasn't the biggest cruise ship he'd seen by far. It didn't belong to any of the major cruise lines, based on the logos painted on the bulkhead. It seemed to do family-oriented cruises to Mexico and the like. Had this ship even been as far as Hawaii? Simon wasn't sure he liked the captain's plan. He wanted to get back to San Diego as soon as possible. It couldn't be destroyed. It just couldn't.

He checked the laundry room, calling for Esther as the cotton piles swallowed sound. The clean scent of detergent masked the charcoal smell of the ash still clinging to his clothes. Where was she? Rationally, he knew she couldn't have gotten off the ship, but panic still clutched at him with every second spent searching.

After ten minutes he opened the engine room door. A loud roaring filled the cavernous space, rattling his eardrums. The big engines looked like windowless cars lined up in the center of the floor. A metal catwalk ran around the outer edge of the two-story room. Simon stepped onto it from the doorway, his footsteps clanking.

A pair of men stood on the catwalk, staring down at the engines. One took a long swig from a hip flask. They must know what was going on outside then.

"Excuse me," Simon shouted above the noise. "I'm looking for a little girl. Pigtails. Blue T-shirt. Have you seen her?"

The man with the flask looked at him, eyes bloodshot, and answered in a language Simon didn't understand. The other man nodded and uttered what sounded like a curse word. Simon gestured toward the machines. The men shrugged and didn't stop him, so he climbed down a flight of metal steps to the lower level.

His feet vibrated with the motion of the engines. He walked along the room, calling for Esther. It was well lit, even though the rest of the ship seemed to have switched to emergency power. The fluorescent lights threw sharp shadows across the machinery.

"Esther! Are you in here, button? It's Daddy."

He reached the end of the room and rounded the big engines. He started back, passing a row of machines with pipes running out of them, perhaps pumps of some kind.

"Esther?"

"Daddy?" Her voice was so small, Simon almost didn't hear it above the growl of the machines.

"Yes, button. It's me. You can come out now."

"What's going on? Are we at sea?"

A pair of large eyes appeared beneath one of the big pipes along the edge of the room. Esther stood. There was a long smudge of grease across one side of her round face, as if she had lain down on the floor. For some reason the sight made Simon want to cry.

"We're sailing somewhere safe right now."

"Where?"

"Hawaii. Doesn't that sound nice?"

"Where are Mommy and Namie? Are they sailing to Hawaii too?"

Simon looked down at his daughter, with her messy pigtails and her blue Thomas T-shirt, and finally let the truth engulf him. He sat on the floor and pulled Esther onto his lap, hugging her close. She felt small and warm in his arms. He would keep this little girl safe no matter what happened next.

"Mommy and Naomi were in San Diego, Esther. They . . . they're . . ." How could he explain this?

What if he was wrong and they got out? "There was a big volcano in Wyoming. It erupted. When that happens, there's lots of ash in the air and it can go really far away if the explosion is big enough and the wind is strong. It's really dangerous, like poison."

"Is that the smoke we saw?"

"Yes. That was the ash from the volcano. If anyone breathes too much of it, they . . . they could die."

"Can't they hold their breath?" Esther asked.

Simon passed a hand over his eyes.

"Not for long enough," he said. "Not when there's that much ash. If it rains it also gets really heavy, and it can make houses fall down on people."

"What if they went far away?" Esther said. "Like us. We got away on this big boat, right?"

Simon cast about for a hundred different reasons why it might be true. What if they found gas masks? A safe basement? Was it possible? What if they had decided to drive to Mexico instead of going to the dentist? Would they be far enough away in time?

"We did. We were really, really lucky. I think most people weren't as lucky as us today."

"Is Mommy dead?" Esther spoke so quietly that Simon wouldn't have heard her if he hadn't been dreading those very words.

"I don't know. I think so."

"And Namie?"

"They were together."

"Can we go back and find them?"

"I don't think we can go to San Diego again for a while. Maybe weeks."

"Did our house fall down?"

"I don't know, button."

"What are we going to do without Mommy?"

"I don't know."

The tears came then. Simon hugged Esther closer and wept into her tiny shoulder. Her Thomas T-shirt grew damp from his tears. Esther didn't cry, but she gripped him tightly with her small, warm hands. The engine vibrated solemnly at his back.

JUDITH

The women in the reception lobby were crying when Judith arrived with her pile of sweatshirts. The older one with lavender hair and the long peasant skirt sat on the floor, rocking back and forth. Judith hadn't realized before how tiny she was. She was holding the hand of the woman lying on the couch, whose eyes were closed.

Blood and fluid matted the cushions. It made Judith's stomach turn, and she looked away. The woman with the cross necklace was on her feet.

Her cheeks were wet and her shirt was covered in blood.

In her arms was a tiny baby. Bright-red hair dusted its head, still glistening with fluid. The woman hummed a hymn over the baby as her tears continued to fall.

"Is she . . . ?" Judith cleared her throat. "Is she okay?"

"They both are, honey. They both are."

Wordlessly, Judith handed over the pile of sweatshirts. She helped the lavender-haired woman, who introduced herself as Bernadette, wrap the exhausted new mother in soft cotton. The other woman cleaned the baby with fragments of her own soiled clothes and then wrapped herself and the newborn in clean sweatshirts.

"There was supposed to be a nurse. Did she help you?" Judith whispered to Bernadette.

"Yes, dear. She was here for the worst of it. She just went down to the clinic to get some supplies. Our girl Constance is going to need stitches. She wouldn't trust anyone else to get the right stuff, and Penelope here knows plenty about looking after babies."

Penelope smiled over the newly swaddled form. "This is an angel. The Lord will look after us. Don't ya'll worry about a thing."

"Stitches?" Judith felt ill. "Should we move her down to the clinic?"

"Best to keep her still. We'll move her some-where safe and clean as soon as she's patched up."

Judith fought down the bile in her throat. She couldn't stand blood, and even talking about stitches made her feel nauseated.

"Umm, I don't think I can help with that."

"Of course not, dear," Penelope said. "We have things under control here. Would you like to hold our little Catalina?"

"Catalina?"

"She'll go by Cally for short," the woman on the couch said, lifting her head slightly. "Like my mother, Calypso."

"Oh, um, no. I don't like ba— "

But Penelope was already thrusting the tiny cot-ton-wrapped bundle into Judith's arms. The baby barely weighed a thing, but Judith held her out in front of her like a twenty-pound sack of rice, both arms stiff. Catalina had a snub nose and ears like mother-of-pearl shells. Her hair looked even redder now that it had started to dry. It was soft like down. Her skin was nearly translucent. Judith could see the veins pulsing on her tiny temples. She swal-lowed a gag and quickly handed the baby back to Penelope.

"I'd better go see if everything's okay back in the plaza," Judith said. She wanted to get out of there before the nurse returned.

"Wait!" A face popped up from behind the computer on the reception desk. "Did the captain make an appearance? What'd he say?"

"Who are you?"

"Nora. I've been trying to access the net. Had to break into the ship's system."

Nora had spiky pink hair and at least a dozen earrings in each ear and two in her eyebrow. She appeared to be in her late twenties. Judith introduced herself and joined her at the reception desk, turning her back on the three women with the baby. She didn't understand how they could sit there and coo over a wrinkly baby with all that blood around.

"Do you have an Internet connection?" she asked. For one wild moment she thought about emailing Donald Herz to tell him she wouldn't make it to her interview. In a way it was easier to think about that than about her family. Captain Martinelli had to be wrong about San Francisco. She would email her parents to let them know where she was. They would answer her. Everything would be fine.

"I've been trying," Nora said. "I've only been able to log on for seconds at a time. It's worse than spotty dial-up."

"Did you check the news?" Judith went around to the other side of the desk to sit beside Nora. The woman was relatively calm. Judith respected that. "The captain was telling everyone some pretty crazy things in the plaza. He said the Yellowstone super-volcano erupted." Judith tried to laugh. "It can't be that bad, can it?"

Nora shook her head. "It's that bad. The networks in New York are broadcasting. Anything based in California or the Midwest is silent as the grave."

"What do the networks in New York say?"

"Apocalyptic headlines. Fear-mongering talking heads. The usual click-bait bullshit."

"You don't think it was Yellowstone, then?"

"Some people say Yellowstone," Nora said. "I don't know yet. Need more data." She twisted the ring in her eyebrow, making Judith feel queasy. "You've seen the documentaries, right?"

"Not really." Judith didn't waste her time with conspiracy theories and doomsday predictions. The chances of that kind of thing happening in her life-time were vanishingly slim. And yet . . . "What do the documentaries say?"

"That it'll get worse before it gets better," Nora said. "The day of the eruption is killer obviously, but the scientists think the US probably wouldn't be able to produce a harvest in the years afterwards because of weather disruptions. It's like climate change on steroids. The big problem is that there might not be any food to get from overseas either if the harvests fail there too. Depending on what happens to the weather, we could go for years without a proper harvest."

"What would we do then?" Judith asked. This was all hypothetical, surely.

"Starve," Nora answered. "That's what the documentaries say at least. It'll happen all over the world."

"This doesn't feel real."

"Tell me about it," Nora said. "Hey, the net's back. Let's see if we can get the BBC. They'll sort out the bullshit."

Her fingers flew across the keyboard. Judith had never seen anyone type so fast.

"Here we go. Fuck."

The BBC page loaded slowly, opening a few pixels at a time. The picture that emerged was a simulated image of North America. The headline, in eighty-point font, said simply, CATASTROPHE. The simulation showed a crater the size of Washington over Yellowstone National Park. Contour lines marked the estimated ash fall range. California had been swallowed up. Lower Canada and the desert in the Southwest. To the east, the disaster squeezed outward like an amoeba. It ate up the Great Plains, the Midwestern cornfields, threatening Pennsylvania, sitting heavy above the Deep South. The Eastern Seaboard looked untouched for the moment.

"Damn," Nora breathed. "It says casualties could be in the hundred millions. That's eight zeros."

They stared at each other for a moment. There was no scope to comprehend this catastrophe. A hundred million was an abstract number, a fiction.

And California was buried. Judith's whole family was there. She hadn't been close to her parents since their divorce. But even when they fought over custody, argued about money, or paid more attention to their work than to her, they had still been there. She could always go home. Now her whole life had been swallowed up in a single morning, and she couldn't do anything about it.

"Isn't anyone sending help?" Judith said weakly.

Nora turned back to her computer screen. Where before she had been purposeful, now her fingers moved clumsily. Judith felt like she was seeing everything from underwater.

"It says the president is in a secure location. Communications are spotty." Nora clicked down through the article and scanned the accompanying headlines. "There's not much real information. Experts speculating about the potential toll. They keep linking to a documentary from a few years back. People in the UK are rushing stores and stocking up on food and supplies." Nora pulled up another page. "Same thing's happening in the rest of Europe. God, I wouldn't want to be working at a grocery store today."

"What about the military?"

"Let's see . . . Highest alert, obviously . . . All bases closed to civilians. Planes grounded all over the world, even air force. Navy ships in the Pacific are heading for a rendezvous at Pearl Harbor."

"Really? That's where we should go." Judith thought of the warship pushing through the boat jam so recklessly, so confidently. She wanted to call in the cavalry, to have men in uniforms move in and set things to right. "The navy will keep us safe. I bet they're already coordinating relief efforts."

"Maybe," Nora said. "Ugh, the net's gone again. I'll see if I can get it back."

"The captain was staying in touch with people via radio up on the bridge," Judith said. Captain Martinelli had called it the end of the world. He may have been right about the volcano, but that didn't inspire confidence. There was no way it was that bad. Things would clear up soon. They just had to give it some time.

Nora pounded at the keyboard in frustration, then pushed back from the desk. "I can't get it to work. All this ash can't be good for the satellite signals." Nora hammered the keys again, but the screen stayed blank. "Nope, it's gone again."

They stared at the blank screen for a few minutes. A hundred arguments for why it couldn't be as bad as the news said rioted through Judith's mind. But she was finding it harder to explain this away. Just a few hours ago she had been preparing to take her first steps into a bright, shiny future.

She had done everything right. But now she sat in a cold cruise ship lobby with a group of strangers, one of whom had just delivered a baby for goodness' sake!

"What are we going to do?" Nora said quietly, almost to herself. She pinched her largest earring, a ball with spikes coming out of it, like the head of a mace, almost hard enough to draw blood. The report from the venerated BBC had brought the true weight of the disaster tumbling down on their heads.

"I don't know," Judith said. She remembered Simon saying they should keep people from panicking. She couldn't process the implications of what had happened, but she had to do *something*. "It looks like we'll be on the ship for a few days. Maybe we should make sure everyone has somewhere to sleep. Do you know how many people this ship can hold?"

"I can probably get a deck plan," Nora said. She tapped at the computer. "Oh, and I found the passenger manifest."

"How many rooms are there?" Judith asked.

"Give me a sec . . . Looks like there's enough space for seven hundred fifty passengers and two hundred fifty crew. Six hundred forty-two passengers were checked in, but I don't know how many of those are still on board, or how many extras we picked up. I think that Simon guy was collecting names."

"There had to be a hundred of us running on from the city, maybe more. I'd be willing to bet there are at least a thousand people on this ship."

"If that's true, there won't be enough passenger rooms for all the runners," Nora said, bringing up a diagram of the ship on the screen. Each room was labeled with a number and occupancy figure. The ship didn't look all that big, actually. Judith had thought cruise ships usually carried thousands of people, but this wasn't that kind.

"We're going to have to put some people in crew cabins," Nora said. "I don't want to piss anybody off, but I think we should move the single passengers into the smaller cabins so we can keep families together and possibly pair a few people up."

"That sounds reasonable," Judith said.

"The cruise guests aren't going to be happy about being kicked out of their cabins." Nora peeked over the top of the computer at the women with the baby.

"It's for everyone's good," Judith said. "People will have to make sacrifices until we get back to shore."

"Yeah, but how do we get them to agree?" Nora thumbed at her mace-head earring. There was a tiny silver tortoise beside it.

"We don't give them any other option," Judith said. "Let's get everyone assigned and sent on their way before they have time to complain."

"All right. We'll need a full list, though," Nora said.

"People will come up for the food," Judith said. "We can get everyone sorted out over lunch."

"Roger that."

The nurse, a squat woman in a floral sundress, bustled back into the reception lobby. She had a threaded needle laid out on a tray. She passed the tray to Bernadette, pulled out a huge syringe, and leaned toward the woman on the couch. Judith blanched. She turned quickly to Nora.

"Let's head down there now. We can let people know what we saw on the news."

"Good idea," Nora said, eyeing the medical preparations. "Let me just shut the computer down. We've got to save power."

They left the reception lobby, Nora clutching printouts of the ship's rooms in her hands, crumpling them slightly. They didn't walk fast enough for Judith, though. The woman on the couch moaned, and Judith put her hands over her ears to block the sound.

6. The Dining Hall

SIMON

HUNDREDS CROWDED INTO THE Atlantis Dining Hall for the meal. Two long buffet counters and rectangular "family-style" dining tables were arranged across the room. A row of windows filled one wall. The sea outside was restless, churning darkly beneath the sullen sky. It was a gray day, already so different from the sunny moment when Simon had decided to walk along the harbor. That had only been a few hours ago.

He turned his back on the windows and focused on the people filling the tables around him. The dining hall didn't have room for everyone to eat at once, and people were already lining up outside, waiting for their turns. Many wore *Catalina* sweatshirts with cheery slogans about islands, vacations, and paradise in shades of turquoise, purple, and sunshine yellow. The dining hall had similarly bright walls and fixtures, incongruous given the dull gray beyond the window.

Ana Ivanovna directed operations by the buffet tables. She served huge trays of fresh California fruits and vegetables and assorted sandwiches. Compared to famously extravagant cruise buffets, it was simple fare. Any complaints about the lack of hot meals and dining options were met with swift dismissals.

"I am not wasting energy when there are refrigerators to run!" Ana said, waving people away with a spoon dripping fruit juice.

Simon thanked her as he filled a plate with sandwiches for himself and Esther. Frank Fordham sat at a larger table alone, so Simon carried their plate over to him. A few people looked up and nodded as he passed them. Esther studied them curiously, unafraid.

"Frank? Can we join you?"

"I suppose." Frank waved his hand vaguely. He scanned the room, perhaps still hoping to find his son.

"This is my daughter, Esther."

"Hello." Esther hopped into the seat next to Frank. "What's your name?"

"My name is Frank."

"Do you like Thomas the Tank Engine?"

"What?" For the first time Frank's eyes landed on Esther, pulled away from his futile search.

"Thomas. He's a train. He has lots of friends, like Percy and Toby and Mr. Conductor."

"I've seen Thomas before," Frank said, a hint of a smile on his lips.

"He's really cool," Esther said. "Sometimes he has engine trouble and his friends have to help him. I like engines. I can fix cars. I'm helping my daddy." Esther took a huge bite of a sandwich.

"Can you?" Frank said. He leaned closer to Esther, his mustache twitching. "I used to make engines. I was an engineer."

"What kind of engines?"

"Ones for moving water. For purification systems, that sort of thing."

"What's purication?" Esther asked.

"Purification," Frank said patiently. "It means taking dirty water and making it clean enough to use again."

"That sounds cool," Esther said, her mouth still half-full of sandwich. "It's not as cool as train engines, though. Those take people places."

"You're right. Trains are cool."

The dining hall buzzed with earnest conversations. Everyone was calmer with a bit of food in them. They were already settling in for the journey, sharing where they were from and exchanging theories about what had happened. The two couples at the nearest table debated how far the volcanic ash could spread, raising their voices over the issue of wind speed.

Simon looked around for the captain, but he was nowhere to be seen. Simon still wasn't sure they should have told everyone about the volcano until they had more information. If the captain was wrong, everyone could be worrying and debating unnecessarily. As it was, it didn't feel like reality had set in yet. They could almost be on a regular cruise.

Judith walked over from the buffet table. She now wore a *Catalina* sweatshirt too. The pink-haired young woman who'd offered to help with the reception computers followed.

"Is it okay if we sit with you, Simon?" Judith asked.

Her question was tentative, but Simon got the impression that Judith was generally quite confident. It was something in the way she set down her tray and pulled back her chair. Her movements were swift and straight.

Simon introduced Frank and Esther. Judith introduced Nora.

"Your hair is pink," Esther said.

"Be polite, button," Simon whispered.

"It's okay," Nora said, grinning at Esther. "My hair is pink as a pony. That's what my mom says."

"Ponies aren't pink." Esther wrinkled her nose.

"You're absolutely right. My mom's a little crazy." Nora laughed, but her voice was raw.

"Where does your family live?" Simon asked.

"Texas," Nora said. "I don't know how they are yet." She thumbed at the row of earrings glinting in her ear.

"Nora got onto the Internet for a few minutes," Judith said. "The news confirmed what Captain Martinelli said . . . about Yellowstone."

"Was your source—?"

"Saw it on the BBC."

It felt like all the air had drained from the room. Simon had been hoping the captain was delusional. But it was true. This could be the end.

"The map might be wrong," Nora said, fiddling with her earring again.

"Did you see any pictures?" Simon asked.

"A simulation of the ash fall."

"Did you get in contact with anyone?" Frank asked. "I need to find my son."

"My webmail wasn't working," Nora said. "The social networks are overloaded. I couldn't get through to any of them." She paused for a heartbeat. "Half of Texas is covered, but they have a chance." She looked down at the sandwich that sat untouched on her plate.

"Where's your family, Judith?" Simon asked.

"San Francisco." She too studied her sandwich intently.

"I'm so sorry. My wife and other daughter were in San Diego."

He thought about Nina, her rich brown eyes, her smile, the warmth of her skin. He remembered sneaking glances at her in the university library, inviting her to study with him beside the greenhouses, taking their newborn baby, Naomi, from her exhausted arms. *Stop. This won't help anyone.*

Judith met his eyes, utterly vulnerable for a split second. Then it was as if a cloud of ash covered her eyes, cloaking the light. Judith cleared her throat and straightened her back.

"Nora got the room plans for the ship off the computer," she said briskly. "If we're going to be here for a few days, we should assign rooms so everyone has somewhere to sleep. We may need to make a few people move to crew cabins so there will be room for all the families, though."

"I'm not sure we should be making people do anything just yet," Simon said, matching Judith's businesslike tone. "We can find places for people to sleep in the restaurants for the time being. There's probably a spa with beds or mattresses too."

"Everyone's going to have to make sacrifices," Judith said.

"True. But I think we've all made enough sacrifices for today," Simon said.

An awkward silence descended on the table. Then Judith nodded.

"Sure," she said. "Oh, the pregnant lady had her baby. It seems fine."

"And the woman?"

"She's getting stitches, but the nurse said she'll be okay."

"That is good news," Simon said. "And terrifying news, to have a newborn in these circumstances."

"There's a baby?" Esther asked. "Can we see it?"

"I'm sure it needs to sleep right now," Simon said. "We'll go see it later."

"Can we name it Thomas?"

"It's a girl," Judith said. "The mother named her Catalina."

"That's a weird name," Esther said.

Judith leaned close to her. "I think so too," she said.

Esther grinned.

"Shall we take a look at those room plans you found?" Simon said, pushing the rest of his sandwich over to his daughter. "I've been collecting the names of the people on board. We can start matching them up."

"Sure thing, boss." Nora unfurled her stack of papers and spread them across the table.

They bent close to the diagrams and started working through the handwritten lists, crossing off those who were still on the ship. It felt good to do this straightforward motor task. The group avoided any further talk of families and focused on the simple puzzle of finding somewhere for everyone to sleep.

JUDITH

They worked all afternoon and late into the evening getting everyone food and a room or a mattress. Their little group began to gather helpers. They still hadn't found a high-ranking member of the cruise staff to take over, but a woman named Willow Weathers, who sang in the lounge every night, knew her way around the ship. She told them about all the additional spaces where they might find extra blankets, sundries, and more space for people to sleep.

Judith and Nora managed the room assignments. They spread out the diagrams on one of the bigger tables near the entrance to the dining hall and ticked off names as people came over to confirm whether they had a place to stay and whether there were any empty beds in their rooms. There were some complaints, but most people were too exhausted by the day's events to protest too much. If anyone didn't know where to go, either because they had still been in the process of checking in or because they were runners, Judith or Nora would give them a room number. Willow Weathers would then tell them how to get to the correct deck or assign a porter or a member of her backup band to help them.

Simon divided people into teams to search the ship for anyone who hadn't been accounted for yet. He dealt with any miscellaneous questions as best as he could, turning to the three women for their input often. Judith kept an eye on him as he delegated tasks and listened to the passengers' concerns. With his quiet voice and unassuming demeanor, he had a calming effect on people. He could resolve conflicts with a hand on the shoulder and a soft word of encouragement.

When Rosa Cordova, the woman they had met earlier in the plaza, demanded additional rooms for her large family, Simon listened patiently and referred her to Judith. The survivor count had climbed past the thousand mark, and Judith explained they needed every room filled to capacity. Rosa grudgingly accepted Judith's verdict. She looked to Simon to see if he had noticed, but he was already dealing with a dispute between two older men. He apparently trusted her to take care of Rosa on her own.

Most people cooperated. They only needed to stay on this ship for a few days, and then they'd be safe. They set their sights on Hawaii.

By the time everyone had been fed and assigned a room, night had descended. Simon picked up his daughter, who had fallen asleep leaning against a support pillar near their table, and told Nora and Judith to get some rest.

Nora invited Judith to bunk with her in her stateroom on the eighth deck. It was about the size of a college dorm room and had a queen-sized bed. The bathroom door retracted like an accordion, and a closet/dressing area separated the bathroom from the rest of the stateroom. The walls were painted sandstone, and large abstract prints hung above the bed in mostly sea green and purple. A small desk with a round cushioned chair sat between the bed and the floor-to-ceiling window. A little square balcony jutted out from the ship, divided by a low wall from the balconies on either side.

"Toilet still works," Nora said, poking her head around the corner of the dressing area.

"That's a relief. Hope it stays that way." Judith sat on the edge of the bed, rubbing her feet. She was thankful for her comfortable running shoes, but it had been a very long day. "Do you think the ship will make it all the way to Hawaii?" she asked.

"It should," Nora said. "We made it out of the ash fall." She sat down on the other side of the bed and began removing her larger earrings.

"How much longer do you think it'll take to get there?" Judith asked.

"Maybe three more days. A normal cruise does it in four to five, and we've been booking it."

Judith studied the other woman. She had tossed her heavy black trousers onto her suitcase, which had been delivered to the room before the chaos began. She had a tattoo of an upside-down tree stretching most of the way down her thigh.

"Nora," Judith said.

"Yeah?"

"Why were you cruising by yourself? Don't people usually do that sort of thing with friends?"

Nora was quiet for a moment. "This is supposed to be my honeymoon," she said finally. "I know I don't look like the cruising type, but my fiancée really wanted to do one. She loved the beach and Mexico and the sea . . ." Nora fell silent.

"I'm sorry," Judith said. "Did she . . . ?" Judith didn't want to complete the sentence, even in light of the fact that most of the people she knew had probably died today. That still didn't feel real.

"Oh, no!" Nora said. "Nothing like that. The bitch got cold feet a few months ago and dumped me. I paid for the cruise, though, so I decided I'd go anyway and have a bang-up time. Guess the joke's on me after all."

"Do you think she made it?" Judith asked.

Nora sighed. "Yeah, she's probably fine. She lives in Boston now."

"Do you think you'd want to see her again?" Judith asked. She thought of her own strained relationship with her parents. Despite everything, she desperately wanted to hear their voices. She wished things had been different between them. She'd even be happy to see her insipid stepfather.

"Sure, why not?" Nora said. "I'm over it. God, I could sleep for a week. I had no idea apocalyptic disasters could be so exhausting." She flipped over in bed and burrowed beneath the covers, so that Judith could only see the bright pink of her hair.

Judith didn't answer. She lay on the bed, still in her borrowed *Catalina* sweats, and pulled the blanket up to her chin.

Scenes from San Diego began to curl in the air above her like smoke. The screams. The pure terror on faces she barely registered as she ran after Simon. Esther's pigtails bobbing like a beacon in front of her. She saw the animal fear in the pregnant woman's eyes. The bared teeth of the tall sailor as he pulled up the gangway behind them. The thick eyebrows of the man in the warship's crow's nest as it shot past them and blasted through the civilian ships. As she drifted to sleep, she imagined the veins pulsing in the little baby's head, changing from blue to red to ashy gray as consciousness fled.

7. Day Two

JUDITH

EARLY THE NEXT MORNING Nora roused Judith from bed and dragged her back to the reception computer. There was no Internet. No matter what Nora tried, she couldn't get a connection. Her eyes grew bloodshot as she stared at the computer screen, trying to find some way to break through to the rest of the world. The blank web browser was worse than static screaming through an old TV.

Judith fetched food and coffee for both of them from the dining hall, where bleary-eyed passengers asked each other if they'd been dreaming. They huddled together and stared out at the empty sea. When they left San Diego, they'd been in the company of dozens of other ships, all speeding away from the shore. But now they were alone. Judith wondered if the other captains thought they'd be able to head back to the mainland rather than sailing straight for Hawaii.

The sky swirled with multicolored clouds. A thick layer of grime coated the windows. Judith couldn't tell if she was seeing real volcanic ash above them or if those were storm clouds. How long would it take the ash to fill the whole atmosphere? Those purple-black skies definitely weren't normal. The sea was unsettled too, and it made Judith queasy to think about how far from land they were. How deep was the sea here? She was so used to being able to look up answers for questions like that in an instant. She had never felt so cut off from the world.

She returned to the reception lobby, balancing a pair of bagels on top of overflowing coffee cups. She sat and sipped at the bitter liquid while Nora tapped away at the keyboard. Images from her nightmares rose before her, but she shook them off like mosquitoes.

When passersby spotted Nora and Judith at the computer, they begged to have a turn.

"My phone's not working."

"My laptop won't connect."

"I paid extra to have Internet on the cruise. What gives?"

"I need to reach my family. Please let me use the computer."

They had to turn everyone away, explaining that there was no connection, they were trying, they'd let everyone know if they got through. Over and over they watched faces fall as the others realized they'd have to wait even longer for answers. One woman burst into tears, and Judith had to search the drawers of the reception desk for tissues. She wasn't sure what else to do.

After more than an hour of trying to access the Internet, Nora pushed away from the desk.

"Impossible. I can't get through. This computer is shitty."

"Do you think there's a better connection in the bridge? Maybe they've been able to get online," Judith said, thinking of the double row of computer consoles she'd seen the day before.

"Maybe," Nora said. "But if the satellite signals aren't getting through, it won't be any better up there."

"It's worth a try, though, right? We could see if they've heard anything on the radio."

"Sure, why not?" Nora said. "I'm not making any progress here."

They followed the same route to the bridge Judith had taken the day before. The corridors were crowded with other passengers. *Should I be calling us survivors?* Most looked as if they didn't quite believe what was going on. One woman wandered around with the cruise schedule clutched in her hand, asking what time the bingo started. A couple of children ran through the corridors, screaming and laughing as if nothing had happened, their parents nowhere to be seen.

The ship felt surreal. Inside, it was like walking down the hallways of a hotel. Judith experienced a jolt of surprise whenever they passed a window revealing the rolling expanse of the sea beyond.

She couldn't help feeling nervous when they pushed through a door marked "Cruise Staff Only" on their way to the bridge. She disliked breaking rules. She wished Manny the porter was with them. She hadn't seen him since yesterday, when he'd delivered a too-short list of crew names to their table for sorting.

When Judith and Nora entered the bridge, the captain wasn't there. The room was nearly empty, and they had a perfect view of the sea in front of them. The skies swirled unnaturally, blue and purple and gray.

The woman with the brunette pixie cut stood up from a computer terminal.

"What are you doing here? The bridge is off-limits."

"It's Ren, right?" Judith said. "I'm Judith. I was in here yesterday. We were wondering if you've had any updates from land. Is the captain around?"

Ren appeared to want to send them away, but then her shoulders relaxed a little. "I don't suppose it matters if I tell you this," she said. "The captain went on a bender up in the lounge last night. He's still sleeping it off. Who's your friend?"

"This is Nora. She's been trying to access the Internet, but we haven't been able to get on at all this morning."

"Computers are down," Ren said.

"I got one working yesterday in the lobby," Nora said. "We even had the net for a few minutes. Checked the BBC and everything." She fiddled with her tortoise earring as she met Ren's eyes.

"How'd you manage that?" Ren said. "The hotel units are password protected."

"I know my way around computers."

"You shouldn't be messing about with ship property," Ren said.

Judith detected a bit of a Canadian accent in Ren's voice when she said "about."

"We just wanted news," Judith said.

Ren sighed. "I guess all the other regulations are out the window. I haven't been able to get a connection today either. We're moving at a good pace toward Hawaii, though. We can get our answers there."

"Can we wait for the captain to come in?" Judith asked. She wanted someone to take charge, someone with experience and authority and a uniform.

"Suit yourselves. Just don't touch anything." Ren sat back down at her computer and put her feet on the next console. Nora and Judith waited hopefully in the aisle. It was hard to believe there weren't more people here, given that the ship was still moving.

"You might as well sit," Ren said. "In fact, wanna have a go at this computer? It's on a different system than the hotel ones. Maybe you'll have better luck than me."

"Sure." Nora moved to the computer beside Ren. Soon Nora's fingers were flying across the keys and Ren was leaning over her shoulder, watching in admiration.

Judith sat in a swivel chair nearby. "What about other ships?" she asked. "Have you talked to anyone on the radio?"

"Vinny is up in the broadcast tower now. He'll let me know on the 'com if there's any big news." Ren gestured at the intercom set in her console, keeping her attention on what Nora was doing.

"What was the last thing he heard?" Judith asked.

"More or less what the captain told you yesterday. Definitely Yellowstone. The eruption wiped out communications to half the world. All militaries are on high-level alert."

"We saw on the net that the navy is gathering in Pearl Harbor," Nora said, looking up from the screen to meet Ren's eyes for a second. A shadow of a grin flitted across her face.

"Yeah? Then you know more than me," Ren said. "Vinny got a warship on the radio late last night, but they wouldn't tell him anything."

"Why not?" Judith asked.

"They don't want to help us."

"What?"

"They're looking out for their own right now. This isn't a US vessel, technically. Most ships are registered offshore for the looser regulations. I guess it's coming back to bite them."

Judith didn't believe it. *That's what the military is for. Of course they want to help us.* She had always found something comforting in the routines and hierarchy of the military. Most of the people on board were US citizens, no matter where the ship was registered. They'd find the help they needed in Pearl Harbor.

Judith and Nora stayed in the bridge with Ren. She was a bit brusque, but she didn't seem to mind their company. Ren and Nora bonded quickly over the computers. Ren showed her how the internal system operated and monitored most of the ship's essential functions. She explained that it actually took very few people to sail the ship now that most things were automated, and the main control room was actually down on a lower level next to the engine room. Ren herself was a navigator, which was why she was stationed in the bridge. Her family was from Toronto, but she'd had no contact with them since the disaster.

Judith studied the logbooks and emergency manuals she found in the bridge. She needed to keep busy. She hated waiting, staring out at the rough seas and angry skies. She bent over the books, where page after page described the official procedures for all likely seabound emergencies. But what had happened yesterday was unprecedented. There were no guidelines for an apocalypse.

When Captain Martinelli finally returned, he squinted at them, then walked unsteadily to the front windows and lit a cigarette. Judith approached him cautiously.

"Sir, we got everyone settled with food and somewhere to sleep last night," she said. "What should we do with the passengers today?"

The captain put one hand to his head and waved the other like he was trying to swat a gnat.

"I don't want to deal with passengers," he grumbled. "I have a ship to sail."

"But we need to tell them something," Judith said. "Maybe you could come—"

"Get someone else. That Simon fellow was keen."

"But he doesn't have any infor— "

"Just sort yourselves out," the captain snapped. He inhaled through his cigarette and squeezed his eyes shut.

How could he just wash his hands of them like that? Weren't there codes of honor or something for ship captains? Judith wondered if he might have cracked a bit. His quick action had gotten them away from the rush of ash, but maybe he should have just taken them south to another port. Did they really have to sail all the way across the ocean to Hawaii?

Captain Martinelli continued to smoke and glare at the waves. Finally, Judith got frustrated and went to see if she could help Simon. As she left the bridge, she vowed that if things ever went back to normal she'd never go on a cruise for as long as she lived.

Simon

Simon had selected an empty crew cabin with two twin beds for himself and Esther. They didn't need much space. They were lucky to have a small window, little more than a porthole in the base of the ship. Esther slept soundly the first night, but she asked for her mother when she woke. Simon held her and allowed himself to picture Nina's soft face and imagine the feel of her hands, the smell of her perfume. Grief threatened to pull him under, but he couldn't allow that, not when he had Esther to look after.

Esther gripped his hand as they headed down the corridor for breakfast. She kept pulling him off to examine things: luggage carts, doorways into service areas, even diagrams of the ship, with emergency exits marked in red. She seemed fascinated by this new world, but Simon worried about how the trauma of what had happened yesterday would affect her. He just had to focus on getting them through the next few days. He held her hand tighter.

As soon as they arrived in the dining hall, people began coming to Simon with questions and grievances: *Where is the medical center? My neighbor kept me awake with her crying all night. My kid is seasick. This asshole is hoarding food. I want to go home.*

Perhaps because he had been the first to stand up and speak, news spread fast that people should go to Simon with their problems. He welcomed the distraction. He picked up the names of his fellow passengers quickly, like he always had with his students. He did his best to mediate disputes and connect people with others who could help them with their problems.

The nurse's name is Laura. She's in the clinic on Deck 4. Ask for Willow Weathers. She can tell help you find more blankets. I don't know about that, but ask for a crewman named Reggie. I noticed a sign for a chapel. Take a look around Deck 7.

Simon tried to get to know the ship quickly so he could help out, Esther tagging along behind him. The *Catalina* was less than six hundred feet long and had only ten decks. She had space for everyone, but it was tight. Many of the runners had found places to sleep in the crew cabins, and a handful camped on the massage tables in the little spa on the fifth deck. The space was a bit claustrophobic, but Simon preferred the depths of the ship to the unnatural sky outside. Most people avoided the outer decks, fearful that the air was poisoned.

Judith found him midmorning and reported that the captain refused to become involved with the passengers. He immediately took Judith's report to Ana Ivanovna, the highest-ranking person remaining from the original hotel staff. Simon found her in the galley with a clipboard balanced on one arm, busy taking inventory of a huge freezer. When he reported the captain's abdication of responsibility, Ana scowled and chewed at her maroon-painted lips.

"I handle the food and rations. You keep the people out of trouble," she said.

"I'm not sure I can do that," Simon said. It was all well and good for people to come to him to resolve arguments, but that was different than keeping the entire ship running. He was a teacher first and foremost, not a leader.

"Is only for a few days," she said. "You treat them like it is summer camp."

"But maybe you could—"

"I am busy up to my eyeball," Ana said. She waved the clipboard at Simon and slammed the freezer door. A rush of cold air swept over them. "You must do this."

Simon had no desire whatsoever to become a cruise director. He left Ana to her work and headed back out to the dining hall. The people at the tables talked in low voices, staring out at the grim sky. But one group looked up and waved at Simon. It was little Adi Kapur with his mother and father. Both parents kept reaching over to touch their son on his head or shoulders, as if to remind themselves that they were still together. They must be scared too, but it was more important to be strong for their child.

Esther waited for Simon at another table, her legs swinging because they were too short to reach the floor. Simon stood a little straighter. Ana was right: it was only a few days. He could keep things running smoothly until they reached Hawaii.

He started out by asking everyone to clean their own cabins and bathrooms. It didn't seem right for the remaining cleaning staff to do it. Some of the passengers objected, but he brooked no argument.

"These people are survivors just like you," he told a particularly combative cruise passenger when she waved her gold frequent-cruiser card under his nose and demanded room service. "We all have to do our part."

The porters did help care for the common areas, though, keeping things relatively orderly, and some of the passengers pitched in with that too. Simon sent extra able-bodied men to help Reggie and the crew clear the ash away from the ship's outer vents. Eventually they'd get to the decks too. Having chores would help keep people from sitting and staring endlessly at the sea, letting their worries overwhelm them.

As the days passed and they started to run out of areas of the ship to clean, Simon encouraged the passengers and crew to make use of the books, table games, cinema, and other kinds of entertainment on the ship. Willow Weathers, the lounge singer, opened up the cruise director's storage compartments to bring out more games and activities. She even led a yoga class in the middle of the plaza a few times.

People were more likely to complain if they had nothing to do, and they were far more likely to despair. When Simon saw Frank Fordham drifting aimlessly around the plaza on the third day, still inquiring whether anyone had seen his son, he asked him to check out the ship's desalination system and report back. Frank had walked away with purpose. Simon himself felt that as long as he kept moving, his own grief wouldn't catch up to him either. At least not yet.

Esther kept close to Simon's heels, and soon she was predicting his answers to the people who came to him for guidance. When she wasn't following her father, she attached herself to Judith, who was proving to be quite capable. She was clearheaded and organized, and she had no qualms about telling people what to do. With Judith's help, Simon got everyone to fall into what was more or less a routine.

In a way they were lucky to be such a small group. The final head count had settled at 1,114. He could only imagine the disorder and panic that must be rolling through the surviving cities back on land, where the sheer numbers would overwhelm. Here it was like they were a small town dealing with their problems together.

It wasn't entirely smooth sailing on the *Catalina*. Each individual was fragile in a different way, whether angry or distressed or just scared. The lack of information was the worst part. The days had a grim, gloomy look to them, and the nights were pitch black. Simon hadn't seen a single star since they'd been at sea. But by the end of the third day Simon felt they had managed the crisis fairly well. No one in their little world had died or gotten into any serious fights. Soon they'd be back on land, and he would find out what had happened to the rest of his family no matter what it took.

8. The Storm

THE EVENING BEFORE THEY were scheduled to arrive in Hawaii, Simon and Judith lingered in the Atlantis Dining Hall after dinner. They'd eaten only vegetables again today. Ana Ivanovna was determined to conserve all the canned and imperishable food and use up anything that wouldn't keep. The ship was stocked for a seven-day voyage, and cruise ships always carried more than enough food for the all-you-can-eat buffets, but Ana wanted to be extra-careful just in case.

The sky had grown night dark. The seas were rough, the ship rolling more than usual. The *Catalina* was big enough that the movement didn't affect them too much, but tonight it felt different, unsettled. The dining hall was warm, though, and they talked about what they'd do when they got to Hawaii the next day if the planes were still grounded.

"I might get a job to tide me over," Judith said. "And then see if I can make my way to the East Coast. Or maybe Europe. I'd like to work in London."

"I'm not sure anyone will be hiring," Simon said.

"It's not going to be that bad, is it?" Judith asked. "They always say things will be worse than they are. Don't you think everything will have calmed down by the time we get to Hawaii?"

Simon's glass of water slid across the table. He caught it and took a sip.

"I don't know, Judith. There's no precedent for this."

"But the worst is over," she said. "Now it's time to rebuild."

The ship lurched. Lightning flashed outside the window, still far away.

"I don't know if the worst is over," Simon said.

"What do you mean?"

"The darkness. The ash. I think there will be repercussions from the volcano that stretch beyond the US."

No one had managed to access the Internet that day. With the communication links down, there was no way of knowing what was going on in the world. They were totally isolated.

Lightning cracked again, closer this time. It lit the sea with shimmers of white and blue. Wind howled against the large windows.

Esther skipped over from the buffet table.

"Hi, Judith. Hi, Daddy. Ana said I could have an extra piece of cornbread."

Simon smiled at his young daughter. She had been exploring the ship more and more. She'd know every nook and cranny soon. It was nice that he didn't have to worry too much about her wandering off, as there was nowhere for her to go.

"That looks good, button. Did you say thank you?"

"Yup," Esther said. "Ana says we can stay on the ship when we get to Hawaii if we want to. She says it's like a hotel."

"That's an idea," Simon said. "Maybe we'll do that."

"Are you excited about Hawaii, Judith?" Esther asked. She was still wearing her Thomas shirt. Simon hadn't had the heart to make her change.

"I guess so," Judith said, grinning at the little girl.

"Oh, I got to hold baby Cally today!" Esther said as she dug her fingers into her cornbread. "She's so small. And she sounds like a kitty when she cries. Her mommy says I can be her ornery sister if I want to."

"Honorary sister?" Simon asked.

"Yeah, that!"

"That's nice of her."

"I want to be a good big sister," Esther said. "Just like Namie."

Simon exchanged glances with Judith over Esther's head. He felt a twinge in his chest at the sound of his other daughter's nickname. Esther still hadn't shed any tears over her mother and sister. He wasn't sure whether he should prepare her more, impress the likely truth upon her. It would catch up to her in a painful way eventually if she didn't accept their loss.

Based on what Simon had seen of the cloud descending over San Diego and the confirmation that it was volcanic ash, he knew no one could have survived in their city. He still held on to the shimmering hope that Nina and Naomi might have driven out of San Diego and headed south in a hurry, but he couldn't think of a plausible reason why they would. He and Nina had been stressed and prone to snapping at each other lately, but she would never have taken Naomi and left him. He almost wished she were the type just so he could hold on to a sliver of hope that they had survived.

Rain had begun to fall. The storm was getting worse. Simon could barely see anything through the windows. The sky was a writhing, living black. The ship rolled hard, and Judith reached out a hand to protect Esther's head from swinging into the back of her chair. Esther smiled brightly at her, unafraid.

"Judith, can you be *my* ornery big sister until we find Naomi?"

Judith looked startled. Simon had noticed a reticence about her. She kept her emotions under tight control. But Esther didn't seem to mind.

"*Please*, Judy."

"Um, I guess I can," Judith said.

The wind picked up, howling around them like a wolf in the darkness. Empty chairs—and some occupied ones—began to slide across the floor as the ship lurched. People around the dining hall exchanged worried looks. This was not good.

Simon stood, holding on to the table. His chair fell backwards onto the floor with a crash.

"Everyone," he called. "I think we should go back to our cabins and wait this out."

The wind shrieked, and the ship rocked more violently still. Plates and glasses crashed to the floor. The heavy tables began to slide back and forth across the room. Chairs banged against each other, and someone screamed. Then people were jumping up, panicking, stumbling toward the doors, grabbing on to whatever they could.

"Be careful of the glass!" Simon yelled, his voice swallowed by the howls of the wind and the sea. "Stay calm!"

He reached for Esther's hand, but she tumbled away from his grasp, rolling like a potato bug as the ship swayed.

"Esther!"

A table shot across the floor between them, cutting him off. Simon crouched low, trying to keep his balance. There was a scream from the other side of the hall as another sliding table pinned a woman against the wall. The lights flickered.

"Esther!" Simon yelled. He could barely tell who was who in the chaos. He clung to a pillar for support. He couldn't lose his other daughter. He had to keep her safe. She was the only thing that mattered now.

The ship tossed like a rag doll in a washing machine. Waves crashed into it, jarring, erratic. People clung to support pillars, the floor, each other. Glass and porcelain shattered. Food tumbled across the floor, which glittered with shards of glass. A collection of dinner rolls bounced back and forth.

Suddenly, a table rolled sideways across the dining hall and crashed through the tall sea-facing windows. Water and wind surged through the opening. Another table pitched through a window further along, shattering it too. Wave upon wave assaulted the opening, the water rushing in and out of the dining hall.

"Esther!" Simon shouted.

He searched the darkness frantically. The crack of thunder and roar of the waves drowned out people's screams. The *Catalina* tipped sideways, dipping into a deep, dark trough. They tilted, the floor tipping past a forty-five-degree angle. An elderly man lost his grip on a support pillar and rolled toward the broken window. He disappeared into the black hole, his screams lost in the howling sea.

"Esther! Where are you?"

Shadows and lightning flashed. People stumbled to and fro. Chaos. Confusion.

"Esther!"

"I got her!" shouted a voice behind him. "Simon! Over here!"

He followed the voice, pulling himself around to the other side of the pillar. Judith had Esther clutched in her bone-white hands. Relief squeezed at Simon's heart. Judith was wedged into an alcove to protect them both from the tumbling furniture, Esther's arms wrapped tightly around her waist. Esther's eyes were bright with fear and excitement. Lightning flashed across her face.

Simon waited for the next roll of the waves and then lurched across the floor and fell to his knees in front of them.

"Are you girls okay?"

"Yes," Judith said, her face white. "Are we going to sink?"

Simon didn't answer. He lodged himself in front of the alcove, his body between Esther and Judith and the torrent of icy water that burst through the broken windows every time the ship rolled. The others were taking refuge by pillars and in alcoves or stumbling toward the relative safety of the corridor.

"Daddy," Esther shouted. "I feel sick."

"We'll be all right. It's okay if you need to throw up."

Esther's face turned green, but she kept her mouth clenched shut. Simon met Judith's eyes over her head and mouthed *thank you*. She nodded, her jaw set and eyes wide. She didn't let go of the little girl.

Simon gripped the edges of the alcove, his whole body tense, trying to protect them from the tossing sea. The dining hall had transformed into a watery hell. The remaining emergency lights swam beneath seawater as wave after wave surged through the broken windows. Each time the water retreated it dragged glass and food and chairs with it. Pale faces peered out from corners, some covered in blood. Several people vomited as the rolling of the ship continued unabated.

There was no way to move, no way to run for a more protected part of the ship—or the lifeboats. They weren't safe anywhere now.

JUDITH

The storm was endless. Judith felt like she had always been there, huddled in that alcove with Esther and Simon, holding on against the sea. She didn't know how long the tempest actually lasted, but it felt like days. She silently begged the waves to abate. She hated the utter lack of control she felt, never knowing which way the sea would toss them next. They had to make it through. She wanted to live.

Hours passed, but eventually she became aware of the waves lessening. They weren't throwing her quite as hard against the walls. She didn't have to tense as much against the churn. Finally—*finally*—the sea was beginning to calm.

Simon put a hand on her arm. "Judith? I think it's safe enough to move." His voice was hoarse, and he was shivering violently.

Judith was almost too numb to feel the cold. Almost. Her sweater and yoga pants were damp and stiff. Salt coated her face from the water that had come through the broken window. The ship still tossed in the waves, but the violence had abated over the hours. Miraculously, Esther had fallen asleep, her chubby arms still wrapped around Judith's waist.

"Is the storm over?" Judith asked.

"It's a bit calmer at least," Simon said. "Let's get everyone out of here."

Judith slowly extracted herself from Esther's grip and stood. Pins shot through her legs like lightning. Simon offered her a hand to steady her, then knelt to wake his daughter.

The sea was still rough, but they were no longer in danger of hurtling out of the broken window. Judith shivered. She had seen two people disappear into the darkness throughout the night. She hoped she never had to see something like that again.

They made their way painfully out of the alcove, keeping to the edge of the dining hall. They roused the people crouched around the room, urging them to take shelter deeper in the ship.

Judith found the woman she'd met in the plaza with her son, Neal, crouched by a support pillar. She shook worse than a sail in a storm.

"Get up," Judith said. "You'll be safer and warmer in your cabin."

"I can't . . ." The woman's teeth chattered so hard she could barely speak. "He doesn't want to move, and I can't carry him. I hurt my knee."

"Tell him he has to move," Judith snapped, more harshly than she intended. They had to get somewhere warm. *She* had to get somewhere warm.

"Neal, honey," the woman whispered. The mousy-haired boy was curled up with his arms around his head, looking like a drowned rat. "Come on, sweetie, we need to get up."

Neal shook his head, trembling.

"Get up," Judith said again. "We have other people to take care of."

"I can help."

Esther appeared at Judith's elbow. Her face had a red mark from where it had rubbed against Judith's salt-roughened sweater. She crouched down beside little Neal and poked him in the ribs.

"Hey, what's your name?"

The boy peered out from beneath his arms. In the semidarkness his eyes looked like luminous jellyfish.

"Who are you?" he asked.

"I asked you first," Esther said. Then she started tugging on the boy's arm. "Let's go. I can show you a safe place to hide. It's really warm down there."

"Where is it warm?"

"By the engines. And they have lots of tools. Do you like tools? Daddy says I can have some of my own when I get big."

Neal stood and allowed Esther to pull him toward the door leading deeper into the ship. Esther seemed to have things well in hand, and Neal's mother needed Judith's help. She draped the shivering woman's arms around her neck and half carried her toward the door. The floor still swayed.

Neal's mother questioned her feebly about how close they were to Hawaii.

"I don't know any more than you," Judith said. "This storm could have tossed us anywhere."

She felt like the numbness had moved from her limbs, which were warming up with the exertion, into the core of her body. What if they had been carried too far away from Hawaii? How much longer could they sail before they ran out of fuel? They had almost made it.

After installing Neal's mother in her cabin, Judith returned to the dining hall. The injured had been moved with the help of the other survivors, and Simon was directing a group of sailors to improvise some sort of patch for the windows. They used whatever they could find, mostly tables reinforced with metal from the few lounge chairs that had been in storage. The other deck chairs had been swept away by the storm.

Simon told Judith he didn't need any more help, so she headed for the bridge.

9. The Captain

JUDITH

BY THE TIME JUDITH arrived at the bridge it was morning. The sky remained dark gray, with just enough light forcing through the clouds to distinguish it from night. Judith couldn't wait to see a real golden sunrise again.

Ren was hunched over her computer console when Judith entered the bridge. Nora sat beside her, swigging vodka from a cracked blue bottle. They must have located the captain's supply. Both women wore the same clothes as last night when Judith left them to have dinner with Simon and Esther. Was that only yesterday?

"Are you guys okay?" Judith asked.

"We've been better," Ren said, reaching for the vodka bottle in Nora's hand.

"Ugh, are storms always like that?" Judith slumped into a chair and put her head in her hands. "Where's the captain?"

"Up in the radio tower shooting the messenger. Poor Vinny." Ren tipped the bottle up and then handed it back to Nora.

"Huh?"

"Vinny finally got in touch with Hawaii," Nora said. Her eyes were the same bright pink as her hair. "About an hour ago."

Judith bolted upright.

"And?" she prompted.

"The storm was bad for us," Ren said. "Longest and worst one I've ever been through."

"Okay . . ."

"Well, we were just on the edge. This thing was massive." Ren rubbed her eyes, pulling her skin tight across her face. She had kept it together so well over the past few days, taking up most of the slack from the captain, but now she was coming undone. It had to be bad if she was drinking vodka at her post.

"We've been blown far off course," Ren said, "and there were huge storm surges across the Hawaiian Islands. We're talking Indian Ocean tsunami, Hurricane Katrina, Typhoon Haiyan on overdrive. This storm is hell-bent on destruction. Hawaii is a disaster zone. Honolulu got it bad, and the little beach towns got it worse. Pearl Harbor is basically a puddle of mud. We can't dock there anytime soon even if we have enough fuel left to get there."

Judith felt the world narrowing to a point. They had been almost there. They were supposed to be sailing into the harbor this very moment. She had pictured the Hawaii of postcards, despite the darkened skies. She had seen them gliding into Pearl Harbor, taking refuge amidst strong and reassuring warships, walking across a clean white-sand beach. She couldn't reconcile that image with what Ren was saying. They were supposed to be safe.

"What about the navy?" Judith whispered.

"Do you know what happens when a storm surge picks up a warship?" Ren asked, her words slurring.

"No."

"Same thing that happens when a storm surge picks up any other ship and throws it onto the beach."

Judith slid to the floor. The feeling had finally returned to her limbs, but now she felt like her head was full of cotton. No Hawaii. No navy. The ship was still rocking, making her feel ill.

Nora handed her the bottle of vodka, teetering on the edge of her swivel chair. "We got the net back for a few minutes," she said. "Apparently the ash from the volcano is spreading in the atmosphere and making it hard for satellite signals to get through. While we were online, we found a site that seems to have the most updated news. It's on a network with a capacity barely out of the nineties. There have been riots in New York and Atlanta. People are scared."

"How long have we been at sea again?" Judith said. She took a swallow of the vodka, a drink she had never cared for in the best of circumstances. It burnt her throat like bile as it went down.

"This is the fourth day."

"What are we going to do?"

"We have to get to land," Ren said. "Problem is we're not exactly sure where we are right now. The storm dragged us around quite a bit. For all we know Hawaii is a thousand miles away. I'm still working on figuring out our position."

"How much fuel do we have left?"

"A little," Ren said. "But it may not be enough to get us back."

"Does anyone know we're out here?" Judith asked. She felt very small. Rain slicked the bridge windows with a viscous film. It was only a trick of the light, but it looked like there was oil dripping down the outsides of the ship.

"Who? The coast guard?" Ren said. "They could be in worse shape than us. I think we're on our own."

The door burst open.

"Captain! Captain, sir!" It was Manny, the young Filipino crewman who had helped Judith on the day of the disaster.

"Captain's in the crow's nest," Ren said.

Nora giggled, reaching for the bottle again.

"The ship. She is leaking," Manny said.

Nora set the bottle back down.

SIMON

Simon had found Esther and the little boy, Neal, wedged beneath an engine again. The humming of the machine was soothing. The engine room was deserted, apart from the children. The remaining crew was still working on covering up the broken windows around the ship.

Simon returned Neal to his mother, whose name was Mona. She was shuddering with fever, and Simon instructed the little boy to go to Nurse Laura for help if she got any worse. Then they headed for their own cabin, hoping to settle in for some sleep. Esther ran ahead, while Simon knocked on a few doors to check on people along the way. It seemed like the right thing to do.

In a cabin on their corridor, one that had been outfitted with bunks for four, he found Penelope Newton, the woman with the cross necklace who had helped during the birth of little Catalina. She had insisted on taking a hotel staff cabin with her sons instead of a larger stateroom. "Give it to someone who needs it," she'd said.

Now the tiny room was full of people. An older woman Simon didn't know opened the door at his knock.

"And if it be your will, Lord, carry us through the . . ." someone was saying.

Simon started to back out again, but the old woman put a hand on his arm to stop him. Penelope sat on one of the lower bunks, holding hands with people on both sides. She was the one who had been speaking. She opened one eye when Simon entered, then closed it again.

Her three towheaded boys sat cross-legged on a top bunk, looking down on the people filling the room. Horace, one of the runners, still wore the suit he'd had on the first day, the sleeves and cuffs rolled up like Robinson Crusoe's. Elderly cruise passengers squeezed together on the other bottom bunks. A family of four from Michigan sat on the floor, one child in each parent's lap. Everyone's eyes were closed, and they held hands with one or two others.

Penelope's voice was a strong, sure drawl. "And be with my Jeb, Lord, and protect our sacred union. Your eye is on the sparrow, and I know it must be on my little boys' daddy in San Diego too. Please guide the hands that sail this ship. And if we are truly living in the Last Days, then Jesus come quickly. Amen."

Amens circled the room. There was something cozy about the scene, but it left Simon feeling desperately sad. God couldn't possibly be with them, not if he wasn't with Nina and Naomi—perfect, beautiful Nina and Naomi on their way to the dentist.

Simon realized that the whole prayer group had turned to look at him.

"I just wanted to check in and see how everyone's doing," he said. "Any injuries during the storm?"

"The Lord brought us through. Didn't He?" Penelope said.

The people nodded fervently.

"I see." Simon faked a smile. He didn't want to think about God, didn't want to allow the anger and despair to rise in his chest. "Good. Well, I'll leave you to—"

"Would you like to join us in prayer?" Penelope asked.

"I'm Jewish actually . . . I don't think—"

"That's all right. Horace here is a Buddhist," Penelope said, gesturing to the suited man. "We don't think Jesus'll mind too much under the circumstances."

"I don't want to pray," Simon said, his breath catching. He tried to slow his heart rate. He could stay calm in other situations. Why not during a simple prayer meeting?

But Penelope wouldn't be deterred. "Would you mind if we lay our hands on you? You don't have to speak a word."

"What? Why me?"

"You're the one who's been watching out for everyone. We were talking before the prayer, and we think you're the shepherd anointed for this voyage."

The two Michigan parents were nodding. The old woman who had opened the door patted Simon on the shoulder.

"I'm not really doing anything, just helping out."

"Even so," Penelope said, "we all feel better with you taking the lead. Don't ya'll think Simon's got a better head on his shoulders than most?"

A murmur of assent went around the room.

"Thank you. Hopefully we'll be disembarking soon, though. I'd better go get some shut-eye." Simon was surprised to see a flash of disappointment on a few faces when he turned to go. He really didn't like to let people down. He sighed. "I suppose it couldn't hurt."

He went to the center of the cabin, a mere two steps from the door, and got awkwardly to his knees. He was exhausted. He hadn't slept the previous night as he sat tensed in the alcove, trying to keep Esther and Judith from tumbling into the sea. But the weariness was deeper than that—bone deep, soul deep. Every waking moment he was struggling against the despair that threatened to pull him under.

Penelope shuffled forward on her bunk, reminding Simon of a pheasant hen. She put her right hand on his head. It was soft and light. The others reached out their hands, some firm, some trembling, and connected.

Then Penelope prayed, her breath ruffling the hair on the back of Simon's neck.

He couldn't identify what he felt as she spoke. There was energy in the room, perhaps because it was small and stuffy and the floor still tipped, perhaps because everyone was coming down from what he had learned to recognize as a fear high. He'd experienced that high too many times in the last few days. But Simon felt warmed by all the hands on his head and shoulders. It was as if they were sending electricity into him through this act of faith and hope. He didn't know if it was God, but when it was over he felt encouraged and a little more alert.

"Thank you," he said as he stood to go. "Uh, take care, everyone."

"God bless you, Simon." Penelope took the hands of the people next to her again and closed her eyes.

Out in the corridor Simon leaned against the wall. Emergency lights along the ceiling lighted the passageway. It was a strange feeling to have people put their trust in him. He'd rarely had anyone except his family rely on him or look to him for leadership. It scared him, but the more they looked to him, the more he knew he wouldn't let them down. He rolled his shoulders, feeling a little looser and lighter, and went into his own cabin.

JUDITH

At Manny's words, Ren jumped into action, turning to the ship's computers to isolate the problem. She should be able to close the flood doors in the problem area to keep the water from spreading.

Manny darted to the crow's nest and whisked up the ladder to fetch the captain. He stopped when his heels were about to disappear from view and then backed down into the bridge. Vinny and the captain followed.

Captain Martinelli's silver hair had lost its sheen. It looked longer, Einstein-like, without the careful comb and plaster job he'd worn previously. His face was darker than the sky outside.

Judith leapt up and helped Nora to her feet. They backed away, hoping the captain wouldn't notice them. He stumbled on the last step, but when he stood, his back was straight. He walked stiffly to the windows.

"We cannot disembark in Hawaii," he said, his voice distant as the moon. "We don't have enough fuel to reach Asia or return to the continent. Little good that would do." He put both hands behind his back and stared outward, unseeing.

"Uh, sir?" Ren said, looking like she might faint. "There's a leak in the hull. What are your orders?"

"Let the ship sink into the goddamn sea."

Judith started. Manny crossed himself and squeezed his eyes shut.

"Sir?"

Captain Martinelli didn't turn from the window, but his voice was as clear as a thunderclap.

"We have nowhere to go. I will not abandon this ship. Let her sink."

Ren and Nora stared at each other, eyes sharp and fearful despite the alcohol. Vinny's mouth worked soundlessly, and he looked like he might throw up again.

"We have to do some— " Nora began.

"You wish to do something?" Captain Martinelli said. "It's taking too long for you, is it? I agree. I shall open the floodgates."

He strode to a computer console and began tapping.

"Sir!" Ren started up from her chair. "You can't do that! The water—"

"The water? The sea? The infernal goddamn ocean can take us. We shall sink like the *Arizona*, like the *Lusitania*, like the *Titanic* herself!"

"We're not just going to give up and die!" Nora said.

"The world is dead already," Captain Martinelli said, hammering at the computer like a piano.

Judith turned to Ren. "Is he really going to—?"

"Yes."

"He's raving!" Nora said.

Ren curled her fingers around the neck of the mostly empty vodka bottle.

"We have to do something," she said.

Nora joined her, a little unsteady on her feet. Vinny shrunk back from them, clapping a hand over his mouth. Judith watched, paralyzed, as Ren and Nora approached the captain, silhouetted against the windows. He mumbled about ship-wrecks and floodgates and doom.

All was still for one razor moment.

Then Ren lifted the bottle and brought it down on the back of the captain's skull. The crack was worse than thunder.

Captain Martinelli crumpled like paper. Nora caught him and guided him to the floor, while Ren took over the computer.

Manny opened his eyes. He took one fleeting look at the captain. Then his jaw set into a firm line, and he walked over to Judith—not to Ren or to Nora; to her.

"What do we do?" he said.

Judith shook herself. No point in gaping. It was done.

"We need to fix the leak," she said. "And then we need to stop wasting fuel. Ren? Nora? Can you shut off all operations that require fuel temporarily? Even the engines. We need to figure out exactly where we are before we make any decisions about where to go. And keep the captain here. I'm going to find Simon. Manny, come with me."

SIMON

Simon had barely closed his eyes when Judith pounded on his cabin door. He stumbled over to it, still groggy.

"Simon, the captain has lost it!" Judith stood in the corridor with Manny the porter, bouncing anxiously on her toes. "The ship is sinking. We have to make some decisions. You need to come to the bridge!"

"Calm down, Judith," Simon said. "Tell me what's going on."

"We can't dock in Hawaii because of the storm," Judith said, "and we're running out of fuel."

Simon glanced at Esther sleeping beneath the periwinkle blanket. She didn't stir. He stepped into the corridor with Judith and Manny and closed the flimsy door behind him.

"What's wrong with the captain?" he asked.

"He wants to let the ship sink," Judith said.

"There is a leak in the hull, Mr. Simon, sir," said Manny. "She is sinking."

"Are you sure?" Simon asked, following them along the corridor. The emergency lights flickered above them.

"I think something is hitting the ship," Manny said. "Maybe another ship."

"Okay. Manny, can you find Reggie and let him know?"

"The captain is saying—"

"We'll take care of the captain," Simon said.

"Yes, sir."

Manny jogged to the service stairwell at the end of the corridor and started down it. Simon and Judith headed for the bridge.

Ren, Nora, and Vinny were gathered around the captain when Simon and Judith arrived. He slumped on the floor against a computer console, eyes closed. A thin trickle of blood made a track down the side of his face.

"What's going on in here?" Simon said.

Judith pranced beside him like a nervous race-horse.

"He tried to open the flood doors," said Ren—a navigator, if Simon remembered correctly. "The ones I engaged to contain the leak."

"He said the whole world is dead," Nora said.

"I hit him on the head with a vodka bottle." Ren looked like she was in physical pain. Nora put a hand on her shoulder and squeezed it gently.

"Is he alive?" Simon asked quietly.

"Yes."

"Okay." Simon let out a breath he hadn't realized he was holding. "Let's try to keep the violence to a minimum. That's the last thing the world needs right now." Ren started to speak, but Simon held up a hand. "I understand you did what you had to. Now, what's going on with Hawaii? Can we disembark?"

Vinny, a flabby middle-aged man with nervous hands, quickly reported what he'd heard on the radio from another ship, who'd heard it from someone holed up in a villa on a mountainside on Oahu. The Hawaiian Islands had endured a devastating storm surge. The ports were clogged with debris and mud. The people left behind by the torrent were only starting to pick through the wreckage. They weren't in any condition to help refugees.

"The navy was supposed to be gathering there," Judith said quietly.

"I'm sure some of them are still out there," Simon said. "Didn't they see the storm coming and head out to sea? I understand that's safer than being in port during a big storm."

"It is safer," Vinny said, "but they didn't see this one coming. We've become too reliant on satellite imaging to predict the weather, but the satellite signals haven't been getting through properly since the eruption. I've basically been living in the broadcast tower because it seems to be the only way to get any news, and I don't want to miss it."

"What about the Internet?" Simon looked to Nora. She seemed a bit unsteady on her feet.

"Getting spottier," she said. "The major US networks are down. I can barely get the BBC to load because of the bandwidth required. There must be a server running somewhere, though, because there's a rudimentary news bulletin site up. It's preaching doom and gloom mostly."

It seemed incomprehensible that they could be so cut off from the global news. In the wake of the eruption, Simon would have expected twenty-four-hour coverage of the disaster. Instead, deafening silence came from the continents.

"Do you know where we are?" he asked.

"Best as I can figure," Ren said, "we've bypassed Hawaii and been thrown pretty far west. We may be able to wait a few days and then sail back once they've cleared the ports and gotten their relief efforts going. Maybe they can send someone to help us."

"Okay. Providing we can fix the leak, that sounds reasonable. How far could we go on the fuel we have left?"

"I don't know yet," Ren said. "That'll take some calculations. We cut the engines to conserve fuel until we have a new heading. Judith's idea."

Simon nodded. He was exhausted. It was hard to think clearly in this state. "That was the right move," he said. "We should have enough food to last us a bit longer. Maybe some of the navy ships that were on their way to Pearl will be able to help us. Vinny, can you stay on the radio? I'll find someone to help you out if you need it."

Vinny saluted.

"Good. Let's all get a bit of rest and then call a meeting to discuss our next course of action. We should let everyone know we may need to hang on for a few more days before landing in Hawaii."

"What should we do about the captain?" Nora asked. He hadn't moved from where he had slumped against the computer console.

"We'd better restrain him somehow," Simon said, "if he's going to cause problems.

"We can barricade him in his quarters until things calm down," Vinny suggested.

Simon felt like he was in a small boat that had just tipped over the crest of a colossal wave. He didn't know what he was doing. They needed the captain, but not if he was in this state.

"Okay, yes," he said finally. "Lock him up for now and make sure he has plenty of food and water." He hoped he was making the right choice.

"We just started a mutiny, didn't we?" Nora said.

Ren blanched at the word. Simon looked down at his hands

"You had no choice," he said. "We'll do whatever it takes to get through this."

10. The Meeting

JUDITH

AFTER A FEW HOURS of sleep, the *Catalina* survivors gathered in the Pearl Theater. Vinny had showed them how to use the intercom system so they could call everyone together at once. A group of teenagers led by Rosa Cordova's daughter Gracie gathered all of the children in the bowling alley, while the remaining adults squeezed into the theater to discuss the situation.

The stage was nearly two decks tall and featured heavy velvet curtains in shades of purple and gold. A garish lighting fixture shaped like an octopus hung from the center of the auditorium. The theater wasn't quite big enough to seat everyone, but it was more conducive to conversation than the plaza.

Judith stood at the edge of the stage beside one of the velvet curtains and watched the survivors trickle in, somewhat the worse for wear after the storm. They looked tired and rattled. Some people had given up on showering in the days since the disaster. They stared around, glassy-eyed. Others had dressed up like they were going to see a show on the cruise's formal night. The muted tap of high heels echoed on the theater steps.

The crew assembled too. Some had already made subtle changes to their uniforms, leaving buttons undone and forgoing their neckerchiefs. The rules no longer applied.

The most bedraggled among them were those who had fled from San Diego. Like Judith, they had now been wearing the same clothes (their own and a miscellaneous assortment borrowed from the shops) for four days. She had never wanted a nice stiff pair of freshly washed jeans more. At least she had her running shoes, but they were still damp after being soaked during the storm.

When every theater seat had been filled and more people crowded outside the double doors, Simon stepped to the center of the stage. He was supposed to take a nap before this meeting, but he still looked very tired. Briefly, he explained how the storm had devastated Hawaii and no one on the islands could help them right away. They had been driven to the west, far out in the Pacific Ocean and further away from Hawaii and the mainland. They had to be careful about making any movements lest they use up their fuel and exhaust their options.

Simon spoke patiently, and Judith could see the teacher in him. He told everyone they had decided to float for a few days to conserve power until relief efforts were underway in Hawaii and someone was able to send help. Judith thought he sounded perfectly reasonable, describing precisely why this was the best course of action for all.

Judith had always imagined her first boss would be a bit like Simon: a wise mentor; someone to help her prepare for her career. Someone who recognized her potential. It had always been important for her to get recognition and respect. Even here she was desperate for it. All her other plans were spinning out of reach, but at least she had Simon's lead to follow. She wanted to show him how capable she was.

She thought the others must admire Simon as much as she did, but as soon as he closed his mouth, the problems began.

"Who died and made you king?" said Rosa Cordova.

"I can't stand being on this ship another day," shouted a man in the front row. "We need to get to land!"

"My whole family is crammed into a two-hundred-square-foot cabin," someone else called.

"We can't take it anymore!"

"We have family all over the US. We have to find out what happened to them."

"Where's the captain?"

"Captain Martinelli is incapacitated at the moment," Simon said. "I'm just filling in."

He tactfully left out the part about Ren hitting him over the head with a bottle. But this only made the people more agitated. Some stood up from their seats to shout their opinions.

"Why do you get to decide?"

"We almost died last night."

"Shouldn't we vote?"

"I want my feet back on dry land."

Simon looked surprised at the onslaught. "I thought it would be best—"

"We should go to Hawaii."

"My wife is too seasick to leave her room."

"We've been here too long already."

"When's the captain coming back?"

"Let's sail back to California!"

"Why does it matter? The world is already ending."

The words assaulted Simon from all sides. The pressure had been building for days, and now it was boiling over. Judith clenched her fists. She wanted Simon to shout at the people, to make them see how foolish they were being. Simon's decision to wait for a few days was obviously best for everyone.

But Simon didn't yell. He simply listened as the frenzy worked itself out around him. He nodded at some of the speakers to acknowledge their comments but didn't say anything.

Judith tapped her foot, growing antsy. *This is ridiculous. These people should listen. Simon is clearly right, and getting petulant about it won't change that.*

But still Simon remained silent, his face giving nothing away.

Answer them! Tell them this is how it's going to be. Why isn't he saying anything?

Slowly the shouts began to fade. Simon stood still, waiting at the center of the stage. He didn't react to the provocations, and a few people began to look sheepish. The crowd quieted, and eventually even the angriest voices ceased completely.

Judith's attention stayed rooted to Simon. The last echoes disappeared, but still he waited.

Finally, after a full minute of silence, Simon spoke again.

"You're right," he said.

The people leaned forward so they could hear him better.

"We're all scared. We're all angry. Things have spun out of our control so quickly. I don't have any right to make decisions for you. We should all have an equal say in how things are done here. For the moment I suggest we regroup and sort out our communication problem without wasting fuel. I think it would be unwise to sail back to Hawaii until we know they can help us, because if they can't, we'll be out of luck. Does anyone have other suggestions they'd like to offer? Would you kindly form a line in each aisle and come to the stage so everyone can hear you?"

Simon's quiet voice and sane questions worked wonders on the crowd. People began to stand and line up in the aisles. Simon joined Judith by the curtain. Sweat ran from beneath his curly hair despite the cold. He must not be as calm as he seemed. He nodded at Judith, then kept his attention on the people lining up to take the stage. They moved in an orderly fashion, waiting for their turns with only the occasional tapping foot or impatient sigh.

One by one the survivors offered opinions and expressed their frustrations. Most, it turned out, agreed that Simon was right and they needed more information before choosing a new course. A sizable minority wanted to return to California, but others in the crowd swiftly disputed this view. They all saw what had happened to California. Returning was not a viable option, at least for now.

Judith thought they should vote to confirm their decision. Simon's plan had to have majority support by now. She suggested as much to him.

"Not yet," he said. "Sometimes voting can be divisive. Give them some more time."

Judith frowned, but she waited to see what he meant.

The conversation turned subtly toward more productive suggestions, mostly based around the assumption that they would be staying on the ship for a few days until things cleared up in Hawaii.

One man volunteered to organize a crew to repair the storm damages. Another offered to lead aerobics classes so people could work off their cabin fever. Bernadette offered to teach drawing for as long as they had paper. Simon encouraged more suggestions like these.

"I can fish," announced the older man who had the floor. "Let's gather some food so our stores will last a little longer."

"Hear, hear!" someone called.

"What about seaweed? Can we eat that?"

"My mother cooked it for me all the time in Japan. I can help."

More people filed into the aisles to offer help. As the suggestions became more practical, Simon showered praise on the speakers. He offered a few contributions himself, and everyone listened closely to him. He always asked for at least one or two other people's affirmation whenever he approved of an idea. It became a call-and-response conversation.

"My sister and I can set up activities for the kids."

"Good idea. I bet some of the teenagers would like to help you."

"I can arrange a clothing exchange so the runners don't have to keep wearing the same thing."

"I'd really appreciate that. What does everyone else think?"

The more Simon sought out people who agreed with him, the more the crowd turned in his favor. A consensus was emerging. Simon had somehow won everyone over to his side by relinquishing the stage to hear them.

Eventually, Rosa Cordova proposed that they come up with a watch schedule so people could work in shifts and make sure everything was running smoothly on the ship. Simon praised her for her contribution, and she actually blushed. Judith was impressed. He had gotten everyone to agree with his decision to wait a few days before sailing anywhere, but he somehow made them feel like they were part of the decision.

"Shall we select a council to guide us over the next few days?" Simon asked after a while. "It might not be practical to gather in here every time we need to make a decision. Perhaps we can choose representatives from each of the major groups: crew, passengers, and runners."

There were murmurs of assent.

Again Simon waited for a few people to stand up and voice their agreement before he asked, "Who would like to volunteer?"

Rosa was the first to step forward, followed by a middle-aged man Judith didn't know. Some of the other passengers nominated Frank, and he agreed after a moment's hesitation. The crew quickly selected Ana Ivanovna, Reggie, and one of the porters as their representatives. Simon asked who would volunteer for the runners.

"You, of course!" someone shouted from the back of the theater. Simon accepted modestly and asked for two additional volunteers.

"All right then," he said when the selections had been made. "Is it okay if we meet in the mornings over breakfast so we're all fresh?"

Everyone seemed to think that was a great idea.

They got down to the nitty-gritty details of assigning roles. Judith ducked into the cramped backstage area of the theater and found some large posters advertising an old dance show. She brought them out to the stage and used the backs to create a neat record of all the duties. By the time they were finished, every healthy adult on the ship had been assigned either a role on the council or a concrete task for the next twenty-four hours.

Judith took the job of cataloguing nonperishable assets—anything that could prove useful in the days to come. When Simon suggested her for the task, she felt a thrill of pride. Simon's recommendation meant a lot to her.

When the meeting finished, people filed out of the theater with springs in their steps. A bit of purpose and direction was exactly what they needed in the face of that day's setback.

As Judith headed up the aisle toward the doors, she noticed Simon sitting down on the edge of the stage. He was a slight man and didn't seem to take up much space against the backdrop of the huge stage. Yet somehow he made people want to listen to him and follow him. She hoped she would be like him one day. And she would show him she was worthy of his trust.

Simon

Simon thought that had gone surprisingly well. As the assembly dispersed to their new duties, they seemed calmer than they had in days. Their situation was worse than it had been since the eruption, but they knew what to do, at least for now.

He was relieved that no one had asked more about the captain. He'd have a hard time explaining what had happened to the man. In retrospect maybe it was good that the captain hadn't been very visible over the past few days. People weren't too used to seeing him around and looking to him for leadership.

A handful of people stopped to shake Simon's hand before heading out of the theater. He wished Nina could see him now. She would be so proud. He had begun to feel responsible for the people on board the *Catalina*. He wanted to protect them, to keep them safe and calm. If he could do that, maybe he could make up in some small way for his failings before all this began.

He remembered how he had jumped to Morty's every demand when he was in the midst of his tenure bid. All that seemed so insignificant now. The simplicity of their battle for survival eliminated any space for his worries and insecurities. They were going to live. He would make sure of it.

11. The Message

JUDITH

THREE DAYS PASSED, AND the *Catalina* drifted. The survivors were enthusiastic about their new tasks at first. The additional duties helped keep everyone's mind off their families on the mainland and the thwarted promise of Hawaii. They ate their first seaweed meal, and even though the taste made Judith gag, it was satisfying that this meal didn't deplete their stores. She began keeping a tally of their days aboard the ship alongside her inventory notes. They had now been at sea for a full week.

Some people had taken to staring at the waves for hours on end, searching for imaginary landmarks that appeared and disappeared with each swell, but Judith would never allow herself to become one of them. She took up running again. She hadn't gone more than two days without a run since she was thirteen, and it made her antsy. She jogged in wide circles around the main deck, wishing for the straight expanse of a California boulevard. It was cold all the time now, but this was better than running inside the claustrophobic little gym, and the treadmills had been unplugged to conserve energy anyway. On the deck she had to dodge people and run up and down slippery steps. Watching out for obstacles made it easier to keep her mind from straying to regrets, the missed opportunities with her family, the life she had lost on land, her potential future.

Sometimes Esther ran beside her for a few paces, full of questions. She always popped up in unexpected places. She had taken to sea life better than most. She would chatter to Judith for a few minutes and then veer off to try to climb the exhaust vents or trail after Reggie and the crew as they went about their work.

When Judith wasn't running or working on the resources inventory, she hung out in the bridge with Ren and Nora. Vinny descended from the broadcast tower every so often to report on the communications (or lack thereof). Simon had sent a woman named Kim Wu to assist him so he wouldn't have to pull such long shifts. She had been in San Diego for an IT conference, but she fit into the bridge team well. The Internet worked in fits and starts, but precious little information came out of Hawaii. The Pacific Ocean was beginning to feel like the Bermuda Triangle.

"Where's the fucking BBC when you need them?" Nora pushed back from the computer that she had adopted next to Ren's console. She started twisting her earrings one by one.

"What's wrong?" Judith asked. She stood at the front window, looking at the persistent gray clouds that hung above the sea. She missed sunshine so much.

"Some nut job says a tsunami took out half the Eastern Seaboard," Nora said. She scowled at the computer screen. "He's the only one who's transmitting a reliable signal at the moment, but his site is full of conspiracy crap and apocalypse porn. It's hard to sift through it for the real news."

"Where is he?" Judith asked.

"Could be on this ship for all I know. He claims to have 'sources,' but I don't see how he could have any information when I can't access a single major news outlet or social network."

"He says there was a tsunami?"

"Let's see . . . triggered by an undersea earthquake . . . he says every coastal city from Boston to Atlantic City got wiped right into the sea by a monster wave."

Judith imagined a map of the US where each section was being systematically blurred out. It felt cartoonish, impossible. The report had to be wrong. They needed a more reliable source.

"Does he know anything about the navy?" she asked. "I'm sure some of them got out of Pearl Harbor before the storm. They would know the truth." Judith had begun to think of the navy as a shining beacon of order and purpose. If they could just meet up with a navy ship, they would be okay.

"Sorry, Jude. This isn't the kind of stuff you want to read about the navy," Nora said. "I'm telling you: he's full of shit."

Judith walked around behind Nora's computer console. "What's he say about them?"

"Nothing coherent."

A white page filled Nora's web browser. It looked like a homemade site from the early 2000s, with a simple index function and no sense of design at all. It contained no images, only a lot of headlines in flashing, multicolored text. Judith read the first few.

NEW YORK DROWNED!
GOVERNMENT COVER-UP OF YELLOWSTONE
RED FLAGS CONFIRMED
RIOTS IN LONDON OVER LIMITED FOOD SUPPLY
ASH PRECEDES SEVEN YEARS OF WINTER

Nora scrolled down. "See, it's all this doom and gloom stuff, but there seem to be nuggets of truth every once in a while. He does have a contact page, and sometimes he'll post reports from people who might actually know something."

"Where's the stuff about the navy?"

"Hold your horses. Here we go: BATTLESHIPS TURN TO PIRACY."

Judith bent closer to read the article.

Sources confirm a coordinated effort by the US Navy to pillage resources from any ships they meet on the high seas. Warships have been spotted surrounding distressed vessels and draining them of fuel and food, like a swarm of locusts. Too much like a Robert Louis Stevenson novel, you think? Think again. The navy is coming, and they want your fuel. Our sources report that the battleships lure their victims with promises of aid. Beware, readers of the seas: the navy is not your friend.

Ren had leaned over from her computer to read alongside Judith. "He seems pretty sure."

Nora snorted. "He's a geek with a decent connection on a power trip."

"But if he gets reports through a contact page . . ."

"He embellishes," Nora said. "There's probably one ship out of thousands that went rogue. He's decided that's not interesting enough, so now we have the entire US Navy turning to coordinated piracy. And the entire East Coast being wiped out by one wave! How likely do you think all that is?"

Judith banished the image of the warship blowing a path through the civilian ships in San Diego harbor. She hadn't told Nora about that.

"Isn't it strange that they haven't issued some sort of statement themselves?" Ren said. "We haven't heard anything from a government source since before the disaster."

"Do you think the government has collapsed?" Judith asked quietly.

"It sure feels like it," Nora said.

"That's just impossible." Ren fiddled with the buttons on her keyboard. "You never think something like this will happen in your lifetime. I mean, we watch disaster movies and joke about the zombie apocalypse all the time. Now that this—whatever this is—is actually happening . . ."

"We're out of contact, that's all," Nora said. "Once we get back to land, things will be better. But you're right. I had no idea how bad it would feel to be off the grid, and I practically live inside the grid."

"It sounds like the US will never be the same, though," Judith said. "Even if that East Coast tsunami didn't happen."

She still sometimes believed that they'd sail into a harbor and find it had all been a mistake. The nightmare would be over. San Diego would still be intact. All of their families would be fine. She could go back to her perfectly coordinated life.

They stared out at the restless, white-capped sea. The clouds were heavy and sullen. Judith hoped there wouldn't be another storm. It had been three days since the last one, and she was still waking up in a cold sweat picturing people tumbling out of the broken dining hall windows.

"What do you think you'd be doing if you weren't here?" Nora asked suddenly, clearly wanting to change the subject. She climbed out of her chair and sat on top of the desk behind it, putting her large maroon combat boots on the seat.

"Studying for finals," Judith said. It was hard to reconcile the image of her old self sitting in the library in front of a stack of neatly color-coded notes with her current reality.

"Lame."

"I'd still be on this ship," Ren said. "How's that for strange?"

"That is trippy," Nora said. "I would be here too, unless I decided to jump ship in Puerto Vallarta. I thought about it, actually. I've always wanted to live in another country."

"I've had my share of wanderlust too," Ren said. "I work on a cruise ship after all. Cruises aren't the most badass places to be a sailor, but I've always loved the idea of being at sea every day, taking shore leave in exotic cities." She sighed. "Now I just want my feet on dry land."

Nora put a hand gently on her shoulder. Ren gripped it for a moment.

"What about you, Judith?" Nora said. "Were you planning a graduation trip or anything?"

"Not really. I was going to start working right away," Judith said. "I guess I'd take business trips eventually. London. Hong Kong. Tokyo. I didn't study abroad in college, because I wanted to focus on internships."

"You were one of those overachievers, eh?" Ren asked.

Judith nodded. "I had it all planned out: work for two or three years and then get an MBA. I've had my eye on a CEO's corner office for as long as I can remember."

"It could still happen," Nora said. "*I'd* hire you."

"I might never even get my degree now. All that work, and I don't even have a BA to show for it."

"At least you're alive," Ren said.

"I guess so," Judith said.

"I don't know how you two decided what you wanted to do so early on," Nora said. "I'm good with computers, but I still don't know what I want to be when I grow up, and I'm twenty-eight!"

Judith frowned. A chasm seemed to yawn before her. She had always been so focused. Her teachers loved to talk about her potential, yet she had absolutely no idea who she was apart from her ambitions. Suddenly all that mattered was surviving—

and the relationships she had never given enough time before. She should have taken more weekend trips to see her parents. She should have spent more afternoons hanging out with Sonya. She should have gone on more dates! All that texting and flirting had seemed like such a waste of effort. Now she wasn't sure why she had spent so much time alone with her goals.

Well, that wasn't entirely true. She'd seen what happened when her financially successful father divorced her mother, leaving her at the constant mercy of alimony negotiations until she met her new husband. Judith always knew she would be self-sufficient, successful in her own right. She never wanted to be vulnerable the way her mother had been for those years. Right now she depended on the other people on the ship, but this wouldn't last. They'd have to find a safe harbor soon.

Footsteps rang out on the broadcast tower ladder. Kim Wu's shoes appeared, then the stained knees of her khaki pants.

"Word coming in on the radio! It's the navy!"

SIMON

The meeting was going well, all things considered. They had decided to meet in the Mermaid Lounge, the nightclub on the ninth deck, because the Atlantis Dining Hall was still damp from the storm and smelled like rotting food. The Mermaid Lounge had a long bar overlooking the sea, round tables, and booths with couches covered in shimmering velvet. Green drapes hung on the walls, along with jewel-toned prints of buxom mermaids with artful hair arrangements.

It was early afternoon, but the light coming through the sea windows was weak. Simon worried about the effect the diminished sunshine would have on morale. He hardly dared think about what it would do to plant life around the world. They'd been able to skim seaweed off the top of the sea after the storm, scrubbing it thoroughly in hopes of avoiding contamination, but he worried about what they would do if it started to die too. *You can't think like that. You'll be back on land soon.*

Simon spent too much time worrying these days. They had been at sea for a week, but already it felt like a decade—or at least like he had aged a decade. He shook his head and returned his attention to the issue at hand: space. They were always talking about space.

"We should be allocated another cabin," Rosa Cordova was saying. "We paid to be on this ship, and it isn't fair for so many children to have to share rooms. The Raines family feels the same way. Their kids are too old to be crammed together like that."

"What do you expect us to do, Rosa?" said Horace, one of the runners. "Sleep in the bowling alley?"

"Hate to break it to you, but you're not on vacation anymore. You can't be so selfish," Frank grumbled.

"It's not selfishness," Rosa snapped. "We need space for the children. Us old folks are fine, but the children need room!"

"The kids are all right, Rosa," Frank said. "They're basically having a sleepover."

"They are all right," put in Ana Ivanovna, "but they are eating like hyenas. Maybe you take less room because you are taking more food, eh?"

Rosa scowled and adjusted the sunglasses hanging from the neck of her shirt.

The arguments bounced back and forth. There was still too much division between the runners, passengers, and crew. It didn't help that many of the crew came from poorer countries and didn't always speak English well. Ana Ivanovna was their primary advocate. She was more than a match for Rosa Cordova.

"You are wanting the crew to bunk together, yes?" Ana continued. "So the runners can live in the crew cabins? You are not thinking that we are still working to make sure everyone has food, and for this work we are not getting paid."

"Well, we're certainly not getting a refund," Rosa huffed. "Do you know how long we saved to take this vacation?"

"Is no vacation," Ana muttered.

"Please, would you shut up about how much you paid for your rooms?" Frank said, not quite under his breath.

Rosa swelled like a bullfrog.

"Let's hang on for a few more days," Simon cut in. "This is all temporary. I think the kids will be okay bunking together for a little while longer. Kids are resilient, and under the circumstances they probably prefer the company." He thought about Esther, who was proving to be even more resilient than he could have hoped. Once again he was grateful that he didn't have to worry as much about where she was in their little self-contained world. "Can we get back to the cleaning issue?" he said. "I think Ana raised a good point about the shifts—"

The lounge door swung open with a bang. Judith dashed over to where the council sat around the largest round table. She still wore her running shoes and her souvenir *Catalina* sweater. She'd found one for Esther to wear too. It had been getting colder since the storm.

"We got a message from the navy!" Judith announced.

"What kind of message?"

"Radio. They're calling for ships in the vicinity to head to Guam."

Simon felt a surge of hope. He sat back in his chair, trying to picture where Guam was. If he remembered correctly, it was about three-quarters of the way between Hawaii and the Philippines, north of Australia and Papua New Guinea. They'd been drifting west since the storm, so there was a chance that they weren't too far away.

"Do they have food?" Horace asked, fingering the rolled cuff of the suit jacket he had been wearing all week.

"I don't know," Judith said. "Vinny and Kim didn't actually talk to anyone. There's a message playing on a loop, and they happened upon the right frequency when they were scanning for signals."

"Can we make it to Guam on our remaining fuel?" Frank asked.

"Ren thinks we can."

"What kind of aid are they offering?" Simon asked.

Judith hesitated. "Well, they're not technically offering anything. The message sounds like it's meant for navy ships in the area, but they'd have to help a bunch of Americans, wouldn't they? If they're gathering in Guam, it has to be in better shape than Hawaii."

"Finally," Rosa said. "This is what we've been waiting for."

"I've always wanted to go to Guam," Frank said. "My son was stationed there once, but I never made the trip."

Simon hesitated. Would the navy really be in a position to help an entire cruise ship full of people if they were still trying to establish contact with their own vessels? No one else seemed to share his reservations.

"I came straight to you so the representatives can vote," Judith said. "Can we set our course for Guam? Ren says we've been drifting in the right general direction."

"I think we should establish contact first and let them know we're coming," Simon said.

"We can do that on the way," Rosa said.

"Yeah, let's head for Guam," Frank said. "I can't wait to get off this infernal ship—and back on US soil."

"Let's vote," Horace said.

"All in favor of Guam!"

Hands were raised all the way around the table. Simon abstained. For some reason he got a sinking feeling in his stomach at the thought of the automated message. What if they got to Guam and no one was there? But Judith's face lit up when the motion passed, and she darted back to the bridge before Simon could speak to her about his reservations.

12. Guam

JUDITH

JUDITH STOOD IN THE bow as they approached Guam. The wind blew her hair back from her face. She'd washed it in seawater that morning, and it felt crinkly and rough but cleaner than it had been in days. They'd been on restricted rations, trying to use fresh water only for drinking and food preparation. The desalination system cleaned the water using energy from the running engines, so as they sailed toward the shores of Guam they were replenishing their supply. Simon had insisted that they store most of the water in case they encountered problems in Guam. It seemed like an unnecessary precaution to Judith. Their journey would end on this little island at the edge of Oceania.

It had been three days since they'd made the decision to head west, ten days since the disaster. Judith had gotten used to a new normal on the ship, following the same routines each day, but she was ready for the adventure to be over.

She fixed her eyes on the horizon. The sky was dark for early afternoon, the sea rougher than it had been since the storm. White-tipped waves cascaded against the hull and stretched outward like strobes of light. Any minute now they'd see the outlines of warships, shorelines, structures, civilization. Their time on the *Catalina* had been surreal, but soon they'd be with the navy. Everything would be okay.

Others joined her on deck. The people were in good spirits, stretching their legs and reaching their arms out toward the obscured sun. It was like they'd been living in a cave for a month and were finally walking toward the opening. They chattered about their plans for when they reached the island.

"I'm going to kiss the ground. I don't care how dirty it is."

"I want to drink a cold beer on the beach. Think the navy has any left?"

"I just want to find a way home . . . preferably on a plane."

"This trip has been long enough for me."

"I'm never setting foot on another boat."

Judith couldn't help thinking that when they reached dry land they'd find out the eruption hadn't been as bad as they'd heard. The world would have stepped in to help, and they'd already be rebuilding. This whole detour at sea would be like a dream.

Simon was up in the broadcast tower, monitoring communications with Vinny, but Esther had been allowed on deck. She climbed up on the railing next to Judith.

"Judy, can we go on a battleship when we get to Guam?" Esther asked.

"Maybe. They probably have strict rules, though," Judith said. "I don't know if they'll let us."

"Frank says all battleships are warships, but not all warships are battleships." Esther giggled. "Did *you* know that?"

"No, I didn't."

One of Esther's pigtails had come loose in the breeze. Judith combed her fingers through the little girl's hair to fix it. Esther grinned up at her.

"Do they have turbine engines or electric prop'uller engines on battleships?"

"I have no idea."

"Can we go to the beach when we get to Guam?"

"Maybe. You're not tired of the ocean?"

"No way. I like the ocean. I want to be a sailor when I grow up. Do you think I can, Judy?" Esther asked, her brown eyes bright and hopeful.

"I think you can be whatever you want," Judith answered.

"That's what Daddy said, but he was distracted. He's always busy, isn't he, Judy?"

"Everyone relies on him," Judith said.

"Yup. That's because he's the smartest man on the ship. Don't you think so?"

"Yes, I think you're right."

Esther nodded proudly. "Reggie's stronger, though. He's the strongest man on the ship. And Frank is the best engineer on the ship. And Mrs. Cordova is the meanest lady. And Mrs. Newton is the best pray-er . . ."

Esther rattled on about the people of the *Catalina*, and Judith only half listened. Was there something on the horizon? That smudge of gray looked different from the cloud-burdened sky. Judith gripped the cold railing. Yes, there was definitely something solid there. Was it the coastline taking shape?

"I see it!" Manny said, joining them at the railing. He had given up on wearing the sailor's collar with his uniform. His shirt was unbuttoned, revealing a silver crucifix hanging on a slim chain. "It is the island."

"Land," Judith whispered. It wasn't a mirage. They were going to be okay.

It took an eternity for the island to grow large before them. The hazy weather kept the details indistinct as they drew close. Judith searched for some sign of navy ships gathering, but everything was amorphous, forming and dissolving in the haze with each shift of the wind.

Then quite suddenly a concrete shape emerged. A small boat sailed directly toward them from the island. A pair of big guns stood out on the prow, and an American flag flew in the wind. There was one painted on the hull as well.

We're saved! Judith thought.

The boat slowed when it was within a hundred yards of the *Catalina*. Then a voice amplified by a loudspeaker droned across the water.

"You are in restricted waters. Turn back, and we will let you go peacefully."

"What does that mean, Judy?" Esther asked.

Surprise and confusion spread across the deck faster than wildfire.

"You are in restricted waters," repeated the voice on the loudspeaker. "Turn back."

"What do we do?" Manny said.

"They can't turn us away!" Judith spun to look up at the bridge. Could Simon hear this?

The *Catalina* rumbled, and then the engines went quiet. They drifted to a stop. The sudden silence was deafening. Were they going to turn around?

"You are in restricted waters. We have no room for refugees. Turn back, or you will be fired upon."

"No," Judith said. "They have to help us."

"Repeat. You will be fired upon."

They couldn't be serious. But the boat still rode the waves in front of them, the deck deceptively empty. The guns waited in the prow.

"Judy? What's going on?" Esther asked.

Judith felt an electric shock go through her when she realized Esther was still beside her, totally exposed.

"Esther," she said quickly, gripping the little girl's shoulders, "you need to go back inside the ship right now. Do you understand?"

"But—"

"Right now. It's not safe here."

"I want to see!"

"No. Go inside and take all the other kids with you," Judith ordered. "Get Neal to help you. Go find Mrs. Gordon and baby Cally and stay with them, okay?"

"But I want to go to Guam!"

"Now!"

Esther continued to complain, but she did as she was told. She gathered up Neal and the other children on the deck and led the way back into the *Catalina*. Judith and Manny exchanged worried looks and turned back to the sea.

Two sailors had emerged and taken hold of the guns on the smaller boat. They couldn't truly be planning to fire on a distressed ship full of civilians, could they? Not when they weren't in any danger. It was impossible. Judith gripped the railing tighter, but she didn't take cover.

SIMON

Simon and Vinny sat in the broadcast tower, headsets clutched over their ears. The radio repeated the same message that was being relayed over the other ship's loudspeaker. Panic simmered in Simon's chest as he looked back and forth between the threatening ship and his daughter on the deck.

"Hold your fire," he begged through the radio. "We need water and fuel. We're desperate."

Down below, Esther gathered the other children and disappeared from view. Simon breathed a little easier, but many of the adults were still on the deck, staring at the ship blocking their path to Guam and safety.

"You are in restricted waters," said the voice on the radio. "Turn back, and we will let you go peacefully."

"We have no weapons," Simon shouted into the mic. "We're American citizens!"

The voice repeated the same emotionless message. *Restricted waters. Turn back. We will fire.* Vinny stared imploringly at Simon, wide-eyed. There had to be some mistake. They couldn't mean it.

The *Catalina* floated like a big, lumbering target in front of the little mosquito boat. She was no match for the other ship, but they had nowhere else to go.

"Please," Simon said. "You have to let us come ashore. We have children aboard."

There was a pause.

"We are under strict orders not to permit any nonmilitary personnel to pass beyond this point."

"Please, it's a matter of life and death."

"We are under strict orders . . ." The voice on the radio sounded less sure, perhaps a bit more human.

"We've stopped our engines," Simon said. "Please talk to me for a minute, sailor. And for God's sake, hold your fire!"

"I'm sorry, sir. We can't let anyone disembark in Guam."

Simon wrapped his fingers around the cord to the headset, casting about for something to say.

"What's your name, sailor?"

"Seaman Michael Williams."

Whoever manned the loudspeaker outside was still shouting warnings at the people on deck. Some crouched low, gazes fixed on the guns. Judith remained standing, her blond hair flying loose from her ponytail.

Simon couldn't let them down. He had to get through to this man.

"Michael, my name is Simon. I have a daughter on board this ship named Esther. Her mother, Nina, and her sister, Naomi, were lost in San Diego. We've been sailing for ten days, and there are over a thousand people on board. We won't last another week without more food, and we don't have enough fuel left to sail for that long anyway."

Simon swallowed hard and took a gamble. "Michael, do you have any children? Or siblings?"

The radio was silent for a heartbeat. Then: "I have a kid brother."

"What's his name?" Simon asked.

"Matt."

"If it was Matt on this ship, you would want someone to disobey orders to help him. Wouldn't you, Michael?"

"I'm sorry. We can't help."

"Please, Michael, we have nowhere to go," Simon said. "And we need answers. We have no idea what's going on in the rest of the world."

The boat still bobbed in front of the *Catalina*, guns trained on the decks. It was small enough to fit inside the Atlantis Dining Hall with room to spare, but those guns made all the difference.

"The world has gone to hell, sir," said the voice on the radio.

"At least tell us where we should sail if you won't help us," Simon said. "Please, Michael, for your brother's sake."

Desperation buzzed in Simon's head. He felt like he was coming down with a fever. He didn't know what to do from here.

"There are no safe harbors," Michael said. "The storms are getting worse. There were earthquakes in China and . . . Sir, I can't speak to you anymore. You have to turn your ship around."

Simon swallowed hard, fighting to stay calm. "I know you're trying to do your job, Michael," he said, "but if this is the end of the world, isn't helping a group of innocents the right thing to do?"

Michael was silent for a moment. "We don't have any help to give you," he said after a while. "Guam is basically ruined. The storm surges have been catastrophic. We're barely surviving ourselves."

Simon leaned back in the chair and let out a long breath. So that was it. Things were just as bad here as they were at sea.

"Thank you for your honesty, Michael," he said. "We won't cross into the restricted zone, but please stop pointing your guns at our people. Is there anywhere we can get fuel to keep us going for a bit longer? We have to keep trying to get back to our families."

There was a long silence on the other end of the radio. Simon wondered if they had lost the connection. They needed help . . . information . . . something. He had no idea what they were going to do.

"Seaman Williams?"

He waited. Still no answer. The men at the guns below hadn't moved.

Then the radio crackled.

"Permission to come aboard your ship, sir."

Simon exchanged glances with Vinny.

"Sorry? Could you repeat that?"

"Permission to come aboard the cruise ship *Catalina*," Michael said. "I'll collect the passenger manifest to add to our records."

"Okay," Simon said slowly. "But please don't bring any weapons."

"Roger that. Let down a ladder from the starboard lifeboat deck. I will be unarmed. Over and out."

Simon pulled the headset down around his neck. "What's that about?"

"Maybe he doesn't want his superiors to hear what he has to say on the radio," Vinny said. "Otherwise, he'd just ask us to transmit the list—or read it out to him."

"But they'll know that," Simon said. "I wonder what he wants. Hold down the fort here, Vinny. I'm going to meet our Seaman Williams."

JUDITH

The loudspeaker on the other ship ceased abruptly. Judith tensed. Would they start shooting? She felt like she was watching the entire scene from underwater. She should duck in case they opened fire, but she still didn't believe the navy would hurt them. What had happened in San Diego was a fluke, an aberration. Any minute now they'd offer to lead the *Catalina* in to port.

The haze had cleared a bit, revealing the coastline of Guam. They were so close. There were definitely warships moored there. She couldn't make out any buildings, though. That was strange. They should see the city by now.

A small speedboat appeared from behind the other ship, apparently launched from its stern. It approached the *Catalina*, manned by a lone sailor. Judith saw the fuzz of a crew cut and thick eyebrows on a high forehead before the boat sped around the side of the *Catalina*. She jogged after it toward the starboard lifeboat deck, Manny following in her wake.

A burly blond crewman—she thought his name was Pieter—was lowering a ladder over the side of the ship beside the foremost lifeboat. The little speedboat bobbed in the shadow of the *Catalina*. It was dark gray, like the sea beneath it, with a powerful-looking outboard motor. The sailor tied the boat to something below and began to climb the ladder. He hunched his shoulders as he ascended, as if every second he expected someone to fire down on him. Judith felt like she had seen this man before. Could it be the same face she had glimpsed behind a gas mask in San Diego harbor? The odds were impossibly slim.

Pieter reached down to help the young sailor aboard, but he waved off the assistance and climbed up by himself. He wore a crisp uniform and carried himself with an obvious sense of assurance, as if he was completely aware of every muscle in his body at all times. Beneath his thick eyebrows he had striking blue eyes, a classic square jaw, and a full mouth.

Judith felt suddenly shy. The sailor was movie-star hot. He looked like a high school quarterback in a teen movie, the kind that was always played by a twenty-six-year-old actor.

Simon appeared in the ship's entryway.

"Welcome aboard the *Catalina*, Seaman Williams," he said.

He moved deliberately, but Judith could tell he was nervous.

"Are you Simon?" the sailor asked.

"I am."

"You're the captain?"

"No. The captain of the *Catalina* is indisposed," Simon said. He stood at a distance from the young sailor, not offering his hand.

"I see."

"Why are you here, Michael?"

The sailor scanned the deck, as if expecting someone to be listening in. He noticed Judith, and his eyes widened slightly.

"I want to come with you on the *Catalina*," he said finally.

"You're deserting?"

Michael flinched at the word. "I'll work in exchange for a lift," he said.

"You won't be any better off with us," Simon said. "We're dangerously low on fuel, as I said on the radio."

"I know where you can get more fuel," Michael said. "Enough to sail on to Asia."

"Why are you here?" Simon repeated the question so quietly, Judith could barely hear it.

Michael's jaw tensed. Finally, as if the words were being torn from him, he said, "We're being ordered to gun people down. Refugees, any ships that get in our way, anyone who won't listen to our warnings. I can't do it anymore."

Judith couldn't believe it. The world had gone mad. The navy was supposed to help them!

"Are they guarding something on the island?" Simon asked.

"We don't have much in the way of food and fuel, but they're defending whatever's left," Michael said. "There's no leadership. The men are fighting each other. They don't know what else to do."

"But why come with us?" Simon asked.

"The navy is supposed to be better than this, sir. I want to do what's right. I have to get back to my family. My first duty is to them. You reminded me of that."

Simon didn't answer. He studied the younger man, but his face gave no indication of what he was thinking. Judith wished she could read his thoughts. Did he believe this stranger? Would he trust him?

"Has there been any news from back home?" Simon asked.

"The East Coast is a shambles," Michael said. "There were riots after the eruption, and then some sort of tsunami. I'm not really sure what happened. All the food's gone, hidden away in people's homes—if they still have homes. Water supplies are tainted. No one knows where the president is. If he's still alive, he's not talking to us."

"What about internationally?"

"Same thing. Panic. Looting. They don't have aid to send. It's the end of the world."

Judith stared at Michael. He seemed to be confirming what that crazy conspiracy theorist said on his website. About the East Coast. About the complete breakdown of order. It couldn't be that bad. It just couldn't.

"Things will have to calm down eventually," Simon said, his face grave. "We need to hold on until then. I'll be honest with you, Michael. You wouldn't be any better off with us."

Michael looked back toward his ship. It drifted silently on the waves, the guns still pointed at the *Catalina*'s decks.

"I can't stay in Guam." Michael turned back to Simon. "If you give me a ride to land, I can help you get more fuel. But we need to move fast."

"We'll have to put it to the council," Simon said slowly.

"There's no time," Michael said. "You just have to trust me. I swear I'll help."

Simon studied Michael for a moment, then walked over to Judith and leaned close to speak to her privately.

"I'm not sure what to do, Judith," Simon said heavily. "What do you think?"

Judith met Michael's eyes. They were a blue so light they made the sky seem gray. His navy uniform looked clean and sure, like order, authority. More importantly, he had an open, honest face. He seemed like he meant what he said. He was trying to do the right thing.

"We need fuel," Judith whispered, "and if he's telling the truth, he might be the only one who can help us get it. I think we should trust him."

"Okay then," Simon said. "I agree." He turned back to Michael and said, "You may join us. What do we need to do?"

Michael nodded, his shoulders relaxing a bit. "There's a wrecked cargo vessel off an atoll that we haven't had time to salvage," he said. "It's carrying a load of fuel tanks, but we need to move fast. They're scheduled to retrieve them at 0900 tomorrow."

"What about your comrades on the other ship?"

"The captain's son is my friend," Michael said. "We were in basic together, and I helped him out of a tight spot. The captain owes me. As long as we don't let on that we're going after the fuel, he'll let me go. I just need to talk to him."

"Okay then. Welcome aboard," Simon said. "Judith, will you take Seaman Williams up to the bridge? I need to explain the situation to everyone, and then I'll join you so we can make a plan. Manny and Pieter, would you get everyone else off the deck, please, just in case?" Simon gave Michael one final, long look before heading off.

Judith jerked her head toward the doorway, and Michael followed her into the ship, leaving the view of Guam behind them. She led him through the corridors toward the bridge.

She wasn't sure what to say to him, so they walked in silence. He was tall and broad shouldered, and the way he carried himself made him seem much larger. Judith was conscious of her seawater-washed hair and sweats. She had grown used to seeing the same faces on the ship, and it was very strange to have a newcomer.

"So," Michael said finally. "You're Judith?"

"And you're Michael."

They climbed a service stairwell, the same one that Manny had taken her through a lifetime ago. She stayed two steps ahead of Michael, and she felt the added height gave her a slight advantage. She still didn't know what to say. How were you supposed to start a conversation with someone who had just told you the world was ending?

"So . . ." Michael tried again. "What's a girl like you doing in a place like this?"

"Seriously?" Judith smiled in spite of herself.

"Worth a shot," Michael said. "Where are you from?"

"San Diego. We escaped from the harbor."

Judith glanced back fast enough to see a flicker of uncertainty cross his face. She stopped short. He took one step up, closer to her, before he stopped too.

"I—"

"Were you there?" she demanded.

"My ship escaped from San Diego, yes," he said.

"You gunned through all those people."

"We couldn't help them," Michael said. "Any ships that stopped would have had their equipment clogged by ash in minutes. We barely escaped."

"But you're the navy! You should be helping, not firing on civilians."

"You're right," Michael said. "When that ash cloud rolled in . . . the officers just panicked. I know we let people down. I was scared shitless, just like everyone else."

"That's no excuse," Judith said.

"No, it's not," he said. "The navy should be better. I never thought we'd do something like that." Michael met Judith's eyes steadily. "I gave my whole life to the navy, you know, to serving my country. I was really part of something, but now . . ."

Judith scowled. "I thought a crisis was supposed to bring out the best in people," she said. "How could they just turn the *Catalina* away when we came to them for help?" She had put so much hope in the navy waiting for them in Guam. Deep down she believed what had happened in San Diego was an accident, a one-off. Now she felt betrayed.

"I don't know," Michael said, "but I want to make it right, do what the navy really stands for, even if my superiors won't. That's why I'm here."

He seemed sincere, but Judith wasn't sure what to believe anymore. The people they should be able to count on had let them down again and again. She felt like she was caught in a whirlpool, grasping for some kind of stability, for an anchor. Tears welled up, and she tried to blink them away.

Michael put a hand on her arm.

"I didn't mean to upset you," he said.

Judith met his eyes, startled by the physical contact, the sudden intimacy with this stranger. His eyes were very, very blue.

"Do you think it's too late?" she said. "Even if we get the fuel from this shipwreck that you mentioned, is the world really—?"

"I don't know," he said, dropping his hand from her arm. "I don't know if the human race is going to last much longer. I don't even know if my family is still alive."

Judith was so close to Michael that she could have touched his face. For a moment she wanted to, here in the half-light of the darkened stairwell. She wanted to reach out to this man, to forget about everything that was going on in the world. But something held her back. She turned around and continued up the stairs. Michael followed in silence.

When she reached the bridge, Ren and Nora looked up from their usual posts at the computers. They stared as the stranger followed her through the door.

"This is Michael," Judith said. "He's going to lead us to some fuel. Simon says to let him use the radio."

"Um, what about Guam?" Nora said. "You know, that bit of land right in front of us?"

"We're not going to Guam."

Judith slumped into a chair and avoided looking at Michael. She was embarrassed by her outburst. He wasn't the navy personified. He had just been following orders, scared like everyone else.

"I was afraid of this," Ren said grimly. "Where to, sailor?"

SIMON

By the time everyone had been pulled off the deck, the patient optimism of the last few days had evaporated. The news about not being able to disembark in Guam spread, filling the ship with despair. When the people had somewhere to go and something to do, they'd been almost cheery. But now the fear and grief of the past week came crashing down like a tsunami.

Simon walked through the plaza before going up to the bridge. People stopped him as he passed, asking him if it was true, if they really had to keep sailing. He hated the way their faces fell when he told them what had happened.

Frank sat straight down on the ground, white and shaking. Constance Gordon, the young mother who was only recently back on her feet, held her newborn and stared at nothing. Little Cally caught her mood and began to cry. People were too stunned to complain. Even Rosa Cordova was at a loss for words. She simply gathered up her children and hugged them close.

Simon didn't know what to tell them. He dug through his inner reserves and found nothing. He'd tried not to lay all his hopes on Guam and the navy, but he too felt betrayed. They had nowhere to go. He trudged up the plush steps of the grand staircase as their little community struggled with the truth. The chandelier above him tinkled softly.

But on the third balcony at the top of the plaza, he found a different scene. A small group gathered around a little gallery full of painted seascapes and photography. They seemed to be leaning in so they could see through the doors of the shop. At its center, someone stood near a large painting of a stormy sea with a single ray of light cutting through the clouds.

A few people in the doorway stepped back so Simon could see who everyone was looking at in the gallery.

It was Penelope Newton. Her eyes were the size of dessert plates, and she clutched her cross necklace so tight that it must be cutting into her palm. She closed her eyes, and the people in the shop crowded closer. Then she spoke.

"I know ya'll are hurting right now, but I think it's time we turned to Jesus. I believe we're living in the Last Days. He is the only one who will get us out of this here mess. Would you join me on your knees as I implore the Almighty to see us through?"

Then she got down on her knees by herself in the middle of the little gallery and began to pray. She looked plump and motherly, but she had a magnetic presence, somehow both zealous and reassuring. And she had a voice like an old-time revival preacher's. It was her confidence, Simon thought, which gave it that quality. She truly and fervently believed that when she prayed the Almighty listened.

Something happened to the tight knot of people in the gallery as Penelope spoke. Movement rippled as some dropped to their knees. Others seemed to draw energy from the woman kneeling in front of the painting, from her voice and demeanor more than her words. As Penelope's voice rang out, soft and strong, the people in her little following seemed to swell with renewal.

Simon reached within himself too, hoping to find some sort of connection to God or a higher power or energy or whatever Penelope was accessing, but still he felt empty. He knew people often turned to religion in times of trouble. He was a little surprised that he couldn't find that connection himself. Why in this darkest hour could he not find some sort of faith to keep him going? The people around him were taking hope; Simon felt only sadness.

"Come quickly, Lord Jesus. Amen." Penelope finished her prayer and turned around to sit on the floor, as if she'd expended all of her energy and given it to the crowd. She looked directly at Simon, and he stepped back, allowing those massing outside the gallery to make their way further in. He didn't fully understand what he'd witnessed. But if it comforted people, he was glad of it.

Unexpectedly, he felt a sense of release at the knowledge that people were looking to Penelope and to God instead of to him. He didn't always have to be the one with the answers, the one staying strong in the midst of everything. He could share the load a little.

He continued on toward the bridge, his steps a bit lighter. He would work out a way to retrieve the fuel from this shipwreck with the young sailor. It was a measureable goal, something Simon could work with. He may not be able to find hope in a seemingly hopeless situation, but he would do what needed to be done. He sensed a thread of calm making its way through his body. It was time to make a plan.

13. The Beach

JUDITH

THE ATOLL WAS INVISIBLE until they were almost on top of it. It was a tiny island, no more than a flat stretch of sand, with a few windravaged trees hanging on for dear life at the center. Debris was strewn across the beach: parts of ships, dead sea creatures, even a four-door sedan. The largest piece of debris was a huge cargo ship, broken into two pieces, sitting halfway in the shallows and halfway on the beach.

"There she is," Michael said. He stood beside Judith as they approached the little island. He had stayed close to her while they made plans to retrieve the fuel tanks from the wrecked cargo ship. He was capable and straightforward, with an easy sense of self-assurance. "I'm glad to finally be doing something," he said.

"Me too," Judith said. She met his eyes and couldn't help blushing and looking down. *Get a grip, Judith. He's not that hot.* It had clearly been too long since she'd met any attractive men. He wasn't the type of guy she usually liked anyway. He was too much of a jock. This was no time to be thinking about his piercing eyes and square-jawed good looks.

"Some of that stuff on the beach could come in handy," Judith said briskly. "We should gather whatever we can when we go in for the fuel."

"There should be plenty of room in the lifeboats."

"How close can we get to the atoll?" Judith asked.

"It gets shallow pretty far out," Michael said. "We'll have to go a few hundred feet at least to get to the beach. We gotta move quickly before the sailors back on Guam figure out what we're doing."

"What will they do if they find out?"

Michael hesitated. "Let's just not let them catch us."

Fifteen minutes later the crew lowered three lifeboats full of storage containers and people into the sea. Each one was partially enclosed and designed to hold up to 150 people. Now twenty or thirty crew members and former passengers climbed into each boat to help with the salvage operation.

Michael followed Judith and Nora into the third lifeboat. She felt keenly aware of him as he reached behind her to hold on to the bulkhead, the muscles in his arms bulging when they hit the water. She almost wished he'd gotten into a different lifeboat. He threw her off balance, and she hated being out of control. He was what she would have called a distraction a lifetime ago.

The lifeboat motored toward the shore. The water was murky, churned up by the recent storm. The clouds, as gloomy as the water, swirled unnaturally with purples and grays. Even the equatorial sun didn't quite shine through. Cold sea spray coated Judith's face, but she couldn't wait to walk on solid ground for a little while.

When their boat reached the sand, Michael and a few others leapt out and pulled it further up the beach amidst the junk. About eighty people had volunteered for the salvage team. They scattered like pigeons to collect usable debris and edible seaweed. Nora headed for what looked like a pile of sandy circuit boards.

Judith walked a little slower, savoring the feeling of her feet sinking into the sand. The ground felt like it was moving beneath her. She made tracks with her running shoes in the shifting sand. Michael waited for her where the wet sand met dry.

"Want to come with me to the cargo ship, Judith? I could use a hand."

"Sure."

"Nothing like a long walk on the beach with a cute girl," he said, stretching his arms high over his head as if he planned to put one around her.

"You've got to be kidding," Judith said wryly. She pulled at the salt-stained sweatshirt she wore over the mismatched yoga pants. Michael winked at her.

She followed him across the sand, picking her way around broken propellers, waterlogged suitcases, and a tangled clump of iridescent jellyfish. The beach smelled of oil and rotting fish. The detritus was a mix of things that belonged on land and things that belonged at the bottom of the sea. There was even the carcass of a small airplane half-buried in the sand.

Judith climbed over part of the plane's wing and stifled a scream. Michael ran back toward her.

She fought nausea as she tried to scrub her shoes clean. She'd stepped directly onto a bloated body in the shade of the aluminum wing. It was a man of indeterminate age. His flesh had gone soft and porous, and his face looked chewed and pocked. His lids were open, but his eyes were gone. Judith refused to look at the place in his side where her foot had landed.

"Come on, Judith." Michael put his arm around her shoulder and turned her firmly away from the corpse. "Don't look at it. We have work to do."

She stared at him, trying to find her voice.

"Don't say 'it.' Say h— "

She couldn't finish. She ducked beneath Michael's arm and threw up on the sand. Tears filled her eyes. Why was everything so horrible? She wanted to wake up, to know for certain that this nightmare was over. She couldn't take it.

"You're okay," Michael said, almost humming the words. He patted her on the back. "Let's focus on the fuel. We can do this."

Slowly she straightened and wiped her mouth on her sleeve, mortified at her reaction. But Michael simply offered her his hand, and they picked their way toward the cargo ship lying further along the beach. He talked to her in that same low hum, almost like he was speaking to himself.

"You're okay. We can do this. You're okay."

The hull of the broken cargo ship loomed above them, barnacles covering it like a layer of crumbs. Judith ran her hand along the hull as they walked toward the opening, feeling the rough creatures under her fingertips. It was cold in the shadow beneath the hulking vessel, but it felt stable, real.

There was a gap midship, as if a giant child had broken the ship apart like a toy and dropped it in two separate pieces, slightly out of alignment. The second piece lay mostly in the water, and the waves slapped against its sides.

The smell of oil was heavy here. The barnacles beneath Judith's fingers became slick and dark the closer they got to the break.

"Will there be any fuel left?" Judith asked.

"Cargo ships have built-in tanks," Michael explained. "Those are busted, and we wouldn't be able to get them out anyway. But this baby was transporting additional fuel in tanks lashed to the deck." Michael bent to roll up the legs of his trousers before splashing toward the partially submerged half of the ship. "A few of them were still okay when we spotted the wreck yesterday."

"How will you get the tanks down?" Judith asked. "They must be really heavy."

"The ship has a crane. If we can get it working, we can lift the tanks directly into the water and tow them behind the boats. If that doesn't work, we'll have to siphon the fuel and carry it in trips."

"That could take days."

"We don't have days."

Judith and Michael were the first to reach the cargo ship, but soon about twenty other crew members from the *Catalina* gathered in its shadow, including Reggie. Nora joined them too but immediately climbed into the cargo ship and disappeared into the deckhouse, muttering about computer equipment. Reggie quickly took charge and designated roles for the crew. Judith kept a lookout on the horizon for any signs of the navy, while Michael and the others climbed into the dark interior of the ship. Water rushed in and out of the lowest level where the break was. It was a dark cavern that must have been one of the ship's main fuel compartments. It was empty now except for the rushing, oil-slicked surf.

Judith could no longer see the cargo ship team from her post on the beach. From this angle she couldn't see the crane or the fuel tanks at all. She surveyed the atoll. The other people from the *Catalina* picked up scraps and called out to each other.

"Can we use this?"

"Is this seaweed edible?"

"Help me carry these tires, will you?"

They looked to be in better spirits than she'd seen them in days, even though their hopes of landing in Guam had been dashed. Having solid ground to walk on certainly improved morale. They had already nearly filled one of the lifeboats with salvage.

The *Catalina* herself floated beyond the breaking surf. Judith remembered when she'd first seen the ship by the dock in San Diego. She was still bright white, but the boarded-up windows of the dining hall scarred her surface. She showed the wear from their journey, just like her people.

Clanging came from within the cargo ship, then a screeching mechanical sound. They must have found the controls for the crane. Someone out of sight swore theatrically.

The dark sky swirled. Wind swept the beach, driving sand into Judith's face. She pulled the arms of her sweatshirt over her hands and held them up on both sides of her face. She shivered, not for the first time wishing for the safety of her little apartment back in San Diego, with its grimy counters and flimsy walls. She missed the simple problems: whether or not she'd get the right job; whether or not her professors would like her papers; whether or not her roommate would wake her up when she came home.

After about fifteen minutes Michael and a few of the others climbed back out of the beached ship. Two of them carried a pile of thick chain between them. They set to work disentangling it on the beach.

"We got the crane to work," Michael told Judith. "But the tanks are tied down good. The crew just got the first one loose."

The team brought the first stretch of chain nearer to the ship. There was a shout from the upper reaches of the wreck. A screeching, creaking sound. Then a massive shape loomed above them, swinging out over the side of the cargo vessel. The fuel tank teetered in the space between ship and sky. Whoever was controlling the crane eased it into position slowly.

"Watch your head."

"It's huge!" Judith said.

"Each one holds over nine thousand gallons, and there are half a dozen of them up there," Michael said. "We should be able to sail for a few more days on that." He called out instructions to guide the tank further out over the water.

Judith held her breath as the massive shape swung above them, swaying in the strengthening breeze. It was about the size of the fuel tanks pulled across the highways of California by big tanker trucks, easily the length of several normal cars.

With a frightening creak the crane eased the tank even further out over the water.

"That's good," Michael shouted. "Bring her down!"

The tank lowered, getting closer and closer to shallow surf beside the broken ship. Judith tensed, afraid to move an inch.

"Release!"

The tank splashed into the shallows beside the cargo vessel. Michael and the others hurried forward to keep it from drifting away. They wrapped some of the chain around it, linking it like a harness. Michael patted the tank affectionately.

"So far so good."

"These things are heavy," Reggie shouted, leaning over the edge of the cargo ship above them. "We better bring the lifeboats over to pull. I don't think we'll be able to push it far even with the whole team."

"I'll work on that," Judith said. "You guys get those things off the ship."

"Roger that," Reggie said, wiping sweat from his forehead with his sleeve. "Let's get the next tank moving."

"Right behind you," Michael said. "This is going to take a while."

"Um, guys?" Judith said. "We don't have a while."

She had just looked up to see a massive storm cloud trundling toward them.

SIMON

Simon watched the storm grow from the bridge with Ren and Vinny. It hovered above them, a roiling, turbulent mass. Funnel clouds spiked down, and the sea rose up to meet them. Simon flashed back to the terrifying moments in San Diego when the ash roared above the city. The sea between them rolled, gelatinous beneath the darkening sky.

"Is it going to hit us?" Simon asked.

"Sure looks like it," Ren said.

"Any chance you can outrun it?"

"This atoll is going to make it tricky. If we get stuck, we'll be in real trouble. To be honest, Simon, I'm not experienced enough to pilot under these conditions."

"You'll have to try, Ren. First we need to get everyone off the beach."

"We should pull up the anchor," Vinny said. Sweat formed rivulets on his brow. "We don't have time to wait for the lifeboats."

Simon hesitated for a fraction of a second.

"No," Ren said, standing up and pushing back her chair. "We can't leave them."

"I agree, Ren," Simon said quickly. "Don't worry. Fire up the engines, but wait for my signal."

"Aye aye, captain," Ren said. She scowled at Vinny before turning her attention back to the looming storm.

"Wait a minute. That's what we need," Simon said. He clapped Ren on the shoulder and headed for the exit.

Captain Martinelli's quarters were located just behind the bridge. His spacious accommodations included his cabin, accessible from the bridge in an emergency, and the elegant Captain's Lounge. There, he would entertain VIPs and perform the public relations part of a cruise captain's duties.

Since being forcibly removed from duty six days ago, Captain Martinelli had been locked in his quarters. Vinny had been bringing him his meals and making sure he had plenty of water. He hadn't been allowed to speak to anyone else. They had left the entryway between his room and the Captain's Lounge open to give him more space, but metal taken from room service trolleys barred the other entrances. Simon removed the interlocking pieces one by one and knocked on the door to the lounge.

"Enter."

"Captain Martinelli? The ship is in danger, and we need your help."

"Simon, how good of you to visit. A drink?"

The captain stood before the huge picture windows spanning one wall of the lounge, swirling cognac in a glass. His uniform was soiled, but every button and fringe was in place. He'd combed down his hair since the last time Simon saw him, but this only served to accentuate the madness in his eyes. There was a stale, putrid scent in the room, like rotting food and illness.

"There's no time, sir. We need you to get us out of the path of a big storm. We're near an atoll, so we don't have much room to maneuver between the shallow water and the storm."

"It's magnificent, cognac. Don't you think so, Simon? My father abhorred the stuff, but my elder brother introduced me to its finer points. Do close the door. No need to let in a draft."

"We have to go now. Ren can't do it on her own."

Simon crossed to the window and looked down at the beach. The people from the *Catalina* gathered around the broken cargo ship, and some had climbed up to its main deck. A huge tank swung dangerously from a crane clinging to the top of the wreck. Another tank was already in the water, with another group holding it steady in the breakers.

One of the lifeboats approached, already piled high with salvage. Judith stood a little apart from the crowd, directing the lifeboat into position. The crew moved forward and began securing the first tank to the lifeboat with some sort of chain. They must be planning to tug it toward the *Catalina*. It looked like a very slow process. Didn't they see the storm approaching?

"My elder brother was a ship's captain too, you know." The captain took a sip of his cognac and reached for a cigarette. It must be one of his last ones. "He got me my first job. That was with Galaxy Cruises on one of their smaller models. I worked my way up from there, for half a dozen different lines, and now here I am. My own ship."

"Your ship is going to run aground if you don't help us sail it away from here," Simon said. He couldn't see the hulking storm cloud from these windows. The sky had grown darker above the atoll. A flash of lightning sent shivers across the water.

"I got her through the Sack of San Diego," Captain Martinelli said. "That has a nice ring, doesn't it? A suitable legacy. If people ever write about these days, I hope that's what they'll call it. Sacked by the insides of our own planet rising up to obliterate us. It's a wonder the human race has lasted this long. If I were Mother Nature, I'd have wiped us off the surface ages ago."

"Sir, we still have a chance to survive," Simon said, turning away from the window. He couldn't believe he'd once thought this man looked like a hero.

"Survive?" Captain Martinelli chuckled. "What is the point of this survival you speak of? The world is ruined. We should go down with dignity."

"I'm not ready for that," Simon said. "There's nothing dignified about sinking in a storm after our own military refused to help us. We have to fight for ourselves for as long as we can. Will you help us?"

The captain sighed and turned away from the window. Lightning flashed behind him.

"What exactly do you expect me to do?" he said.

JUDITH

The salvage team loaded up their spoils and brought the lifeboats closer to the wrecked cargo ship. They secured the first huge fuel tank to it with the chains they'd found on the cargo ship. Then one group gathered around the tank to hold it still while the second tank was being brought forward and secured. Judith stood apart from the group and directed the operation. The tank was too big for the people on either side to see each other. They stood knee-deep in the water, holding it steady until the second tank was in position. It was a miracle they could get the huge things to move through the water at all.

When the two tanks were secured, the first group piled into the lifeboat and fired up the motor. The tanks bobbed heavily in the waves, creaking against their chains. The lines tightened. Would it work?

Water and spray churned around the motor. Judith held her breath. Then the lifeboat began to move. It chugged slowly away from the beach, pulling the tanks behind it like a pair of trailers. Its progress was laborious, but it was moving. The teams remaining on the beach cheered.

Judith kept an eye on the storm and the *Catalina* lurching just beyond the surf. The weather was getting worse by the minute, and they still had a lot of work to do.

While the first lifeboat inched toward the *Catalina*, everyone else returned to the cargo ship to start the process over again. Reggie's crew was already lifting the third tank off the deck with the crane.

It took ages, but eventually they got two more fuel tanks down from the cargo ship and secured to the second lifeboat. Another group sailed slowly toward the *Catalina*, their precious cargo in tow.

The storm was larger now, floating like an evil presence above the waves. Waterspouts rose from the sea. A wall of rain swept across the beach, instantly blurring the world. There were twenty people and one lifeboat left on the atoll. They sheltered from the rain in the shadow of the cargo ship.

"We should go now," Judith said. "There's no time for two more tanks."

"If we leave all this fuel behind, we won't get far," Reggie said.

"But when that storm hits we'll never reach the ship," Judith said. She didn't like the look of those funnel clouds.

"Come on, people, don't just stand around arguing," Michael said. "Let's move one more tank and then get the heck out of here."

"Fine," Judith said. "But hurry!"

Reggie climbed back up to the crane to get the fifth nine-thousand-gallon tank. Nora finally emerged from the deckhouse and darted to the last lifeboat, arms laden with circuit boards. Wires trailed behind her. Soon she was running back through the rain to assist the team guiding the final fuel tank off the cargo ship.

"Got enough hardware to build the ship a new brain!" she called. "I think I can fix our communication problem."

The wind picked up, driving the rain horizontally. It couldn't be past four in the afternoon, but the sky was growing progressively darker. The team freed the next tank from the deck above and worked to secure it to the crane. It was becoming harder for them to hear each other above the wind.

Beyond the waterline the *Catalina* was a stark shape against the darkened sky. The first lifeboat was already being lifted up the side of the ship with the winch. Judith had forgotten how tall it was. How were they going to get all the fuel tanks up there?

"Wait! Something's wrong!" Michael shouted, bringing her attention back to the cargo ship.

The fifth tank was teetering over the edge of the ship above them, swaying dangerously. The crane strained, trying to lift it high enough to make it over the rail. The crew struggled to keep it steady in the strengthening wind.

"The crane is stuck," someone shouted.

"A little higher."

"It's slipping!"

"Shit!"

There was a loud crack. The tank lurched and slammed into the deck of the cargo ship. Then it seesawed over the edge and plummeted downward.

"Look out!"

Michael leapt back, flinging out his arm to push Judith further away. The tank hit the water with a huge splash, drenching everyone within twenty feet.

Judith picked herself up off the beach, an angry retort on her lips. She hadn't been underneath the thing! But Michael was gritting his teeth, and a muscle throbbed in his jaw.

"You okay?" Judith asked.

"Landed on my foot wrong," he said. He tried putting some weight on it. "Damn, that hurts." Sweat coated his forehead.

"I was fine, you know," Judith said. "But thank you. Can you walk?"

"If I have to, I'll run."

Michael nodded at the sea. The heart of the storm was closer. The funnel clouds whirled, sucking water up from the sea in spouts. The second lifeboat had reached the *Catalina*, and it was being lifted up the side of the hull. The four fuel tanks bobbed in the roughening waves, apparently tethered to the ship somehow.

"Let's push this thing into position," Reggie said, jumping out of the cargo ship with the last of the crane crew. Veins stood out on his forehead.

"How are we going to get the tanks onto the ship?" Nora asked, wiping the rainwater out of her own eyes.

"We're not for now," Reggie said. "We need to get away from the atoll before the storm hits."

The final tank had landed closer to the waterline than the others, and it had become wedged in the sand. The team worked together to push it further out into the water as the last lifeboat motored forward.

Once it was out of the sand, they had to hold on to the tank to keep it from moving in the waves. Michael took over manager duty, and Judith went down to the water to help the others hold it still against the increasingly rough waves. Reggie brought the lifeboat in closer. It was getting harder to maneuver against the tossing of the waves.

"Steady!" Michael called.

"It's too rough!"

"We can't hold it."

The lifeboat got closer. Judith moved forward to make sure the chain was ready. A few of the men released their grip on the tank to help her with it.

"Come on, guys," Judith said. "We can do this."

Lightning cracked across the sky. The waves battered the team around the tank. They dug their feet into the sand, bracing their shoulders against the rivets and slick edges. The men were having trouble securing the chain around the tank so they could link it to the lifeboat.

"Almost . . . there . . ." Judith said.

Suddenly, a harsh wave knocked some of the team off their feet. The tank slipped sideways. It began to roll, pushed off balance by the waves. More people lost their hold. Then it was loose, tumbling in the breakers. It slammed back against the hull of the cargo ship. The team shouted, stumbling over each other to try to get a grip on it without being crushed.

The waves crashed. Then the tank was being sucked back toward the sea, pulled along by the current rushing dangerously around the hull of the broken ship.

"We're losing it!" Michael shouted.

But Judith wasn't going to let that happen. She dashed through the water, staying even with the tank as the waves pushed it to and fro. There was nothing she could do to stop it. It was far too heavy. But they couldn't lose it now. She would not let it float away when they were so close.

She darted past the tank. She would win this race. The cold shock of a wave doused her face. She splashed through the surf until she was waist deep. She found the dangling edge of the chain and clung to it, trying to keep her grip without allowing it to bowl over her.

Then the natural pressure of the waves slowed the tank's momentum. If it hadn't, Judith would certainly have been crushed. She held on to the chain around the tank and planted her feet deep in the mud, trying to keep it from floating further out to sea. The waves pushed her back and forth like a rag doll.

Michael appeared beside her. "Easy. Let's keep hold of this thing."

"I've got it," Judith said.

A wave filled her mouth with salt and sand. As she spluttered and coughed, Michael stayed calm.

"You're a champ," he said. "Reg! Bring that boat closer, will you? The girls are doing all the work."

Nora and another crew member had already attached another chain to the lifeboat. It was piled high with salvaged objects, mostly suitcases from the plane wreckage. Reggie sailed it in closer to Michael and Judith, and they linked the two chains together with a hook the size of her hand.

"The other boats are already back at the *Catalina*," Nora shouted. "Climb aboard!"

Together, Judith, Michael, and their team clambered aboard the lifeboat. Reggie gunned the motor. They pulled away from the cargo ship and the beach, the fuel tank bobbing behind them like an overgrown mastiff.

The sea roughened. Their lifeboat dipped into troughs, making Judith's stomach plummet, and then rose up high on peaks of surging water. She lost all sense of perspective as the waves grew. Swells obscured the fuel tank behind them half the time. The lifeboat's motor strained against the drag of the tank and the pressure of the rough seas.

Nora's eyes were wide, and she kept both arms wrapped around her circuit boards. She smiled at Judith from across the boat, but her face had gone a little green. Michael sat beside Judith, holding on to a pile of suitcases to keep them from being tossed overboard.

"Almost there," he said, and flashed her a quick smile. "We can beat this storm. And it'll keep the navy off our backs."

Lightning flashed across the sky. The whistling of the wind grew to a howl. Judith checked the chain again. The tank trailed behind them. It was slowing them down. They hadn't crossed half the distance between the beach and the *Catalina* yet, and the storm was getting worse by the second.

The ship heaved in the growing waves. It was hard to tell over the roar of the wind, but Judith thought the engines were running.

"There's no way we're getting the lifeboat back onto the ship," Reggie shouted over the wind.

"Can we secure it until the storm is over, like the tanks?" Judith asked.

"We can try. No guarantee it'll survive a battering like this."

Judith grabbed the seat in front of her as a dip in the sea made her lose her balance. They had to get the fuel to the ship. But then how would they get back on board themselves? Judith cast about for an idea, holding on so hard her fingers ached.

Lightning and thunder cracked together.

Then the *Catalina* started to move.

14. Escape

SIMON

SIMON ENTERED THE BRIDGE with Captain Martinelli. Ren paled and began a sputtering apology, but the captain ignored her. It was like he had flipped a switch on his reason. He barked out orders so swift and complex that Simon couldn't follow half the words. Ren leapt to obey.

Simon hung back as the captain and Ren did their work. He was profoundly grateful that they hadn't ended up on this ship without any of its original crew, even though they were severely understaffed.

The captain didn't seem too worried about the storm and their proximity to the atoll. He asked about the weather and the news. Vinny and Ren did their best to fill him in. They explained that the storm had come out of nowhere.

"Goddamn weather patterns," the captain muttered. "They've never been predictable, truly, but we used to make better guesses."

"What do you mean?" Simon asked.

"A storm like this doesn't come out of the blue. We used to be able to track them on the satellites for one, and we'd get updates from ships at other coordinates. Even then we got hit with surprises sometimes. Storms went north when they should go south, stayed in one place longer than expected, all but disappeared. It was getting worse. Global warming, you know? But this is madness."

Simon didn't answer. Nothing at all surprised him anymore.

He couldn't see anyone left on the beach. Vinny reported that one of their lifeboats had made it back onto the ship already and they were lifting the other now. The crew would be climbing aboard, unloading the salvage, and hopefully hauling in the lifeboats.

The sea was growing ever darker, wilder. A shift of the waves revealed the final lifeboat struggling toward them. A huge fuel tank dragged behind it.

"We have to get those people on board," Simon said.

"It's too late," Captain Martinelli said. "We need to get away from the shore before the waves get any worse."

"We can't leave them," Simon said.

Ren started up too, but he gestured for her to remain calm.

"Are you insane?" the captain said. "If we run aground here, it'll be impossible to launch again."

A crack of lightning illuminated the ghostly broken cargo vessel lying in the shallows. The *Catalina* would end up like that if they didn't get away from the atoll soon.

"Give them a few more minutes," Simon said.

"Are you giving orders on my ship?"

"This isn't a ship anymore, sir. This is a survival operation, and I'm in charge. We are not leaving those people behind. Take us closer to the beach."

JUDITH

The team was exhausted. Judith felt like she'd been in the lifeboat for hours. The boat tossed them about so much they could do little more than hold on. Reggie had a death grip on the motor controls. Michael winced with each shift of the sea, bearing up well despite his injured foot. He had planted his feet firmly against the lifeboat floor to keep from pitching forward. He must be in agony.

The *Catalina* started moving toward them. Judith felt a mixture of relief and fear. What if there were rocks underwater? How close could the big ship get to the atoll without getting stuck?

The lifeboat fought the waves, trying to get closer to the *Catalina*. She sailed nearer, cutting the distance between them to a hundred feet. Almost there. But as they approached the towering hull of the cruise ship . . .

"They're going to hit us!" someone yelled.

The lifeboat lurched forward on a wave, and the hull of the *Catalina* was suddenly a solid wall. The four other oil tanks were chained to the hull somehow, and they tossed about dangerously. With each surge they got closer to a collision.

"Look!" Reggie shouted. "They tossed down the ladder. Let's swim for it."

"What about the salvage?"

"Leave it, or we're not making it out of this alive."

He abandoned the controls and began pushing people over the side. They disappeared beneath the boiling black sea and then emerged, gasping and splashing their way toward the *Catalina*. The ladder swung pendulum-like, scraping across the slick white paint of the hull.

Judith gripped Reggie's arm when he reached her, digging her fingers into his skin.

"We can't leave the fuel. I'll stay with it."

"Don't be stupid," he shouted, trying to force her into the water.

Judith stood her ground. "Get up there and throw me a rope or something," she said. "We need as much of it as possible."

"It's on your own head," Reggie said, then waved to Michael. "Let's go, man."

Reggie dove cleanly over the side of the lifeboat, but Michael didn't follow. Nora hesitated for a moment and squeezed Judith's arm. A flash of lightning sparked off the metal post in her eyebrow. She held her breath and jumped into the sea after Reggie. Her pink hair popped up a moment later.

"You're right. We need this," Michael shouted to Judith above the wind. "Grab an oar and help me stay close to the ship."

She complied, helping him to retrieve the long emergency oars from the bottom of the boat. She gripped one so hard her hands hurt.

The first struggling swimmer reached the rope ladder. He climbed it slowly, holding on for dear life, but his weight kept it a bit steadier for the next person to swim toward it. Judith counted the swimmers climbing up the side of the ship. Unseen hands helped them aboard. The ladder swayed dangerously as they climbed. One by one their team reached the safety of the *Catalina*'s deck. But something was wrong.

"We lost one," she shouted.

"What?" Michael leaned toward her, his breath a shock of warmth on her cheek.

"There were twenty of us left on the beach. Only seventeen made it up the ladder."

Michael didn't respond. Judith struggled against her oar, her eyes stinging from the salt water and wind.

Suddenly, Michael dropped his oar and lunged sideways, forcing Judith down into the boat to get out of his way. When she lifted her head, he had both hands around a thick rope trailing down from the *Catalina*. Someone had tossed them a lifeline.

Michael swayed wildly, trying to keep his balance. Judith dropped her own oar and wrapped both arms around his waist to hold him steady.

"Get to the stern!" he said.

They scrambled backward to where the fuel tank was chained to the lifeboat. Mercifully, it was still attached. Judith kept Michael balanced as he pulled at the line trailing down from the *Catalina*.

"Can you tie it?" she shouted.

"I need more slack. Pull!"

They heaved at the rope, bringing more of it into the boat. Another wave pushed them dangerously close to the *Catalina*, making their task easier. Judith held on to the excess rope and climbed underneath the nearest bench to wedge herself more securely into the boat. Her hands were raw, so she wrapped the rope beneath her arm. Water cascaded around her.

Michael worked at the chain. Judith couldn't see what he was doing. She hoped he wouldn't have to cut the lifeboat loose in order to secure the oil tank.

The muscles in his calves tensed as he braced himself against the pitching of the boat. She watched his feet, praying they'd stay firmly planted. The lifeboat tossed about like kindling.

A crash. The rope ripped out of Judith's grasp, taking a thick layer of skin from her arm and side as it wrenched away. The jolt knocked her teeth together so hard she saw stars.

They'd collided with the *Catalina*. Michael's feet disappeared. He had gone overboard.

SIMON

"We need more time," Simon said.

Manny reported on the intercom that most of the salvagers from the final lifeboat had come aboard, but they were still trying to secure the fuel tank. They weren't sure the others would stay attached to the ship.

"This whole thing will be a waste without them," Ren whispered.

"I know. Damn it." Simon pressed his face against the glass. The atoll loomed. They were far too close.

"We're going to run aground if we don't move now," Captain Martinelli said, his voice emotionless.

"A few more minutes."

JUDITH

Salt water stung Judith's eyes as she clung to the bench. The rope was secure, but she couldn't see Michael anywhere. She couldn't do anything to help him now. A wave pushed the boat further away from the *Catalina* again. The rope tightened, but it held. The lifeboat, with the oil tank in tow, was now firmly attached to the *Catalina*.

Judith dove into the sea.

She was so cold and wet already that it almost didn't matter when her head went beneath the waves. The water swirled around her, dark, consuming. Fear flashed through her with each bolt of lightning. She flailed blindly toward the *Catalina*, swallowing seawater with every stroke.

A surge lifted her up, knocking her roughly against the hull. She felt along the cold steel surface for something to grab on to as the surge carried her, aware of a stinging sensation across her side and arm.

As the wave ebbed, she plunged deep beneath the water, thrashing her arms as she tried to find her way. Another wave pushed her into the hull again, knocking the last breath out of her.

The surge of the sea was endless. She could barely see. Couldn't breathe. She kicked and stroked, trying to get closer to the *Catalina* without letting the waves bash her against it.

The sea surged again.

Judith scrabbled at the frigid hull. Then there was a change, an edge. Her fingers closed around slim metal. It was the rung of the ladder. She hung on, gasping for breath each time the waves abated. She reached up. Grabbed. Next one. Her head cleared the water again.

She climbed a few rungs up the side of the *Catalina*, then looked back. The lifeboat had overturned. It whipped at the end of the rope like a fishing lure. Further out the fuel tank still hung on. There was no sign of Michael or the twentieth member of their party.

She clung to the ladder, her last ounce of strength gone.

SIMON

"We really ought to move now," Captain Martinelli said calmly, "if you wish to survive. We're too close. We'll get stuck in the sand if we don't hit a rock and sink first."

Simon stood beside him, trying to pierce the heavy gray curtain beyond the window. He couldn't see the lifeboat from here. He didn't know whether or not they'd made it. The captain stood still, hand on the helm.

"Any word?" Simon asked Vinny, who sat glued to the intercom.

"Nothing. They're not answering."

"Okay. Let's go," Simon said, avoiding Ren's hard gaze. "And pray that everyone made it back on board."

JUDITH

Judith felt the engine kick into high gear. They began to move away from the island, slowly at first. The propellers beneath the ship would be sucking at the water. It would be impossible to swim against that. Where were the others?

She should keep climbing the ladder, but all she could do was hold on. She had stopped shivering. *That's a bad thing, right?* she thought vaguely. Shapes rose and sank in the water. Debris, seaweed, bodies. She couldn't be sure what she was seeing.

Suddenly, a head popped up above the waves much further forward than she expected.

It was Michael.

He flailed about, taking gasping, panicked breaths, but he didn't swim toward the ship. He trod water where he was. His eyes were closed, and he dragged a hand over them, as if trying to clear them of salt water. He still wasn't swimming toward the ship. *He must have salt in his eyes. He can't see!*

"Over here!" Judith didn't have the strength to move, but she could shout. "Michael! Swim toward my voice! Hurry! The ship is moving!"

She was afraid the howl of the wind would drown out her words. She screamed louder, and Michael responded. He was a strong swimmer. He headed in her direction, stopping every few strokes to listen for her voice again. She shouted and screamed, guiding him to her.

Michael stopped swimming, but he kept getting closer. A current was sweeping him forward. He was moving too fast! He was going to be sucked beneath the ship.

Judith wrapped her legs around the bottom rung of the ladder and dove forward, launching her body back into the water. She grabbed Michael by the arm just as he was about to be swept away.

Judith had no strength left to pull him to her, but he grabbed hold of her arms and dragged himself toward the ladder. She simply hung on as he felt his way to the ladder and seized it too. Now she was the one clinging to him as he hoisted himself out of the sea.

"Can't see," he wheezed. "Salt."

"You're okay," Judith said. "You're on the ladder."

"Let's get on board."

"Can't," Judith gasped. "Give me a minute."

"I'll help you. Tell me where to go."

Judith clutched Michael's arm and maneuvered around so that he could have both hands and feet on the ladder. She clung to his back and talked to him as he climbed.

"Halfway there. Careful, there's an irregular bit here. Reach over it. That's good."

When they reached the top, hands appeared out of the darkness to pull them to safety. Together, Judith and Michael collapsed onto the deck.

15. Aftermath

JUDITH

JUDITH BECAME AWARE OF people moving around her. The ship must be rocking, but she was too disoriented to be sure. There was water on her face, and her clothes were soaked. She lost her grip on Michael. Fog closed in around her.

Some time later a stinging sensation brought the world back into focus. Someone had moved her out of the rain. She was lying on one side with her arm stretched over her head. There was a blanket over her legs, and feeling was returning to them. Pain.

Judith's arm and side hurt too, scraped raw by the rope. The nurse was dabbing her with iodine. A sharp chemical smell cut through the air. Each touch of the nurse's cloth stung. From her position on her side, Judith saw that she was in the reception lobby, perhaps on the very same couch where little Cally had been born just over a week ago.

She couldn't see Nora or Michael or any of the other people who'd been in the boat with her, because a round, matronly figure was blocking her view. Penelope was helping the nurse, Laura, to clean her scrape. Judith coughed, her throat raw from the salt water.

"Where is everybody?" she asked.

"Now, now, dear. You keep quiet," Penelope said. "You've been through an ordeal. You'll be fine when we get you cleaned up."

"Did we get the tanks?" she asked.

"The men are keeping an eye on them. They won't be able to bring them up until after the storm. You secured that last one well."

"That was Michael. The storm's still going?"

"Yes, of course. Can't you feel it? You were only out for a few minutes. You should get some sleep soon, though. Nurse Laura can take you down to the clinic in a bit if you like."

There was a falseness to Penelope's voice. It was determinedly cheery—incongruous given the circumstances.

"Did everybody make it back?" Judith asked, remembering that she had only counted seventeen people climbing the ladder, plus her and Michael. There had been twenty in the boat. Penelope hesitated long enough for Judith to know the truth.

"Who was it?"

Penelope glanced up at the nurse, then back at Judith, shaking her head sadly.

SIMON

When the news arrived on the bridge, Simon's heart sank. Odd to think about sinking after so long at sea. It had taken on a whole new meaning.

Manny brought the news. He had run up from the lifeboat deck to report on the team of twenty, now nineteen. Captain Martinelli didn't react at all. He didn't know her. Simon suspected he had lost all capacity to care.

It was Ren's reaction that surprised him. Simon hadn't realized that Ren and Nora were so close.

Ren turned as white as week-old ash. "Are you sure?" she said, her voice so quiet it was a wonder Manny heard her.

"Nora is the only one missing," he said. "She was helping with the salvage. She was in the last life-boat and could not swim to the ladder. We are thinking she hit her head . . . maybe on one of the fuel tanks."

"Can . . . can we search for her?"

"We are far away now. We are sailing away from the island." Manny looked over at Simon, seeking support.

Ren stared at Manny, digging her fingers into her keyboard. Her computer began emitting a piercing sound.

"Thank you, Manny," Simon said. "Ren, I'm sorry. Are . . . are you okay to . . . ?"

She removed her fingers from the keyboard, silencing the wailing note.

"I'll see us through the storm."

She quickly repaired whatever damage she had done to her computer, and soon she was responding to the captain's instructions, helping to guide the *Catalina* safely away from the atoll and the funnel clouds. But she moved in a trance. As she deftly adjusted their coordinates and set a course for where the captain predicted the storm would break, tears began to drip down her cheeks. Simon didn't know what Nora had been to her, but he could see that this loss cut deep.

Simon himself felt a sense of complete and utter failure. He had believed that if he could see this group to safety he'd somehow redeem himself for not being with Nina and Naomi in San Diego. There was no way he could have stopped the volcano, but he had begun to think he could keep the people on the *Catalina* safe.

He was wrong.

JUDITH

Judith pretended her tears were from the pain in her side and arm. The rope had scoured layers of skin away when it jerked out of her grasp. The injury was raw and ugly, but it was mostly skin deep. Bruises were emerging on the rest of her body from being bashed against the hull. She couldn't move without pain, but she desperately wanted to be alone. She didn't want to break down in front of the nurse and Penelope.

Nora was dead. Drowned. Lost.

She couldn't process it any more than she could process the fact that her entire family—everyone she'd ever known—was likely dead as well. She had been in Nora's position, floundering in the sea just a moment ago. It had been terrifying, but she was safely back on the *Catalina* now. Why wasn't Nora? Why couldn't Judith pop into the bridge and find Nora sitting there, holding hands with Ren or trying out some new idea on the ship's computers?

Judith wondered if Ren knew what had happened yet. It was cowardly, but she didn't want to be the one to tell her.

She sat up, every stretch and tug of her skin an agony.

"You should stay here, Judith, dear, until Nurse Laura can take you down to the clinic," Penelope said. The nurse was checking on the rest of the group. The remaining eighteen. "The storm's still tossing us around like a corn husk doll." Penelope tried to force her back down without causing her further injury.

"I just want to go to my room," Judith said.

"I need to check on my boys," Penelope said. "I can't take you there now."

"I'll go alone."

"That's not a good idea."

"I'll help."

Michael had appeared behind Penelope. He was completely drenched and still hadn't rolled down the legs of his trousers. He limped toward her.

"No, that's okay. I'll—" Judith began.

But Penelope leapt on Michael's offer.

"Would you? That's ever so kind. She has to be so tough all the time, but she could really use a hand. Let this nice young man help you, dear, and I'll send someone round to check on you."

Penelope didn't wait for a reply. She pressed Michael's hand warmly and then handed him off to Judith.

"Here, put your arm around me," Michael said.

"I can walk," Judith said. "You're the one with the broken foot. It's my arm that's hurt."

"We'll keep each other steady then," Michael said.

As if to punctuate his words, the ship rolled violently, and Judith lost her balance. Michael caught her by the uninjured arm to keep her from falling.

"Okay. My cabin is on the eighth deck."

Michael didn't speak as they walked slowly to the stairs. The elevators had been switched off permanently in case they got stuck. He held her left arm loosely, offering support only when the floor tipped. The storm was in full swing now.

On the stairs every step was agony. The act of moving one foot after another pulled at Judith's ravaged skin and took all of her concentration. Michael's presence was calming, though he must be in as much pain as she was. They hobbled along together, giving each other strength, wrapped up in the simple act of walking home.

At the door to Judith's room, Michael didn't hesitate. When she said, "This is me," he opened the door and helped her inside, making sure she didn't scrape her arm in the narrow doorway.

She avoided looking at Nora's side of the bed, which was strewn with her spare clothes. Outside, the little balcony was slick with rain. The sky beyond it was pitch black, even though it was still late afternoon or early evening as far as she knew.

Michael walked Judith to the bed and helped ease her down onto the comforter. Without a word he knelt down and began to untie her shoes.

"You don't have to do that," she said.

"You shouldn't bend over too much. You can help with mine next."

"You must be hungry. You should get some food. The dining hall's not far."

"When the weather's better," Michael said. "I'm okay for now."

He eased the running shoe off Judith's foot. It was soaking wet and filled with sand. She should have kicked off her shoes when she ended up in the sea. It might have made the swim easier. She wondered if Nora had still been wearing her big combat boots.

Michael carried the shoes to the shower and returned with two dry towels.

"Do you have running water?"

"Yes, but we're rationing."

"You might want to take a hot shower to warm you up," Michael said, looking pretty cold and wet himself.

"You were in the water longer than I was. You can use my shower if you want. We're allowed five minutes."

"Let's get you settled first." He carefully removed her socks—also full of sand—and then handed her one of the towels. "Here, hold this. Um . . . do you mind if I . . . ?"

His cheeks flushed, making the chiseled angles of his face look young. He probably wasn't much older than Judith.

"I'm wearing shorts under these," she said.

Her *Catalina* sweater was gone. It must have gotten ripped pretty badly by the rope. Penelope or the nurse had taken it off, leaving her in the tight black sports top she'd gone running in what seemed like a lifetime ago. She'd have to see if there were any clothes left in the gift shop.

Michael helped her stand and carefully peeled the cold, damp yoga pants down her thighs. She couldn't bend down without hurting her side and arm, so she put both hands on his shoulders to keep her balance. She felt his hot breath on her legs as he bent lower to ease the wet fabric off her skin. When she sat down again, she avoided his eyes.

Michael wrapped the dry towel around her legs and rubbed them briskly. Warmth returned to her. She began to shiver, which she thought was a good sign.

"Do you have anything else to put on?" Michael asked.

"This is all I had when I ran to the ship," Judith said. She glanced at Nora's clothes piled on top of her suitcase, then looked away quickly. Nora was— had been—a lot shorter than her anyway. She wrapped the towel tighter around her legs and pulled the blanket up around her shoulders.

"Sit down and give me your foot," she said.

Michael obeyed, pulling up the chair from the little desk and lifting his foot to Judith so she wouldn't have to bend over. She began to work at the stiff laces.

Michael winced as Judith pulled the shoe off, followed by his sock. Deep-bluish bruises had begun to appear across the top of his foot. He must have twisted it badly when he leapt out of the way of the fuel tank.

"Where are you from?" Judith asked, trying to keep him talking to take his mind off the pain. She felt the bones in his foot gently. She didn't think they were actually broken, but she wasn't sure.

"A small town outside of Oklahoma City," Michael said through gritted teeth.

"Do you think it was far enough away to escape the ash fall?"

"I'm more worried about folks running out of food. If the crops fail, it's going to be rough for a while."

"Is your family there?" Judith asked. She wrapped a hand towel gently around his injured foot and gestured for him to give her the other one.

"Yeah. My kid brother graduates from high school this year. He's a star football player. On his way to college on a scholarship. Everything I wasn't."

"You didn't go to college?" Judith asked. She eased the shoe and sock off his other foot.

"Nope. Straight to the navy for me. Grades weren't good enough for anything else."

"You look like a football player too," Judith said, bending lower over Michael's feet. She tried to rub some warmth into the uninjured one. It helped her fingers regain some of their feeling.

"I'm nowhere near as good as my brother Matt was—is," Michael said.

He frowned, meeting Judith's eyes. She thought of her half siblings, wishing she had spent more time with them. The older one hadn't been born until she was on her way to college, and she hadn't really made a point of bonding with him, if you could even bond with a toddler. She should have been a better sister. The regret ached, a chronic pain that she'd been trying to ignore.

"So, did you live in San Diego?" he asked after a while.

"Yeah. I go—went—to college there. I was jogging along the boardwalk when the disaster hit."

"I'd finished my shore leave the day before," Michael said. "My buddies and I went up to LA to see the Avenue of Stars. Even spent a day at Disneyland. I'd never been there before. And now here I am."

He removed his feet from Judith's lap and began peeling off his own sodden clothes. He had all the muscles of a football player too. His broad, chiseled stomach was tanned but lighter than the deep, permanent tan on his arms and face. Judith looked down at her towel-wrapped legs. A small-town football player bound for the armed services, though? She didn't even have crushes on that type of guy when she was a teenager. She supposed a lot had changed since then. Everything had changed.

When Michael went to dump his wet clothes in the bathroom, she noticed an anchor tattoo on his arm. There was something sweetly cliché about it. She felt a light flutter in her chest, soft as moth wings. No, there was no denying she was attracted to this man.

"Any trick to the shower?" he asked. He wore only a pair of boxer briefs now.

"What? Um, no. I can't promise the water will be hot."

"Long as I can get rid of the sand and salt, I'll be happy. Will you be okay for a minute?"

"Of course. This is my room," Judith said.

He gave a trace of a smile and then closed the bathroom door.

Judith shook her head. *Pull yourself together!*

She needed to rest. She'd be able to think more clearly in the morning. She eased herself back on the bed, still wrapped in the towel, and brought the blanket up to her shoulder on the left side. She couldn't pull it any higher on the right because her skin was too raw. She felt exposed, lying partway uncovered and sideways so her battered skin wouldn't come in contact with the bed.

She tried to doze, but she felt too wired from her dunking in the sea. It was still stormy, though not as bad as last time. The sounds of the shower came through the thin walls of the stateroom. It occurred to her that Michael had nowhere to stay.

Was he expecting to sleep here in her bed? She wouldn't mind the company, but she'd already shared an unusual level of intimacy with this man. They'd been through a crazy ordeal together, but that didn't mean she knew him. At all.

The water shut off. Judith couldn't see the changing area outside the bathroom or the stateroom door from where she was lying. If Michael thought she was already asleep, he might slip away quietly. She lifted her head so he'd see she was awake. She didn't want him to go.

"Hey." He came around the corner from the changing area. "You were right about no hot water, but it feels good to be clean. I rinsed my clothes too."

He had a towel wrapped around his waist. Water droplets made tracks down his chest.

"You might find some extras in the shopping arcade."

"I'd like to wait until the storm's over." He stood in the doorway expectantly.

"You can stay here," Judith said, perhaps a little too quickly. She blushed. "Until the storm's over, I mean."

He nodded and hobbled back to the bed. He gathered up some of Nora's things and moved them to the end. The mattress creaked when he sat.

"How are you feeling?" he asked.

"Like my side is on fire," she said. "Helps with the cold, I guess."

"You did well out there. You're pretty brave."

"We'd better still have those fuel tanks after this is all over."

Michael grinned. "I tie a mean sailor's knot. We'll have one at least."

"Good," Judith said. "I don't know where we'll go with it, though." She shivered. They'd been turned away from Hawaii and from Guam. They had to find refuge somewhere. "Where do you think we'll end up?"

"Maybe nowhere," Michael said after a moment. "At least not right away. Moving around probably takes up eighty-five percent of this ship's energy. The fuel would go a lot further if we weren't trying to get anywhere."

"You mean if we just floated along until things calm down?"

"Something like that," Michael said. "Things don't seem to be any better on land, if you believe the reports."

"We just don't know," Judith said. "That's the whole problem, right?"

"Yeah. No, we'll have to go somewhere. I need to get home. Maybe there will be news in the morning."

They were quiet for a moment. Michael lay back and lifted his battered foot onto the clothes piled at the end of the bed. He put his hands behind his head and stared at the ceiling, preparing to sleep.

Judith wanted to hear his voice for a little while longer.

"How long do you think we could last, floating along like that?" she asked.

"Depends how good we got at fishing," Michael said. "And how long we could avoid scurvy."

"We've been eating a bit of seaweed already. That has plenty of nutrients."

"Blech. I hate the stuff, but you're right."

"Hmm . . . staying on the *Catalina*," Judith said. She did not like the idea one bit. She wanted to get her feet back on land. Real land, not just a patch of sand in the middle of the ocean.

"It's probably just the hypothermia talking," Michael said. "We'll be able to disembark somewhere. There've got to be relief organizations on the move by now."

"I hope so. Maybe Nora can—" Judith fell silent abruptly. She'd forgotten.

"She was your friend who . . ."

"Yeah. She was kind of a computer genius. She was helping us keep track of what was going on in the world." Judith swallowed and looked over at the window. The wind howled against the panes, rattling them like ghosts.

"How close were you?" Michael asked.

Judith let out something between a sob and laugh. "I only knew her for a few days. It seemed like a lot longer."

"That's how it works in traumatic situations," Michael said. "That's why war buddies are for life. I'm sorry about Nora."

"It's stupid," Judith said. "She made it out of San Diego. We were the survivors. But she just couldn't swim well enough." Judith wrapped her fingers around her blanket, as if squeezing it would somehow ease the enormous pain in her chest. "It's not fair." She could barely hold in the tears.

"Nothing's fair anymore," Michael said. "The world has gone to hell."

"It's stupid," Judith said again. She really was crying now. She hated crying.

Michael sat up and reached across the small gap between them to put his hand on top of Judith's fist. His warmth relaxed and calmed her. Almost involuntarily the tension in her body eased. Michael reached out to wipe the tears off her face.

"I'm sorry," he said again.

He stayed like that, one hand over her hand, the other hovering near her face, like he was ready to block out the rest of the world. She felt like she was holding her breath and Michael was leaning forward, offering an oxygen mask, but she couldn't quite bring herself to take it.

Then the exhaustion of the day tumbled onto her. She closed her eyes, relaxed. With Michael's hand still covering hers, she succumbed to sleep.

SIMON

When the storm finally calmed, Simon looked out at a changed sea. He had no idea how long it had been, but suddenly the water was as flat as glass. Clouds still swirled above it, milky and chilled.

Ren had finally gone to bed. Vinny and Kim were up in the radio tower, trying to figure out where the storm had brought them and if there was anyone else out there. Captain Martinelli had returned to his quarters. As soon as they were far enough away from the atoll to be safe, they'd shut off the engines and allowed the sea to toss them where it willed.

The navy had forsaken them. They were being pushed away time and again. They couldn't communicate with the outside world. They had lost another of their number. They had nowhere to go. Simon felt the clutches of despair in his heart. When was this going to end?

16. The Shops

SIMON STROLLED ALONG THE plaza in the early-morning hours, surveying the damage. The plaza had been decorated to look like a boardwalk, with tropical-themed shops along the perimeter. In addition to the huge cruise gift shop, there were boutiques selling patio clothes, over-priced artwork, sunglasses, and swimming trunks. There was even a bookstore, and this was where Simon stopped.

The first storm had sent books and merchandise cascading to the floor. Some effort had been made to clean up the mess, but they'd had the sense not to put everything back on the shelves, stacking the books on the floor to prevent them from being damaged further. This storm hadn't been quite as bad as the first, but the books had still scattered as the ship tossed.

Simon began shifting books, clearing a path through the shop. The sound of paper against paper whispered through the air. One bookshelf had tipped over. On the other side, Penelope Newton sat on the floor sorting through the children's section.

"Hello, Simon," she said brightly.

"Penelope."

"How are you holding up?"

"It's been a rough night," Simon said. "For all of us. What are you doing?"

"Just picking out a few stories for my boys. I can't approve of the content of some of these so-called children's books." She held up a book with some sort of sorcerer on the cover. "Gotta narrow it down a bit."

"You look out for them."

Penelope sighed. "I'm not sure if it'll matter in the end."

"What won't matter?" Simon asked. He had come to expect Penelope's persistent optimism. He might not agree with her on many things, but she always seemed so cheerful.

"Whether they read one more story with magic or too much sex," Penelope said. She frowned at the small pile of books she had stacked in front of her. "I want to keep the same standards despite everything, but sometimes I don't know if it'll end up being all that important."

"I think it's important," Simon began slowly, "that you continue to parent them in the midst of all of this. And you're trying to be a good parent."

"Yes," Penelope said. "You're right. It just gets hard sometimes."

She met his eyes for a moment. There were new lines in her face, and her gaze was vulnerable and sad. Her eyes were quite pretty, really. There was more to Penelope than Simon had thought at first.

Then she gave a little sniff and resumed sorting through books.

"Do you need any help?" Simon said.

"Not with this, but it sure is a shame to leave all these books lying around like no one cares about them," Penelope said. Her voice was determinedly cheerful again, though she still sniffled every once in a while. "That's why you're here, isn't it?"

"I needed somewhere to think," Simon said. "This seems like the most sensible place for it."

"What are you thinking about?" Penelope asked politely. She shifted the stacks of books across the floor, back to her usual bustling self.

"What to do next," Simon said. "After Guam didn't work out . . . I don't know where to go from here." He knelt on the floor of the bookshop and began picking up paperbacks. "We have the fuel tanks now, and we salvaged a few extra things that might be useful. I just don't know when it's all going to end. If we were going to hold on for another week, I could take it. If we were going to hold on for exactly two months and four days, I could take it. It's the not knowing that worries me. Should we be rationing for the long haul? If so, things are going to get a bit less comfortable around here."

"Well, the Lord always said we wouldn't know the day or the hour of His coming," Penelope said. She took a book with animals on the cover out of Simon's hands and added it to her small stack. "I believe we're seeing signs of the End of Days. We don't know when the Second Coming will be, so we've got to hang in there. The apostles believed the Lord would come again during their lifetime. That didn't happen, but I think it's a good bet He'll come again in ours, what with all the signs. I've been doing some reading . . ."

Penelope stood and retrieved a worn Bible from where she'd placed it on a now-empty display counter. It was in a carrying case made of some sort of quilted fabric, and the corners were frayed. The tome overflowed with sermon notes and pretty bookmarks printed with inspirational sayings.

Penelope opened the Bible to the very end.

"Seven years, Simon!" she gushed. "That's what we're looking at. Seven years of tribulation before the last battle. I've always been in the Pre-Trib camp myself. I thought we'd be raptured before the Last Days because I didn't think Jesus would want his people to go through all this. But I've been faithful, and he wouldn't have left me and my boys behind, so we must be looking at a Mid-Trib—that's three and a half years—or a Post-Trib scenario."

Penelope explained the signs and portents she believed heralded the Last Days. She catalogued the events, referenced verses. Simon didn't think they were living in some cosmic end-time, but Penelope's voice was calming. The order and methodology of her words soothed him. She was carving out meaning for herself in the madness of the last week and a half. It must be easier than questioning why all this was allowed to happen in the first place. Even if she was completely wrong, her soul was more at peace than Simon's. He wished he too could simply study the right passages in a book to find the answers to his doubts and fears.

It was one of the things he had always liked about being Jewish. He hadn't followed the rules to the letter for years, but there was a consistency and staidness to his heritage that he appreciated. Regardless of whether or not he was personally religious, the tradition was something to study and to practice. But now he wanted an explanation for why all this had happened.

Penelope noticed he had fallen silent. "I'm sorry to babble on like this, Simon," she said. "It . . . it helps that we might be able to work out what's coming next."

"I almost hope you're right, Penelope," Simon said. "But like you said, we won't know the hour, so we need to focus on what to do in the next few days."

"How far d'you think we can get on that extra fuel?" Penelope asked.

"Ren thinks we should be able to get all the way to Southeast Asia on it . . . or all the way back to Hawaii. We can't do both. We don't want to make the wrong choice." He hesitated, then voiced the doubt he hadn't shared with anyone else yet. "I'm not sure we'll find solace in either location."

Penelope gasped. "You don't think they'd help us? Of course they'll help us!"

Simon smiled. Despite everything, she still had faith in humanity as well as in God.

"No one else has helped us so far," he said. "I hope they will, but they're dealing with problems of their own. We're almost better off sailing around for a little while."

"We have to get back on dry land, Simon," Penelope said. "We can't raise our kids on this boat."

"Maybe it's like the Ark," Simon said. "Maybe the *Catalina* will keep us safe."

Penelope smiled. "It already has."

They returned to sorting through the books. Simon arranged them by topic and author, even though he knew another storm could pick them up and toss them about again at any moment. It made him feel better to find order in the midst of the chaos.

JUDITH

Before Judith opened her eyes, the pain reignited in her side and arm, reminding her immediately of what had happened. Her dreams had been filled with dark waves, ropes tangled around her like snakes, and Nora disappearing beneath the ship again and again.

The next thing she became aware of before she opened her eyes was deep, heavy breathing. Warmth touched her face with the sound of each breath. She remembered this part even more clearly. She opened her eyes.

Michael lay beside her, partially on top of the covers. He had fallen asleep holding her hand instead of climbing beneath them. Judith sat up slowly so as not to disturb him. Each movement hurt worse than the last. She must have pulled every muscle she had.

She eased herself out of bed and tiptoed to the bathroom. She managed to undress without crying and took a cold, head-clearing shower. She scrubbed her hair and winced through each drop of water that fell on her wounded skin.

She thought about the man sleeping in her bed, recalling the feeling of his hands on hers the night before, the way the muscles rippled in his stomach. His strength was positively seductive.

But she reminded herself these were extreme circumstances. They had been through a very intense day. She had latched onto him in the midst of the crisis. It didn't mean anything. It was the danger, the adrenaline. She didn't even like jocks! They spent too much time in the gym and not enough time doing useful things, like homework. But that gym time paid off . . . Judith let the shower water course over her face, her sore muscles forgotten for a moment. *Stop it! Just because the world is ending, doesn't mean you need to throw yourself into the first muscular pair of arms you find.* They'd be getting off the ship soon anyway.

Judith turned off the water and stepped out of the shower. She wiped the fog from the bathroom mirror to reveal her reflection. She looked like a drowned golden retriever. She grabbed the spare towel from the rack to dry her hair, then ran her fingers through it, trying to make it look tousled and beachy. *Get a grip, Judith. When have you ever used the word "beachy"?*

She yanked open the bathroom door. Michael was standing right outside it in the changing area.

"What are you doing?" she gasped.

She quickly swung the towel around herself. In her haste, it scoured against the scabs forming on her damaged skin. The pain made her angry, as well as embarrassed.

"I wanted to see if you were—"

"What? Naked?" Judith shrieked. "Yes, genius. I was showering. Get out!"

"I was just trying to—"

"Out!"

Michael shrugged and ducked back around the wardrobe.

Judith finished drying herself off. There was blood on the towel now from where it had rubbed against her raw skin. What was he thinking, lurking outside the door while she showered? Obviously, he could hear the water running. Judith realized she didn't have any clean clothes to put on. That made her even more annoyed.

She wrapped the towel tightly around her body and stalked out of the changing area. Michael was sitting on the chair, slowly putting on his shoes.

"Sorry about that," he said breezily. "I was worried you were having trouble moving and thought I'd see if you needed help."

Face burning, Judith sat down across from him. She had overreacted. It was not like she'd never been naked in front of a man before. They were both adults.

"Look, if you want to make yourself useful you can do me a favor," she said stiffly.

Michael grinned. "What kind of favor?"

Judith fought a smile and scowled unconvincingly. "You can go to the plaza two decks below us and find me some clothes from the shops. Just take them. No one will stop you."

"Sure. Any particular requests? Lingerie or—"

"Leave them outside the door when you come back."

"I'm just jok— "

"If you can't find the plaza, someone will direct you. And get something warm, if you don't mind."

Michael chuckled. What did he think was so funny? He retrieved his now-dry undershirt from the bathroom and came back into the room to put it on. He did it slowly, reaching his strong arms above his head and pulling the hem slowly over the muscles in his stomach. Judith pretended to look the other way.

As soon as he was gone, Judith wished she could call him back. She hadn't meant to snap at him. She'd been embarrassed. It was not like he could hear what she had been thinking about him. She should really apologize.

No, it was probably just as well. Michael was a distraction, one that would never go anywhere. And he had no right to flaunt himself in front of her like that! She ran her fingers through her hair and gingerly began to check her wounds.

SIMON

When Simon left the bookstore, he felt calmer about their next course of action. They'd have to press on and find somewhere to make landfall in Asia. There was no point going back. He needed to talk to Ren about the particulars, and he wanted to run the idea by Judith too. He had come to rely on her judgment.

As he walked toward his cabin, he ran into Michael. The seaman was limping, and he seemed to have some sort of hand towel bound tightly around one foot. But he straightened to attention when he saw Simon.

"Sir," the younger man said, nodding at him. They stopped on the grand staircase for a moment.

"Hello, Michael. Did you find somewhere to stay last night?" Simon asked.

"Temporarily. But I might need more permanent quarters, sir. Are there any spare crew cabins available?"

"I can find out where Nora was staying. That will probably have to do for now."

Michael made an odd face that Simon couldn't read.

"That might not . . . Thank you, sir," he said. "Can I take clothes from one of the shops? I can't pay for them now but—"

"Yes, of course," Simon said. "I should have offered sooner. We've been using whatever we need."

"Do you have a system for it, sir? Like a rationing station, so that everyone gets an equal share."

"Not an official one yet, but that's a good idea," Simon said. "We may need to rotate through what we have here. Some people have their own luggage."

"Some of you came on with nothing, right?" Michael asked. "Judith said . . . Never mind."

Simon raised an eyebrow. "Yes. I've been wearing the same thing for a week and a half, and so has my daughter." His navy-blue trousers were looking quite washed out from their repeated drenchings in salt water. "Let me show you the shops. They're a mess, but you should be able to find a few things that fit."

"Thank you, sir."

"Please call me Simon. And I'll keep calling you Michael instead of Seaman Williams if that's okay."

They walked together along the second level of the plaza. Simon was still trying to get a read on Michael. He treated Simon like a superior officer and on the surface showed the disciplined carriage you'd expect from an enlisted sailor. He seemed like a navy man through and through. And yet he had deserted on the off chance it might help him get home to his family sooner. Perhaps it was a sign of how much the world had changed.

Simon and Michael went into a boutique filled with stylish patio clothes. Simon figured he'd pick up a few things for himself and Esther while he was at it.

"How old is your daughter?" Michael asked.

"Six," Simon said. "She's a wild one. She loves the ship. She keeps pestering the engine crew, trying to get them to teach her things." He picked up a pair of green board shorts that would fit Esther nicely.

"It's not that safe for a little kid in an engine room," Michael said.

"Nowhere is safe," Simon said. "But she's smart, and she knows not to get into anything that'll hurt her."

"That's great that you have her here with you," Michael said.

He had gone straight to the women's clothing section. Simon didn't comment on it as Michael sorted through a stack of sweaters, holding them up to compare the sizes.

After a while Michael asked, "Where's her mother?"

"She was in San Diego with my other daughter, Naomi."

"I'm sorry."

"I don't know whether I should assume they're dead or hold out hope that they're alive," Simon said. "Neither perspective is helpful right now."

"You don't think anyone survived in San Diego at all?"

"I don't see how they could have," Simon said. "There was so much ash. It may look light and fluffy, but it would cling to the insides of your lungs and throat. Anyone who breathed it in wouldn't stand a chance. And if they've had any rain, the weight of the mud would collapse the roofs of the buildings. I can't imagine they could have lasted long."

"What about hiding in basements?"

"Wouldn't have made the air any cleaner," Simon said.

He had gone through these arguments before. Each time he ruled out a possibility, it felt like a tiny betrayal of Nina and Naomi. He wanted to keep hoping, but how could they possibly have made it?

"Does your daughter know?" Michael asked.

"Not sure she grasps it," Simon said, "but I'm trying to make her understand. The sooner she can accept it, the better."

"I don't grasp it myself," Michael said.

He had selected two piles of clothing. One would fit him; the other was obviously for a woman. A small puzzle piece clicked into place. Perhaps he had found somewhere to stay after all.

Simon and Michael shook hands at the door.

"I'm calling a meeting this afternoon to discuss our next course of action," Simon said. "We'll gather in the Mermaid Lounge on the ninth deck, if you'd like to join us."

"I'll be there," Michael said.

"Good. And would you please make sure Judith comes too?" Simon said.

The look of surprise on Michael's face confirmed Simon's suspicions. He smiled and clapped the younger man on the shoulder, leaving him gaping as he headed back up the stairs.

17. Decisions

JUDITH

JUDITH ARRIVED IN THE Mermaid Lounge wearing the outfit Michael had brought for her. He had simply knocked, called to her through the door about the meeting, and left the clothes on her doorstep. She had been more than ready to apologize for snapping and invite him back inside, but he just left, making her angry all over again. She should have pulled him straight back into her room.

The slim-fit trousers were exactly the right size, and he had also brought her a gray sweater that might have been cashmere. She was lucky it was soft because her side and arm still burned from the rope. She'd only managed to make it through an early lunch before she had to return to her room to clean her wounds again.

Now she joined the other members of the informal leadership council to hear what Simon thought they should do now that Guam was no longer an option. There were about forty people there already, more than usually attended the meetings. The lounge was somewhat the worse for wear after the storm, and everyone pitched in to pick up broken glasses and overturned chairs before the meeting.

Judith tried to help, but her injured skin still pulled at her. She went over to the bar overlooking the ocean and leaned on her good side. The sea outside was remarkably calm, but the sky was much darker than it should be. Would they ever see the sun again?

There was no point thinking like that. They'd press on and be back on land soon. This couldn't last much longer.

Judith scanned the small crowd for Michael but spotted Ren instead. She was sitting in a corner of the lounge, her face withdrawn and her eyes red. Judith knew she should go over, but she didn't want to talk about Nora. She hadn't been to see Ren at all today. She couldn't face her friend's grief as she tried to stamp down her own. She kept trying to remind herself that she'd only known Nora for a little while and they probably wouldn't have met or become friends in other circumstances, but it didn't matter. She felt her loss like the cut of a razor.

Michael arrived, limping, with Reggie and a handful of men from the crew, many of them carrying leftovers from lunch. They were laughing and shoving each other jovially. They chose a booth on the far side of the lounge. Michael sat in the outermost seat and put his elbows on the table. He'd obviously gotten his clothes from the same shop as hers. He wore white linen trousers and a polo shirt underneath a navy-blue sweater, like a banker on his way to the Bahamas. It was an illusion, though. There was something homegrown about him. He fit in better with Reggie and the crew than he would have with the guys from her university.

Michael glanced up and spotted Judith. He looked her up and down and gave a thumbs-up. She folded her arms—or tried to, until it made her rope burn hurt—and stuck her tongue out at him. She regretted it instantly. *Ugh. Why can't I just act like a normal person?* But Michael just laughed and pretended to take a picture with an imaginary camera. Judith giggled in spite of herself.

Reggie noticed the exchange between Michael and Judith. He said something that made the whole table laugh. Michael chucked a bit of a roll at him. Judith scowled at Reggie and scooted further around the bar toward the sea, her face reddening.

When she peeked at the group of men again, Reggie held everyone's attention. The conversation had turned serious, and the men were leaning in to listen. People were really beginning to look up to Reggie, especially after his efforts on the beach. He was becoming more and more of a leader each day. If Judith wanted that for herself, she couldn't have Reggie catching her flirting.

But no one was more in charge than Simon. He worked the crowd, speaking softly, patting backs and pressing hands. That's what Judith aspired to. She would never command the sort of respect Simon got if she allowed herself to be distracted by a guy. Maybe she shouldn't open herself up to another friendship anyway. Losing Nora was too recent, too raw. And it would never last.

"Whatcha doin', Judy?" said a voice near waist level.

"Oh, nothing. Hi, Esther," Judith said.

The little girl had come up beside her.

"Are you hiding?" Esther asked.

"No."

"Then why are you standing over here?"

"I'm just . . . I thought it would be easier to see from over here."

"Me too," Esther said. "But I'm short." She climbed up onto a bar stool. She had a clump of seaweed in her hand, and she was pulling pieces off and chewing them thoughtfully. "You look pretty, Judy. Where'd you get those clothes?"

"A friend got them for me."

"What friend?"

"Oh, no one. You're wearing new clothes too, aren't you? Where's your Thomas shirt?"

"Daddy said we had to wash it again," Esther said. "I didn't think it smelled like fish, but he got me this *Catalina* shirt to wear instead."

"I like it," Judith said.

Esther crossed her legs so she was perched like a little genie on the bar stool.

"What's Daddy going to talk to everyone about?" she asked.

"I don't know."

"Doesn't he tell you things? I thought you were his assistant or something."

"I guess I sort of am. He hasn't told me, though."

It made Judith smile to hear that Simon apparently thought of her as his assistant.

Across the bar, Simon stepped to the middle of the room. There were about fifty people here now, and they all quieted immediately.

"Good evening, everyone," Simon said. "I hope you all came through the storm all right. You've all been doing a lot to keep the ship in order. I think it's really helpful and a great habit to get into." Simon scanned the room, stopping often to look individuals in the eyes. He smiled at Judith when he saw her standing by the bar. Then his eyes landed on Esther and he smiled wider. "I think it's time that we talked through our options and decide our next course of action," Simon continued. "Ren tells me we're about three days out from Southeast Asia in one direction and four days from Hawaii in the other. We've already established that Hawaii has its own problems. It may not be the best place to go. We just don't know if Asia will be any better. If we go back to Hawaii, we'll be in a disaster zone, but we'll be in our own country. If we make landfall in Indonesia, for example, we may be better off, but we'll be foreigners. We'll just have to hope they'll help us."

"So you want us to pick a direction?" Reggie asked.

"Unfortunately, we don't have enough fuel to sail for more than four or five days, though yesterday's salvage expedition helped a lot," Simon said. He hesitated for a moment. "I'll be honest with you," he said. "I think we should keep moving forward. We'll have lots of options to disembark somewhere in Asia. We'll likely reach the Philippines in a few days, but if we end up with more weather problems we could try Japan or Indonesia or even China. If we sail back to Hawaii, we may overshoot, just like last time. And we'll be out of luck if they still can't help us. I say we go west—to the East."

"I agree!" said someone sitting at the table nearest to Simon. "Hawaii's a bust."

"The further away we get from the volcano, the better."

"Simon's right. I say we do whatever Simon thinks is best!"

"Hear! Hear!"

Simon waited until everyone had voiced their opinions and then took a vote. Sailing west toward Asia won by a significant margin. No one wanted to sail back the way they'd come from. It was too late to go back.

"Thank you for voting, everyone," Simon said. "Now there's another issue I want to raise. We don't have visas obviously, and we have no idea how welcoming of refugees whatever country we end up in will be. I think we should prepare for a longer time living on the ship, just in case we need to use it as a floating hotel offshore for a little while. Let's fish. Let's make better use of the cruise stuff and divide up clothes and personal items so everyone has a fair share. Let's salvage whatever we can find floating on the water. Anything at all. We never know when we'll be able to use it."

"What about water? And electricity?"

"Good point. We should conserve as much as possible."

"I just want to get off this godforsaken boat," Horace said from one of the tables.

"So do I. But let's take these precautions just in case. It'll give us something to do over the next few days while we're on our way."

Most people seemed to think Simon was overly cautious, but he persisted. It was getting late, and they were growing restless and hungry. Finally, they agreed to indulge him. By the time the council meeting broke up, it was past dinnertime. Judith wondered if Simon held the meeting late so that people would be eager to agree with him so they could head to dinner. Could Simon be that shrewd? If not, it was certainly a tactic he should make use of in the future. She made a note to remind him.

Judith stood up from the bar, the pull of her skin reminding her of her injury. She scowled at the pain and then glanced up to see a look of surprise on Michael's face. He'd been limping toward her, but he turned around again at the sight of her scowl. It hadn't been directed at him! Judith started to go after him, but Simon was heading her way.

"How are you feeling, Judith?" he asked. "Manny told me you had a rough time in the storm."

"My arm and side got scraped up and I pulled a muscle or two, but I'll be fine. It just hurts to move too much."

"I'm sorry about Nora," Simon said quietly. "I know she was your friend.

"Thanks," Judith said. "It's harder on Ren than on me." She looked over at her other friend. She should go and console her, but she felt a fierce flash of panic at having to confront Ren's pain directly.

Simon just nodded and offered his arm to help her toward the door. He seemed to sense that she needed assistance without her having to say so. His presence was comforting, as always. Why couldn't her father have been more like him? Judith had tried so hard to get him to recognize her capabilities, and he had barely noticed. But Simon took her seriously.

"What did you think of the meeting?" Simon asked as they walked.

Esther had hopped off her stool and darted ahead to pester Frank with questions.

"You're obviously right about Asia being the only sensible choice," Judith said. "But you don't think we'll be getting off the boat anytime soon, do you?"

Simon was silent for a moment. They ambled along, Judith unable to move too fast. A few people skirted them in the corridor as they headed for the dining hall.

"That's partially it," he said.

"You want everyone to get used to following a system, just in case the worst happens," Judith guessed.

"People need to stay busy," Simon said. "If we follow a routine every day, they will already be in the habit, and they'll have something to look forward to each day. I'm concerned about what will happen to this group if their hopes are dashed yet again and they don't have anything to do on top of it. Better to get some routines going first."

"That's smart," Judith said.

"It's necessary, unfortunately. Do you think it's too calculating?"

"Even if it is, it's for everyone's good," Judith said.

Simon gave her a cautious look. "Perhaps."

If she was honest, Judith thought he was probably worrying too much. Someone *would* help them. Basic human decency had to prevail eventually.

When they reached the dining hall, they joined Esther and Frank at their usual table. Judith was easing herself into her chair when Michael walked up, managing to saunter despite his limp. He addressed himself directly to Simon.

"Is it okay if I sit with you and your family, sir?"

"Of course, Michael. You know Judith," Simon said. *What's that grin on his face about?* "And this is our resident engineer, Frank Fordham, and Esther, my daughter."

SIMON

Simon wondered if he'd misjudged whether something was going on between Judith and Michael after all. They looked like a couple, both young and good looking, wearing clothes borrowed from the same plaza shop. Michael angled himself toward Judith and looked over at her often as he chatted with Frank about his engineering work.

But Judith barely said a word, answering Michael's questions with one-word answers whenever possible. Her natural confidence that had first caught Simon's attention was temporarily suspended. Simon had rather liked the prospect of young love amid these circumstances, but it didn't look like that was on Judith's mind. Maybe her injuries were distracting her. Or perhaps she was shy.

Esther wasn't shy though.

"Are you from a battleship?" she asked Michael.

"Nope," he said. "I worked on a destroyer. The navy doesn't have battleships anymore."

"Really? Why?"

"They're too big and old," Michael said. "We—they—use destroyers, cruisers, and frigates now."

"But those are still warships, right?"

"Yes, they are," Michael said. "You know a lot about ships."

Esther grinned gleefully and tugged on Judith's sleeve to make sure she had heard. Judith winced, probably at the pain, but she always had a smile for Esther.

When everyone was mostly finished eating, Reggie came over to their table. He carried a large black guitar case.

"Found this down in the theater," he said. "Want to jam, Mike? It might help cheer people up a bit. It's like a funeral in here."

"Sure," Michael said. He jumped up, glancing at Judith before following Reggie to the center of the dining hall.

Reggie climbed onto a chair and shouted to get everyone's attention.

"Yo, hope you folks don't mind. This here is Mikey, and he was telling me earlier that he used to play a bit of guitar. I happen to have a few hidden talents myself, so I thought we'd try something out. It's getting gloomy around here."

Reggie climbed down to confer with Michael for a few minutes as people turned their chairs to listen. Simon glanced at Judith and noticed she was looking intently at Michael. She kept almost smiling and then quickly schooling her features back to neutral.

After a moment Reggie said, "Right, here's an oldie we both know. It seems about right for today."

He climbed back onto the chair, and Michael drew up another one beside him. He took out the guitar and strummed it a few times. Then he began to play.

Simon didn't recognize the song, but a few others around the room did. They started tapping their feet. Michael was very good. Then Reggie sang in a raspy, soulful baritone.

Seabird

See pretty bird
Seabird blue
Seabird
See pretty pretty
Seabird blue

My girl is a pretty bird
Seabird blue
The sea sings
Pretty bird
Seabird blue
Alone with pretty bird
Seabird blue

Michael joined in, adding a bit of harmony. The young men held their audience captive. As they played and sang, more people around the dining hall began to smile and tap their feet. The rhythm drummed around the room like gentle rain. On the next chorus, Willow Weathers, the lounge singer, who had just arrived, sang along.

Seabird
See pretty bird
Seabird blue
Seabird
See pretty pretty
Seabird blue

Blue sea is a pretty song

Sea song blue
My girl sings
Pretty song
Seabird blue
With me sings pretty bird
Sea song blue

Judith had stopped trying to maintain an indifferent expression. She stared at Michael, mouth slightly open. Michael looked up at her and missed two notes because of it. After his second mistake, Judith started to smile. Simon grinned. They'd be all right.

Come home, sweet pretty bird
Blue sea blue
I miss my
Pretty bird
Seabird blue

Seabird
See pretty bird
Seabird blue
Seabird
See pretty pretty
Seabird blue

Come home, sweet pretty bird
Seabird blue

When the song finished, Reggie took a bow and everyone in the dining hall applauded. Willow joined them by the table, along with a handful of others. Simon thought he heard mention of drums and maybe a violin. In addition to the eager musicians, a group of younger women crowded around Reggie and Michael. Reggie leaned jauntily against the table, enjoying the attention, but Michael squeezed through and returned to their table.

Judith leapt out of her chair as if she'd received an electric shock. "I'm going to get some air on deck," she said.

"I can walk you," Michael offered.

"No need. I can find my own way."

Judith turned and walked gingerly away. She looked back at the table before disappearing through the far door, but Michael didn't see it. He sat down, looking dejected.

"Young man, you're in trouble." Frank chuckled deeply.

"What?"

"You're trying too hard with that girl—and not hard enough!"

"I don't know what you're talking about," Michael said, bending over his empty plate.

"Yeah, what *are* you talking about, Frank?" Esther asked. "Why is Michael in trouble?"

Frank leaned toward her conspiratorially. "He has a crush on Judith."

"A crush. Ewwwww!" Esther hopped down from her chair. "I'm going to see if Ana will give me some more shrimp. A crush. Gross."

She darted away, pigtails swinging.

"So, how about it, Michael?" Simon said. He leaned his elbows on the table, and Frank mimicked him.

Michael stared between the two older men, looking cornered.

"We know Judith's something special," Frank said. "If you're man enough for her, I've got a lot of respect for you, but you have to be careful with a woman like that."

Michael coughed theatrically. "No idea what you're talking about."

"Don't let her push you around," Frank said, "but don't try so hard to help her all the time. Women don't like that. She can take care of her own damn self."

"She was hurt," Michael protested.

"Yes, and it's nice for you to play knight in shining armor, but she won't be hurt forever. You've got to have more to offer." Frank was now jabbing his fork at Michael to emphasize each point.

"I—"

"For starters, you should be chasing after her!" Frank said. "Don't let her walk off by herself just because she says she doesn't need help. Damn right she doesn't need help, but I bet you she wants company. If she didn't, she'd have gone back to her room, not mentioned something as romantic as fresh air." Frank jabbed the fork at Michael again. "Learn to read the hints, son, especially when they're written all over her face!"

Michael looked to Simon for help, but he just shrugged. Michael seemed to take that as agreement, because he tipped back his last gulp of water and stood.

"Thanks."

Frank chuckled as Michael limped for the door, looking over his shoulder as if he expected Frank to chase after him with the fork.

"They make 'em more clueless every year," Frank muttered. "You'd have followed her right away, wouldn't you, Simon?"

"Yes," Simon said quietly. "If she was Nina, I'd have followed her across the world."

JUDITH

It was cold on deck. Judith walked slowly, trailing her fingers along the chilled rail. She'd have expected it to be warmer here, even at night. They weren't far from the equator by their last reckoning, but it got colder every day. Maybe the crops really would fail. She wondered if sea life would be more resilient.

The sky was dark, and she prayed for the moon to pierce the sullen night clouds. It had been calm since the last storm, but the skies wouldn't clear. The water was black and still as obsidian. The deck barely moved beneath her feet.

Uneven footfalls sounded behind her. She continued her slow walk along the promenade.

"Judith?"

That deep Oklahoma voice sent a thrill right through the bottom of her toes. *It's about time!* She waited for a few heartbeats. She didn't want to seem *too* happy to see him.

Michael didn't speak again until he was almost close enough to touch her.

"Judith?" he repeated.

She kept her face turned toward the sea, but she could sense him. She wrapped her fingers around the railing.

"Thought you might want some company," he said.

"I'm fine," she said briskly. She wished she could take some of the sharpness out of her tone. Did he have to talk to her like she might break?

He was silent for a moment. The *Catalina* creaked in the darkness.

"Well, I want company," Michael said, "if you don't mind. I'm new around here and all. It'd be nice to have someone to talk to."

"What do you want to talk about?" Judith said.

"Oh, I don't know. Movies . . . the weather . . . whatever you normally talk about when you're getting to know someone. Politics, religion, the meaning of life. You name it."

This was silly. What was the point of getting to know anyone in these circumstances? What did she expect to happen? She'd lose him like she'd lost Nora, or push him away like she was doing to Ren if she let this continue. Then words were tumbling out of her, harsh ones that she couldn't keep back.

"Why don't we talk about how everyone we know is dead? How we can't find a safe harbor and our own people have sent us away. How we aren't going to last another week."

Instead of being taken aback at her tone, Michael just nodded. "That works," he said. "It sucks. It's okay to talk about how much this sucks." He put a hand on her shoulder. The weight of it anchored her to the deck. "With all the shit that's going on right now, it's okay to be angry."

"That's not—"

"Yes, it is. It's okay," Michael said. "Hell, I'm angry too. I walked away from my naval career on the slim chance that my family might be alive somewhere. I swore to be loyal and to sacrifice everything for my country, but it turns out I didn't mean it. I couldn't be loyal to superiors who'd give up their honor like that."

"So we should, what, shout about it?" Judith said. "That won't do any good."

"I don't know," Michael said. "Maybe just acknowledge it. Say, 'Dude, this is the pits' or something. I'm sure you've got a more sophisticated line. I don't want to pretend it all didn't happen."

Judith let out a long breath. "I'm sorry for snapping at you," she said. "Everything's just catching up to me. But seriously, you say you want to get to know me. But do you honestly think anything will come of it? Is that why you followed me outside?"

"I don't know, Judith. I'm going straight to the States to search for my family first chance I get. You know that. I just thought we could be friends, maybe be there for each other a bit."

"I don't need—"

"I need you just as much as you need me."

Michael removed his hand from Judith's shoulder and turned toward the ocean. She felt colder immediately. She ached where his hand had been, as if some precious lifeline had been torn away. She had to grasp it before it was gone. She wrapped her long, thin fingers around his wrist. His pulse beat in time to the lapping of the waves.

"I'll tell you something about me," she whispered. "I'm scared all the time. I'm sad and scared, and I feel like the world will collapse the rest of the way if I lose control for one minute. And my best friend just died. I only knew her for a week, and she was still my best friend. Maybe I just shouldn't make any more friends."

"It's okay." Michael took her face in his hands. He ran his thumbs over her cheekbones, tracing their shape. Then he leaned down and kissed her, touching his lips to hers for the briefest moment. "It'll be okay," he whispered.

Judith stepped into the circle of Michael's arms and put her head on his chest. She still felt sad and scared, but she let herself lean into him. His heart-beat quickened against her ear, unbearably sweet.

She pulled back. "Look, I'm not sure it's a good idea to start something here," she said. "This'll all be over soon. I don't want you to get any ideas."

Michael would search for his family. She would find some way back into the life she'd been about to start. There were no prospects for a relationship here. To entertain the idea would be admitting that their world had truly changed forever.

"Hey, don't worry," Michael said. "I won't follow you home. Maybe something not serious is just what we need." He tapped her on the nose and grinned.

"Yes," Judith said, pretending not to notice the way his thumb brushed her face when he dropped his hand, the way his warmth lingered on her lips. "We've had enough seriousness lately. Race you back to the dining hall?"

"With your scraped side and my smashed foot, it'll be a contest for the ages. You're on."

18. Contact

SIMON

FOR THREE DAYS THE *Catalina* sailed west. Simon roamed the ship, checking on the progress of the cleanup effort, monitoring the new rations stations, and making sure people knew their duties. There was a sense of industry and purpose on the ship that was even better than he had hoped. The melancholy and tension of previous days began to subside.

It made Simon proud to see everyone working hard and following his advice. It felt like when a recalcitrant student turned in a truly excellent research paper. The closer they got to making landfall, the more sure he was that they would be okay, even if they had to stay offshore for a little while before disembarking.

Esther thrived. She kept getting underfoot in the engine room until Reggie and the crew gave her tasks like sorting through bolts and oiling pumps. She had the run of the ship by now, and she'd taken her young friend Neal and some of the other children on tours of the lower reaches of the *Catalina*.

More and more debris floated on the water the closer they got to Asia. They salvaged anything they could, even if they didn't know how it could be used yet. Metal. Plastic. Fabric. The items often came wrapped in seaweed, and they saved this too, spreading it out on the deck, coaxing it to dry in the occasional weak sunlight. Ana and her team invented new ways to prepare the seaweed, adding it to their diminishing diet of nonperishable food items.

They stored the salvage in the shops around the plaza and sorted through the remaining merchandise. They began working out a system so that everyone would have the same number of outfits. Those who still had their luggage donated their excess clothes, or at least some did. Simon was pretty sure others were still holding back. The porters raided the hotel supply for uniforms, towels, and sheets and distributed them evenly. Manny discovered a windfall in the form of bowling shoes. Some people had boarded the ship with nothing more than flip-flops. Soon the hard-toed orange and blue shoes could be seen tramping about the deck on people of all ages.

Simon visited the bridge regularly, but there was little news. No one had been able to connect to the Internet since the last storm. It was as if Nora had taken their last hope of contact with her to the bottom of the sea. They were cut off from the rest of the world. Vinny and Kim tried to find out more information on the radio, but so far they'd only managed to reach a lone Japanese speaker and once heard a barrage of shouts in a language no one recognized. They were alone.

To compensate for the lack of communication with the outside world, people began gathering each night to mingle and chat. They told stories and sang a cappella—everything from campfire songs to sea chanties to Christmas carols. Sometimes Michael would bring out the guitar and others would join him, Reggie, and Willow Weathers in entertaining their fellow Catalinans. The divisions between the passengers, runners, and crew became less distinct the more people pitched in. When everyone was working and eating and sorting through salvage, it was easier for them to forget how they had ended up at sea.

There were arguments, of course, but they were sent to the council whenever possible. Simon tried hard to remain impartial. Decisions were put to a vote, a practice he hoped would stave off politicking and hard feelings. He considered how the council's operations could be made even fairer. Maybe serving on the council should become a rotating duty too.

The high morale and general industriousness lasted until they reached the waters around the Philippines and saw the first bodies.

JUDITH

Judith flipped over a clump of damp seaweed. Manny worked beside her, spreading the dark, oily plants across the foredeck. Michael came over to them and dumped another pile onto the deck from a laundry basket.

"How's it looking?" he asked.

"It takes forever to dry," Judith said.

"We are thinking it will need two more days," Manny said. He scratched at the scab that was peeling away from the cut above his eye. He might have a scar.

"Let's hope we'll be back on land in two days," Michael said. He knelt beside Judith and began spreading out the new seaweed load.

"Yes, but like Simon says, people might not just hand us food right away." Judith moved on to the next pile, putting a hand on Michael's shoulder as she shifted around. Her rope burn was healing well. It itched more than hurt now.

Michael's sprained foot was taking longer to heal, but he claimed the pain wasn't too bad. He'd been working hard alongside the crew, very serious about pulling his weight. He and Judith had spent a lot of time together over the past few days. They tried to keep it light, but they were hanging out pretty much whenever they weren't working. He was sweet and kind and reassuring. Even though this flirtation of theirs wasn't supposed to be serious, he was already the brightest spot in Judith's life. She didn't want to think about what would happen when they reached land.

Michael grinned at her. "Maybe we can sell them some of our seaweed. It's so tasty." He lifted a clump of the stuff toward her face.

"Yeah, delicious," Judith said, avoiding his hands and ducking to poke Michael in the stomach.

He tried to tickle her with his seaweed-covered hands.

That's when they heard the scream. It was an ugly, earth-rending sound, reminding her of those terrible moments in San Diego, of the fear and the ash. The three of them leapt up and ran to the starboard lifeboat deck.

Bernadette, the lavender-haired woman Judith had first seen cooing over the pregnant lady, was the one who had screamed. She leaned over the railing, trembling like a scared puppy. Michael put an arm around her shoulders and pulled her away from the edge. Judith and Manny exchanged glances and looked down together.

The water below was a murky brown. Debris floated thick here: mattresses, chairs, wooden street signs, plastic dishes, even canned food. A bloated body bobbed amongst the detritus. It was face-down, but it was clearly a woman. The wind swirled, stirring up the aching, nauseating scent of decay.

Further out to sea the water was thick with floating junk and rotting corpses. It looked like an entire town had washed out to sea and then drifted on a current straight into their path. Judith held her breath, wishing she could keep holding it forever. People around the ship began to notice what was going on. Some joined them at the railing to stare. Others fled for the safety of the *Catalina's* depths.

"Where's all this coming from?" Judith asked. "We're getting close to the Phil— "

She turned and saw Manny's face. His dark skin looked gray, drained of blood. Of course. They were entering the waters around the Philippines. This was Manny's home. She had endured the horror of seeing California buried in ash. Now it was Manny's turn.

He stayed very still. While the others moved around the ship, discussing where the debris had come from in low voices, Manny simply stared, face impassive. He must have gone into shock. Judith put her hand on his arm, but he shook it off and stayed where he was.

Simon came onto the deck. He shook people out of their stupor with quiet, measured words.

"I'm sorry, folks. Let's take a few minutes of silence. I'm sorry, folks." He repeated the phrase like a mantra. "Let's take a few minutes and then see if we can make our way through. I'm sorry, folks."

As he walked among them, the people turned to him like he was a prophet. Some touched his arms as he passed, as if to draw strength from him. He stayed calm. Judith couldn't imagine how. They sailed further into the flotilla of the dead. She tried to imitate his stance, his facial expression, anything that would grant her some of his poise. She caught sight of Michael, who had returned to the deck after depositing Bernadette inside. He, too, looked at Simon as if he were an apparition.

"I'm sorry, folks. I don't think we'll find solace in these islands. We need to make sure nothing gets caught on the ship. We don't want to carry any diseases with us. I'm sorry, folks, but we need to get to work."

As if in a trance, the people followed Simon's lead. They lowered the lifeboats until they hung a few feet above the water so they could use billiard cues, curtain rods, anything they could find to push the rotting, potentially disease-ridden bodies away from the hull.

After some debate they decided to pull up any sealed food items: bags of chips, canned vegetables, even packages of noodles. They risked bringing disease aboard, but they were becoming desperate. They would run out of food soon. Even if they managed to reach land, they had to get what they could from these waters. There was no guarantee there would be any food left for them on land.

When the groups had been down for long enough to fill their boats, they hoisted them up and unloaded the salvage, piling it on a sectioned-off portion of the deck to be examined and scrubbed clean with laundry detergent. Then they dropped the lifeboats back down toward the water.

Judith joined the unloading crew, while Michael climbed into one of the lifeboats. He and the others covered their mouths and noses with clothing before they approached the putrid water. Michael met Judith's eyes before disappearing below the ship.

Manny didn't join the crews in the lifeboats. He wasn't the only crew member from the Philippines by far. Some cried, lying prone on the decks. Some wept as they worked. But Manny just stared at the sea.

They worked in near silence. A few of Judith's scabs opened, staining her blouse in a pattern like bird tracks. Her hands grew sore from lifting the slick items. They smelled like fish and death.

After an hour a new group of Catalinans, organized by Simon, took over for the salvage crew. He instructed the first workers to scrub themselves down with laundry detergent on deck, then go inside, get some food, and try to find some peace. Judith tried to get Manny to come with her, but he stayed exactly where he'd been since they first saw the bodies.

Judith didn't think she would ever eat again, but she picked up her ration from the dining hall—bread made from some of their last remaining flour—and brought it up to Manny. She offered him the bread, but he didn't react. He just stared at what had once been his home. Judith didn't know what else to do.

It grew colder. Judith tried to get Manny to come inside or even to sit down, but he didn't acknowledge her. So she stood beside him instead, joining his silent vigil.

SIMON

The only coherent thing Simon felt was relief that he'd stopped Esther from going outside.

When the first shouts filtered through the corridors, he'd told her to gather Neal and the other children and see if they could figure out how to get the projector in the cinema deep inside the ship to work. That would keep them occupied for a while. He'd found Bernadette at the entrance to the deck looking as frail as a baby bird and asked her to go down to watch over the children.

On the deck the cool night air carried death. Simon forced away all feeling, clinging only to the relief that his daughter was protected from this. There were too many things he couldn't protect her from, but this was a sight she didn't need to carry to her grave.

Despair lurked among his people. They stared, rigid, at the bodies in the water, or broke down in tears. They'd seen too much, had their hopes shattered too many times. Simon couldn't allow that despair to touch him too. So he walked among them and voiced the sorrow he refused to feel.

"I'm sorry, folks. I'm sorry, folks. I'm sorry, folks."

Then he made them get to work.

The process was both cathartic and traumatic. They had to move, act, sweat. They had to feel that they were doing something, anything, in the face of a world that had spiraled so far out of their control. He told them to gather everything that might have a shadow of a possibility of being useful one day. Even if their fuel ran out and they never found land, they could feel like they were preparing for something better.

Simon himself felt nothing.

When he saw the first child-sized body, he nearly lost the tenuous grip he had on himself. So he followed his own advice and returned to the in-

terior of the ship to coordinate a new shift of
workers. Figuring out who would need a break and
who was available was soothing. He made sure everyone scrubbed their clothes and hands thoroughly
before going inside. They couldn't risk contaminat-
ing their little world. The work helped to consume
his attention, and eventually he was able to climb
to the top deck and survey their position with a
clear head.

From a higher vantage point, he could see the
hunched shapes of islands sprinkled around them.
At first he'd mistaken them for low-lying clouds. It
was getting darker, but there were no man-made
lights. Where were the warm, humming windows?
The coastal campfires? Where were the people?
Could it be that whatever storm surge or tsunami
had swept through the islands had scoured them of
all life?

He walked along the top deck to the broadcast
tower. It had an entrance through the bridge, but
also one directly from the deck. Vinny sat in his
crow's nest, staring out at the silent islands.

"Hey." Vinny didn't respond when Simon entered. "Do you have anything on the radio?" Simon
asked, already dreading the answer.

Vinny didn't turn around. "Thought we should
be there by now," he mumbled. "Didn't want to say
anything. Thought we should have been picking up
signals from the Phils by yesterday evening. Maybe
we were just moving slower than I calculated, or we

were wrong about our position after the last storm. There's so much fucking silence on this radio. I thought we'd hear something by now."

"Maybe they don't have the capacity—"

"Simon. Radio is old. It's basic. If someone out there were capable of broadcasting, they would, at least within this range. Whatever happened here did enough damage to take down the towers and whoever is out there to send a message. I expected this kind of radio silence at sea but not when we're within sight of land."

"What are you saying?"

"If there's anyone left in these islands, they're in more trouble than us. We're not going to find help here."

Simon had hoped they'd reach someone in the mountains, someone on a rescue mission here. Someone.

"So we keep going," he said. His voice was hollow and he knew it. "We keep sailing and hope they'll help us when we reach China."

"Yeah," Vinny said. "We keep sailing. And God help us all."

19. The Harbor

JUDITH

MICHAEL AND JUDITH BROUGHT Manny back to his cabin. He was freezing and feverish after watching the sea carry away the ruins of his homeland for hours. When he grew too weak to protest, they guided him to the crew quarters deep down on the third deck. His roommate, also from the Philippines, had been huddled in his bunk already, and he didn't look up when they brought Manny inside.

"Manny, you have to eat." Judith had instructed, rather than coaxed.

She felt too raw and tired from the events of the day to display any sympathy. She focused only on what Manny needed: food, warmth, and sleep. When he didn't respond to her, she got Michael to force him to sit, and then she pulled pieces off the stale bread she had brought from the dining hall and fed them to him bite by bite.

"Come on, Manny. Swallow."

Manny ate, staring at nothing and following her instructions like a machine. When he finished the final hunk of bread, she took the shoes off his feet herself and made him lie down. She covered him with a blanket and tucked it tightly beneath the mattress.

"Sleep," she ordered. Then she took Michael by the arm and guided him toward the door.

"Wait, Judith," Manny said hoarsely. "Thank you."

She nodded at him and left the room without another word.

Judith and Michael stood in silence in the corridor outside Manny's door. The dim emergency lights bathed Michael's face in a haunting glow. His clothes were still wet from being scrubbed down with detergent after his shift in the lifeboat. Judith felt fragile, like a porcelain cup that had been dropped too many times. If he said a word, she might shatter.

"Are you okay?" he asked.

"No," she answered. "None of us are."

"Yes."

"Would you walk me to my room, please?"

They had to climb five flights of stairs to get to her little stateroom. The cabin Michael had shared with another crew member for the past few nights was on the fifth deck, but they passed it without slowing and continued toward the eighth. Judith reached out to take his hand.

At her door Michael made no pretense of saying good night. He merely stepped back to let her enter first and followed her into the room.

They undressed each other slowly, gently, not unlike that first night. This time they were in a different kind of pain. Michael ran a finger along the tender patches of her healing skin. His hands were icy from the seawater. She took them between her long, thin fingers and kneaded warmth into them. He kissed her forehead, traced silent tears down her cheek.

"It'll be okay," he breathed into her ear. "We'll be okay."

Judith didn't answer. She simply wrapped her arms around his neck and pulled him close.

It was the first time they'd spent the night together since their trip to the atoll. Maybe they would part ways. Maybe the world would truly end. But right now Judith wished she hadn't wasted a single minute.

It was still early when she awoke to the sound of Michael's steady breathing and his arm pillowing her head. The weak morning light struggled to break through the clouds outside her cabin window. Judith drank in the warmth of Michael's body beside her. She felt sore from the work of the day before, but some of the heaviness in her heart had eased.

She slipped out of bed and got dressed in the second outfit she'd acquired through the rationing operation a few days ago. She opened the door to her tiny balcony and slipped outside, expecting to see the usual stretch of dull sky and turbulent purple sea. But the emptiness was gone. From the balcony high in the *Catalina*'s side, Judith looked out on a city.

SIMON

Simon had found Esther and the other children curled up in the projection room of the cinema. The projector made a low clicking sound, sputtering ineffectually. Mangled film lay around it like a giant bird's nest.

Esther slept with her head on a film canister. Bernadette had fallen asleep in the projector operator's chair. Simon left her alone and lifted Esther into his arms.

"Daddy, we broke the movie machine," Esther mumbled.

"That's all right, button."

"I tried to fix it, only I got tired."

"We'll try again tomorrow," Simon said.

Esther's response was lost in the folds of Simon's jacket as she snuggled closer to him. He carried her to their cabin and pulled all her extra clothes over her head before tucking her into bed. It grew colder every day.

Simon lay awake for hours staring at the ceiling. He wanted to scrub the sights of the day from his brain, but they floated, bulbous, in front of his eyes. If Vinny was right about the lack of radio signals from the Philippines, he feared what would happen when they reached China. With over a billion people, China would have to have *someone* they could talk to. They had been at sea for nearly two weeks, most of that time without news. Who knew what the world would be like when they finally managed to reenter it?

Simon rose before dawn the next morning, knowing it wouldn't take long to arrive at the next coast. He wasn't sure where they'd be exactly. He hoped to assess the situation—and maybe even make contact—before most of the ship awoke. Esther was sleeping soundly, wrapped up in all of her clothes. She stirred a bit as he eased the door open, then settled back to sleep, burrowing further underneath the periwinkle sheets.

The slumbering *Catalina* was an eerie place. The new duty roster ensured that someone was always up and keeping watch, but Simon didn't see anyone until he reached the bridge.

He found Ren overseeing the woman she and Vinny had recruited to help out in the bridge and radio tower. Kim Wu, Simon remembered, had worked in IT, and she was a runner. Simon had encouraged Ren to select a few additional people to teach about the ship's operations. If nothing else, he hoped training them would keep her mind off of Nora. Keeping people busy wasn't a sophisticated leadership strategy by any means, but Simon would use it until it stopped working or someone else was ready to take charge.

"How's it going up here?" he asked quietly.

"We should be able to see the coast any minute," Ren said.

"Has Vinny heard anything?"

"I don't know," Ren said. "He hasn't reported in a while. Kim, go up and check on him, would you?"

Kim jumped up and disappeared into the radio tower. Simon wondered if she was Chinese, and if so whether she could help them speak to people when they finally disembarked.

"Do you know where we are?" he asked.

"According to the map, we should be making landfall somewhere near Shantou," Ren said.

"Know anything about it?"

"It's a Chinese coastal city in Guangdong," Ren said, shrugging. "Not much to know. Port. Hundreds of identical skyscrapers."

"Let's hope they're friendly to refugees."

"Ren! Simon!" Kim stumbled back down the ladder. "It's Vinny. He's . . . I think he decided to . . ."

She trailed off, gesturing up the ladder. Then she marched to the other side of the bridge, as far as she could get from the radio tower.

Ren looked up at Simon, her eyes already filling with tears. She must have guessed the same thing he had. It was bound to happen eventually, but Simon didn't think Vinny would be the first.

It only took a brief glance into the radio tower to confirm his suspicions. Vinny had hung himself from an air-conditioning pipe on the ceiling. His body was angled away from the windows facing the sea. With everything they had endured, Simon had feared someone would take this way out, but it was still a shock to see his fear realized.

Simon didn't look at Vinny's face as he climbed onto the communications console to disentangle the wire. He had to touch Vinny's fleshy neck, and he discovered that his body was still warm. He must have stared out at the sea all night long before deciding to do this.

The radio headset still sat on top of the console by the window. Had Vinny heard something that tipped his hand? What could they have said to him?

Kim was quickly promoted to head of communications. She refused to go into the radio tower until Simon and Ren had carried Vinny's body out. As they maneuvered him down the ladder, Ren spoke softly over his limp form.

"He's been more withdrawn lately, ever since he started bringing food to the captain. I should have known—"

"It's not your fault," Simon said. "No one could have known."

"I bet the captain did," Ren said. "He as good as said this is what we should all do."

"He's wrong."

"I know," Ren said. Tears sat in her large brown eyes, threatening to fall at any moment. "I should have sent someone else to bring food to him sometimes. It wasn't fair to put the whole burden on Vinny."

"We have to keep moving forward, Ren. Vinny let it get to him."

"I kind of understand wanting to take this way out," she said

"Let's just focus on getting this ship to shore," Simon said.

He was surprised to realize that he had never once contemplated ending his life over the past few weeks. It was something he had considered in his darkest moments years ago, after he lost his first tenure bid and during a difficult stretch in his freshman year of college. He knew how despair could creep into you, like an oozing, oily mass. He knew what it was like to feel utterly paralyzed and empty, when even getting out of bed was a Herculean task. But here he hadn't fallen into the downward spiral. Despite everything that had happened, he felt more sure of himself and what he had to do than at any other time in his life. The battle for survival, both for himself and the people counting on him, was all that mattered anymore. It had freed him.

Simon looked up at Ren. "We can't do this without you."

"It's okay, Simon." She wiped her nose on the shoulder of her uniform. "I'm with you. I won't give up."

They left Vinny's body in the little chapel. Simon sent a passing porter to get Penelope. He didn't know if Vinny had been religious, but it seemed like someone should speak words over him. Simon himself had to focus on making contact with land. With any luck they'd be able to bury Vinny, so he wouldn't have to stay at sea any longer.

Simon and Ren returned to the bridge, and then Simon climbed back up to the broadcast tower. Kim had gotten to work quickly, sending distress signals out to any frequency she could find. Kim was Chinese, as Simon had hoped, but she was a third-generation immigrant. She told Simon her Mandarin skills were rusty at best.

Simon waited beside her as she trawled the airwaves for voices, requesting help or information in both English and Mandarin. There had to be someone who could finally tell them what was going on in the rest of the world. She searched and pleaded. Finally, someone answered.

"They say to go away," she said.

"Are they threatening us?"

"No, at least I don't think so." She pulled the headphones off one ear. "They say there's no food. They say we can't stay."

"We have to keep trying," Simon said. "See if you can get someone else."

As the sky lightened, a thin strip of coast and the outlines of skyscrapers began to appear on the horizon. Simon couldn't help feeling hope leap in his chest at the sight. The silhouettes on the shoreline grew in the minimal light breaking through the clouds. Simon pressed his forehead against the window. Land. He just wanted to set foot on the land.

Warning messages crackled through the radio, but no one challenged them directly as they sailed closer to the city. Simon had instructed Ren to get as near to the shore as she could, unless someone actually came out in force to stop them. They weren't going to let mere words turn them away. They had to be allowed to come ashore. They had to get off this ship.

Wrecks began to emerge from the sea around them. A crane rose from what he thought was a giant cargo ship submerged on their port side. A large steel structure stuck out of the water to starboard. Was it the keel of another ship? Simon wasn't sure. They eased carefully through the water, trying to avoid the wrecks with their massive hull. Simon held his breath.

Up ahead there was something strange about the coastline, but he couldn't put a finger on what it was. Something about the hazy skyline looked wrong.

JUDITH

Judith studied the silent obstacles in the water as they drew closer to the city. The *Catalina* sailed slowly and carefully through the jutting wrecks. It felt like they were approaching an alien spaceport. Those were just buildings, but after the most harrowing weeks of her life had been spent staring out at a nearly empty view, it was like she had suddenly been transported to another planet.

Land.

Michael joined her on the balcony. He wrapped his arms around her and held her close as the city approached. They didn't speak. There was something solemn about this morning, this moment.

Suddenly, Michael tensed.

"That's not the coast."

"What?"

"I mean, that's not where the coast is supposed to be. Look at the waterline. The water is actually lapping against the windows of some of those buildings. The sea has risen a lot here." Michael went to the edge of the balcony and leaned as far forward as he could. "We're almost on top of the old port. We need to stop. This is a minefield. We could rip a hole in the hull."

As he spoke, the *Catalina* shuddered.

SIMON

Simon finally realized what was strange about the coast. He vaulted down the radio tower ladder and back into the bridge.

"Stop! We have to stop moving!"

"What? We can't just . . ."

Ren threw the propellers into reverse and tried to slow the ship. The *Catalina* groaned. But it was too late. They hit something. The shock wave from the impact reverberated through the ship. With a sickening shriek the *Catalina* stopped. All was still.

"Can you check the hull?" Simon asked.

"Something's wrong with the computer system," Ren said, striking rapidly at her keyboard. "I can't tell if there's a leak. I don't know if I'll be able to shut the water doors."

"Can it be done manually?"

"Yes," Ren said. "I'll get Reg on the intercom to check everything out. But we can't sail any farther."

"The important thing right now is that we stay afloat."

Judith

Michael pulled on his shoes and headed out the door to find Reggie. People stuck their heads out into the corridor and asked what was going on. Judith stared into their worried faces for a moment and remembered Simon from the day before.

"It's okay, folks, we're fine," she said, trying to mimic his calming voice.

But no one listened. They thronged into the passageway, the volume of their voices escalating. Their worry echoed around the narrow space, building up.

Judith took a deep breath and shouted, "Shut up, everyone! Panicking isn't going to help. We're near the coast, and we hit something. If you know anything about fixing the ship, get to your posts. Everyone else, go back inside your cabins and stay out of the way."

"Well!" Rosa Cordova huffed, but she obeyed.

She sent her husband off down the passageway and herded her offspring into their assorted cabins. The others began to disperse back to their rooms.

Judith felt a brief thrill of pleasure as everyone did what she had told them to do. Then she rushed up to the bridge.

SIMON

"It's okay, Simon," Reggie said on the intercom from the engine control room. "The leak ain't that bad. It's mostly contained in the lowest level by the propeller. We already shut the flood doors."

"Okay, good. I knew you boys would have everything in hand," Simon said.

"We took some damage on our main propeller, though," Reggie said, voice crackling in the static. "We won't sink, but we aren't going anywhere in a hurry."

"I see. Thanks, Reggie. Let's hope we won't need to. We're close enough. I think it's time we organize a landing party. Would you choose a few men and send them to the starboard lifeboat deck?"

"Sure thing. Over and out."

JUDITH

When Judith reached the bridge, Ren was at work on the computers. The view of the city was much better from here. Lights burned in a few windows. Someone was alive there, or had been recently enough to leave the lights on. Structures jutted out of the dark water all around them, blocking their path.

"We hit something. Are we going to sink?" Judith asked.

"If we do, we can swim to land," Ren said.

She didn't meet Judith's eyes. They had barely spoken since Nora died. Judith knew it was her fault for not reaching out to her.

"Someone's alive over there, right?"

"Kim got some traffic on the radio," Ren said. "None of it's friendly."

"Where's Vinny? I'd think he'd want to be up here for this."

"Vinny's dead. Hung himself."

Judith didn't answer. She barely registered her response as sad. Surprised maybe. She didn't have enough emotional energy left to be sad.

"Where's Simon?" Judith asked.

"Went down to get the landing party on their way. We're sending a boat over to check things out before we all disembark," Ren said. Her voice seemed to come from a great distance. Detachment must be easier. It was the way to get things done.

"Who's on the team?"

"Not sure. Simon's sorting it out," Ren said. She finally turned to meet Judith's eyes. "I don't think he should go over there. We need him here."

"I agree," Judith said. "I'll make sure he's not on that boat. I want to go, though. I want to see."

Ren nodded. "Be careful."

"I will. And . . . Ren, I'm really sorry for not coming around lately. And for . . . for Nora. I should have come to talk to you."

"I understand," Ren said heavily. "There's nothing to say really. Look out for yourself, Judith."

SIMON

Simon wrapped a green scarf around his neck and prepared to board one of the smaller lifeboats. He had to find out what was happening on land. This could be the place where they would finally disembark and try to make their way home. It was time to see what their new lives would be like.

Michael had already climbed into the boat, which swung gently above the water. Reggie had selected him and Pieter, a burly blond sailor Simon thought was from the Netherlands, to make the trip. Reggie himself would stay on board to fix the propeller that had been damaged in the collision, just in case they had to keep moving.

"Wish we were armed," Michael said.

"If they don't want us to stay," Simon answered, "I doubt that would do much good."

"Still, if they're hostile—"

"It'll be better for us to appear nonthreatening."

Simon held on to the railing and dropped one foot into the lifeboat. His head wobbled with vertigo as he glanced at the water forty feet below him. It was a long way down.

"Simon! Wait!"

Judith burst out of the ship with Kim Wu in tow. Simon clambered back onto the deck of the *Catalina*, limbs shaking slightly.

"What's wrong?"

"I don't think you should go to the city," Judith said. "It could be dangerous."

"I'll be okay, Judith," Simon said.

"The *Catalina* won't be okay if something happens to you."

"But I want to see—"

"It's not fair to us for you to risk yourself." Judith crossed her arms tightly, her lips in a thin line. She looked positively formidable. "You need to keep people calm so they won't go running off to the city until we know it's safe. They'll listen to you. I'll go in your place and report back."

"It's too dangerous," Simon said.

"Exactly why you shouldn't go. The *Catalina* needs you. Esther needs you."

Simon didn't want to put Judith in any danger, but he would not leave Esther an orphan no matter what. He'd been caught.

"Maybe you're right," he began.

"Of course I'm right. I'm taking Kim with me too," Judith said, gesturing to the woman hovering behind her. "It'll be more useful to have a Mandarin speaker in the city in person than as an anonymous voice on the radio, especially if we have to negotiate anything."

"You're probably right about that. Okay, Judith, let's do it your way."

Judith nodded as if she had expected nothing less. Michael offered her his hand and helped her into the lifeboat. Simon didn't like sending Judith into danger, but he trusted her judgment. And Michael and Judith would look out for each other.

A few minutes later the boat was lowered away from Simon. A strong breeze swept across the water, bringing with it the smells of land. City smells, earth smells. He wished he could go along, but Judith was right: he had to make sure everyone on the *Catalina* didn't try to go into the city before it was safe.

The team of four waved at Simon as the lifeboat dropped into the water. Pieter started the motor. They would try to keep the expedition short, just long enough to determine whether it was safe for the Catalinans to take refuge in the city. Simon prayed this would be the end of their voyage.

20. The City

JUDITH

THE LIFEBOAT MOTORED THROUGH a shallow wasteland of sunken boats. A minefield of masts and shards of metal threatened to rip into the hull. Oil lay thick on the water in places. The whole harbor could burn at any moment.

It took an eternity to reach the shore. Judith tucked her hand into Michael's. It made her nervous that it was so quiet here. She would have expected people from the city to be out on the water, salvaging the wrecks. Now that the sun was all the way up—though hidden behind clouds—the city lights were no longer visible. She wondered if they had ever been there at all.

The vacant windows of the skyscrapers stared at them as they crossed what must have been the border between land and sea before. The former shore, a ghostly line marking the drop from water-front to harbor, passed beneath them. The water level had risen at least five feet, possibly more. It was deep enough for them to sail across the onetime boardwalk and up to the steps of the first building. The doors yawned open in front of them. Inside they could see the polished marble lobby of a hotel.

Judith and Michael crawled forward to climb out. The lifeboat bobbed under their weight as they moved to the steps. But when they set foot on the first dry patch, gunshots greeted them.

"Get back in the boat," Pieter shouted.

The shots pinged against the steps about ten feet away. Judith and Michael jumped back into the boat and ducked beneath the awning that covered part of the stern. Kim crouched in the bottom, and Pieter bent low near the idling motor.

"Is anyone hit?" Michael asked.

"We're okay."

"Who's shooting?" Kim wailed.

"I saw someone inside," Pieter said. "They're gone now."

Silence rippled around them. No more shots, no shouts, no movement.

"They obviously want us to leave," Michael said. "Let's pick a different spot to disembark."

"Wait," Judith said. "They're probably just scared. I don't think they were trying to hit us. Maybe we should try to communicate with them."

"We've come too far to be gunned down now," Michael said. "Pieter? Let's keep it slow and quiet."

Pieter reversed the lifeboat away from the steps. He sailed along the waterfront, looking for another place to land. The gaps between the buildings revealed empty streets stretching away from the harbor. Glass glittered across the pavement. Wrecked and abandoned cars, broken signs, and garbage marred the streets. They passed what must have been a busy commercial avenue leading right down to the water. Every single window had been broken.

"Let's stop here," Judith said. "Looks like a main street."

"We can tie the boat to that street sign," Kim said, peeking over the top of the gunwale. "I don't know all the characters, but one of them means 'sea,' and one means 'street.'"

They motored up to the sign, and the boat bumped a bit against the sidewalk.

Michael got out first. Worry clutched at Judith's heart as he stepped out of her reach. He walked a few paces, but there were no shots this time. The city was deathly quiet.

"Okay, I think we're good. Someone should stay behind and watch the lifeboat," Michael said.

"I'll do this," Pieter said.

He and Michael secured the lifeboat to the sign. Kim and Judith climbed out too, looking nervously around the deserted street.

"Stay out of sight unless someone tries to mess with the boat," Michael said to Pieter. "You're big and scary looking. They should leave you alone."

Pieter nodded solemnly. He climbed back into the lifeboat and disappeared beneath the awning.

Judith, Michael, and Kim walked a few paces across solid ground. The street was silent. A cat tiptoed across the way, but even it didn't make a sound. Judith stayed close to Michael, willing herself not to cling to him. She tried to project a confidence that she didn't feel inside.

They walked on, but no one stopped them. There were no signs of life at all.

"Well, I hope someone in this town speaks English," Michael said after a while. His voice sounded far too loud, but conversation was better than this horrible silence.

"They will," Kim said. "And my Chinese is okay. Wish I'd spent more time practicing with my grandma, though."

"Have you ever been here before?" Judith asked.

"Not to this city. I went to Shanghai when I was a teenager," Kim said. "I hear it's changed a lot since then."

Judith nodded. She was surprised at how sleek everything looked, despite its abandonment. Unfamiliar characters adorned the buildings, but there were English signs too. Designer names graced the looted shops. A stray high-heeled shoe lay on the pavement outside one. The modern architecture and gleaming advertisements made the emptiness that much more garish. They walked beneath an imposing chrome-and-marble high-rise.

Suddenly glass shattered directly in front of them. Judith jumped, reaching for Michael's hand. Someone had thrown a bottle from a window above them.

A voice called down in an urgent whisper-shout. "Are you people crazy? Get out of the street!"

A man was leaning out of a fourth-floor window of the high-rise. The group stared up at him in surprise.

"Who are you?" Michael called.

"Did you hear me? Move! The patrols could come by anytime."

They exchanged glances and darted toward the building where the face had appeared. The lock had a keypad, but as they were about to touch it, there was an electric buzz and the door opened automatically. They stepped inside.

SIMON

Simon paced back and forth across the foredeck. Others had joined him, some wrapped in their blankets against the cold. They asked why they weren't moving closer, why they couldn't see any-one in the city, what had happened to all these half-sunken ships.

"I don't know yet. We've got to wait a bit," he told them. "We sent in a team of scouts."

Simon stopped to gaze at the city, then shook his head and resumed pacing. He was keenly aware of the damaged propeller beneath the ship. He didn't know how bad it was. What if they had to move on? It could take them days and more equip-ment than they had to repair the damage. And if they had to keep moving, where would they go?

He'd seen the lifeboat stop and three people climb out, but they had disappeared from view into the city. He wished they had a walkie-talkie or something. On a whim he tried turning on his cell phone, which had a few minutes of juice left that he'd been saving, but he couldn't find a network. He allowed it to roam about, searching for a signal, until the battery died for good.

"How much longer, Simon?" the people asked. "When can we go ashore?"

"We've waited this long. Let's be patient for a lit-tle while longer."

Suddenly a large speedboat shot out from be-hind a wrecked cargo ship. It sped across the har-bor, expertly dodging sunken obstacles. It halted between the city and the *Catalina*, blocking their path to the shore. They had been spotted.

The speedboat had the red flag with a yellow star of the People's Liberation Army painted on its side. It floated near the *Catalina*, not approaching or making any attempt to communicate. Whoever was on board stayed hidden behind the cockpit. They didn't seem to have noticed the lifeboat bobbing by the shore. But now the Chinese military knew that the *Catalina* had arrived.

"We'd better get off the deck," Simon called to the people gathering to gawk at the speedboat.

"I want to have a look!" Horace called.

"We don't know what they'll do," he said. "It's not safe."

"But they're survivors!"

The people were desperate to see other humans who had survived the catastrophe. They had been isolated for too long.

"We can't risk it," Simon said. "Come on, everyone. Inside quickly!"

As the people on deck obeyed, Simon hurried up to the bridge. He had a very bad feeling about that speedboat. If it wanted trouble, they might not be able to get away in time.

JUDITH

The lobby of the building was an explosion of gold and polished marble. The high ceilings featured twin chandeliers. A full-length mirror along one wall magnified the light, bouncing it around the lobby and making it look bigger than it was.

Judith caught sight of herself in the mirror and was shocked to see how thin she had become. She'd always been trim, but now her bones jutted out from her hips. Her face had developed a pinched quality, and there was a permanent furrow between her eyes. She looked like she'd aged ten years.

The group looked around the deserted building, unsure what to do. Then a shrill ding announced the arrival of the elevator, making them jump. Polished golden doors opened to reveal a man in his fifties with salt-and-ginger hair and wide, light eyes that matched his hair. He wore sweatpants and an expensive-looking peacoat. There was a meat cleaver in his hand.

Michael stepped forward, putting himself between Judith and the wild-eyed man.

"We don't want any trouble," he said.

"Damn right you don't," said the stranger. "Are you people crazy? Curfews not up yet."

"There's a curfew?"

"You fresh off the boat or something?"

"Yes."

The man took in their wet trouser legs and mismatched clothing. His almost-orange eyes didn't miss much.

"I guess you are. All right, you can come up if you promise not to kill me."

The three assured him they would do no such thing and crowded into the elevator, staying as far from the meat cleaver as they could. The man's gaze bore into them, but he didn't speak. Mellow instrumental music played in the background. The elevator stopped on the fourth floor, and the man gestured for everyone else to get out first. Michael exited the elevator backwards, keeping an eye on the stranger with the cleaver.

"Name's Quentin," he said. "I'm in the shipping business. Born and raised in Chicago, but I've been here in Shantou since the early 2000s."

Everyone introduced themselves. Quentin took a key out of his coat pocket and opened one of the four doors on the floor. They followed him inside.

The apartment was spacious and modern, with marble floors, black leather furniture, and a bar that occupied much of the living space. Dirty clothes and food wrappers were strewn over the couches, as if the place hadn't been tidied in weeks. Tall windows looked out over the street, and one was still partially open. Quentin gestured to the row of high stools and walked around to the other side of the bar. He set the meat cleaver on the counter behind him, keeping it within reach, and studied them. Judith felt like a student looking over a principal's desk. She fidgeted on her stool.

"So what's your story?" he said finally. "Lost backpackers?"

"We just arrived on a ship," Judith said. "From California."

"Come again?"

"Our ship is out in the harbor. There was nowhere for us to disembark in the US after the eruption, so we sailed here."

"You navy?"

"I am," Michael said. "But the ship's a civilian vessel. A cruise ship."

"We need food and water and help," Judith said.

"Doesn't everyone?" Quentin said. "You won't find it here. They were talking about throwing out all the expats last week. I don't think they'll take kindly to new ones arriving this week."

"Why?" Kim asked. "What happened here?"

Quentin snorted. "What didn't happen? It all started when we got news of the volcano. I take it you haven't been at sea so long you don't know about that. Anyway, the experts get on TV and start preaching doom and gloom, telling everyone the crops are going to fail for five, six, seven years. The local government tried to keep the news outside the Great Firewall, but some of the broadcasts and a lot of the rumors made it here anyway. Everyone panicked, started smashing store windows and hijacking delivery trucks. I've never seen anything like it. Before the satellites failed, it sounded like people were doing the same all over the world."

Quentin was talking so fast it was almost hard to follow him, to process what he was saying. Judith gripped her stool, as if it were tossing in a storm.

"I haven't heard anything from outside the borders in a week," Quentin continued. "There were earthquakes to the south, and I expected to see tanks rolling down the street any minute, but then we got hit with a typhoon like you wouldn't believe. Made me regret renting a place so close to the sea, believe me. Everyone pretty much battened down the hatches—those who hadn't already made a run for the countryside, that is. That's when the PLA swept in and restored order. By the time the rain let up, they'd implemented a strict curfew and rationing system. Everyone gets fed, but if you're outside anytime except between two and four in the afternoon, you're shot on sight. Obviously, there's not much you can do in that window."

"What are you going to do?" Judith asked. She glanced at Michael, who had balled his hands into fists on the counter.

"They've got to let up eventually, so we're pretty much waiting it out," Quentin said, tugging at the pockets of his coat. "The expats have a message system going for noncurfew times, but we try to stay hidden. Like I said, there's been backlash against us because we're here eating up Chinese resources. Word is that we'll get deported if we go into a full-blown famine, but I don't think it's any better else-where."

Quentin stopped talking to open a Tsingtao beer he'd pulled from beneath the counter. He poured the whole thing down his throat, his Adam's apple beating like a heart with each gulp. He must have been bottling up that story for days. He had to be lonely and stir-crazy—and possibly actually crazy, judging by the meat cleaver and sweatpants.

"All right," he said, smashing the can against the bar counter. "Your turn."

Judith gave an abbreviated version of what they'd been through and finished with, "So we came to check things out before we bring everyone else ashore."

"How many people are on this cruise ship of yours?" Quentin asked.

"Over a thousand."

Quentin whistled through his teeth. "There's not a chance in hell. Sorry, folks. They're not going to let a thousand foreigners into the city with re-sources as squeezed as they are. You'll have to find somewhere else."

"We can't get much further on our fuel," Michael said. "I don't know if we'd even make it up to Tai-wan."

"Don't bother with Taiwan," Quentin said. "I heard the PLA took over three days ago. Now *that's* something I never thought would happen in my lifetime. The same with other cities. The People's Republic doesn't do anything halfway. I'm sure the curfew and general sentiment toward foreigners is the same everywhere. You won't find any help in China."

Judith felt like the walls of the apartment were closing in around her. Nowhere to go. How was that possible? The government couldn't just turn them away. Why would no one help them?

But she remembered that their own government had done exactly that—and threatened worse. She'd expected great acts of human compassion and altruism in the face of disaster, but they couldn't count on anyone. Didn't countries usually send aid when storms and earthquakes hit? Why was it so different this time? Was this truly the end?

Judith placed her hands flat on the cold granite counter of Quentin's bar as the world shifted around her. She wanted to go back to the *Catalina*.

They couldn't count on anyone but themselves.

SIMON

Simon watched the PLA speedboat from the radio tower. Chinese words came through on the radio. They had been repeating for hours, an automated message like the one their own navy had put out that had enticed them to Guam.

Simon couldn't see their lifeboat from this angle. It had been too long. The others could come back any minute. He was afraid they wouldn't see the speedboat until it was too late. What would happen if they were caught?

He studied the harbor, worrying about Judith. How long could they wait if the boat didn't come back? They should have agreed something ahead of time. It didn't matter while the propeller was damaged, but as soon as it was fixed they'd have to make some hard decisions, especially if that speedboat called in reinforcements. If worst came to worst, would he be able to leave Judith and the others behind?

The radio crackled. A voice speaking in perfect English, but with an obvious accent, burst into the room.

"You are not welcome here. Please sail away from the harbor at your earliest convenience."

Simon grabbed the microphone. "Hello? We need help. We are refugees, and we need a safe place to come ashore."

"You are not welcome here. Please sail away from the harbor at your earliest convenience."

"Please," Simon said. "We're running out of food and fuel."

"We are sorry. You are not welcome here. Anyone coming ashore will be shot. You are welcome to leave peacefully at your earliest convenience."

"We have nowhere to go."

The message repeated like a record, but Simon was sure it was a human being at the other end. After the third "not welcome," he slammed the microphone down onto the computer console. Not again. They had to get off this ship somewhere. Simon slumped into the swivel chair and put his head in his hands.

There was a knock at the trapdoor.

"Come in."

"Simon?"

It was Mona Mulligan, the delicate woman whose son, Neal, had become friends with Esther. He didn't know Mona well. She'd been ill for most of their voyage and had kept to her cabin. Now, however, she was tugging Neal up the ladder behind her in a firm grip.

"This isn't a good time, Mona."

"Neal has to tell you something." She pushed her son in front of her, holding him firmly by the shoulders. "It's about your daughter," Mona said.

"Esther?"

Little Neal stared at his toes. He was wearing a pair of orange *Catalina* bowling shoes. A purple bruise swelled beneath his eye.

"I tried to stop her!" he said. "She hit me and made me promise not to tell anyone. I'm sorry!"

"Promise not to tell what?"

"She went to the city," Neal mumbled.

"What?" Simon felt his world narrowing to the point of a pin.

"She wanted to see the city with Judith, so she hid in the lifeboat. She said there was a secret box for food and stuff."

"Are you sure?"

"Yes, sir," Neal said. "I tried to stop her. Honest!"

JUDITH

Quentin offered everyone beverages and snacks, chatting as if they'd come over for an after-work cocktail. Judith felt antsy. Despite the many times she'd imagined being on land, she wanted to get back to the *Catalina* as soon as possible. This apartment, with its sleek couches and huge bar, felt wrong. She wanted the warmth of the Atlantis Dining Hall, the sea-slicked decks, the comforting coldness of the rail beneath her hands.

"We should go soon," she whispered to Michael.

Quentin had launched into a discussion with Kim about the Chinese diaspora that seemed weirdly normal in light of their circumstances.

"I agree," Michael said. "I don't like this."

"Should we wait until curfew's up?"

"That's hours away. We don't know what will happen when they notice the *Catalina*. I think it's time to go." Michael wrapped his hand gently around her elbow, spreading warmth through her arm.

"Okay. Quentin," Judith said, not caring that she was interrupting his conversation with Kim. "Can you tell us how to get back to the harbor without walking right down the main street?"

Quentin took out another beer and popped the top. He took a long sip before answering. "Why don't you stay here for a few hours? I wouldn't mind the company."

"We left a man in our lifeboat," Michael said. "He doesn't know about the curfew."

"Fair enough. What are you going to do?"

"Keep sailing, I guess," Judith said.

Quentin took another long drink of his beer. Judith wished he'd hurry it up.

"I'll show you the back way out of the building, but I can't promise it'll be safe."

"What about you?" Kim asked.

"Yes, why don't you come with us?" Michael said.

"I've got a decent setup here." Quentin gestured around his chrome-and-glass apartment. "It's more comfortable than any ship."

"But didn't you say they'd deport you?" Michael said.

"He doesn't want to come," Judith said. "We should get going."

The shadows were lengthening outside. Simon and the others would be wondering where they were.

"I'll be fine," Quentin said, sounding less sure.

But Michael stood his ground. "It's not right. I can't leave a fellow countryman. You're in danger here, and we can help you. At least you won't be alone."

Quentin tipped his beer back, finishing it off.

"You know, why not? That was my last beer, and I'm sick of having a curfew anyway. Let me grab some stuff."

Within a few minutes Quentin had filled a backpack with clothing and bid farewell to his houseplant. The four of them left the apartment building and jogged down a back alley littered with broken furniture, trash cans, and bicycles. It smelled curiously clean, despite the debris. Judith guessed that even rotting food must have been consumed when people realized a famine was coming. They must hoard every scrap now.

Michael took the lead. He checked every entrance to the alley before Judith and Kim reached it to make sure no one was lurking. Quentin warned them to be as wary of civilians as they were of soldiers. The government was offering food rewards for anyone who reported curfew breakers. But they still hadn't seen another soul.

The alley was quiet. Only their footsteps echoed between the buildings. They could have been the only people in the entire city.

Suddenly Michael stumbled, sending trash cans clattering across the alley. The sound was like thunder. Judith ran up and knelt by Michael's side. His face twisted in pain.

"Are you okay?" she asked.

"Thought my foot was starting to get better after the beach," Michael said. "Guess I was wrong."

"Can you walk?"

"Have to." Michael gritted his teeth as Judith helped him into a standing position. He leaned heavily on a barrel that had stayed upright when the cans around it fell. "Give me a sec," he said, working his ankle in a slow circle.

"We need to keep moving," Quentin said. He fiddled with the buttons on his peacoat and looked around anxiously. The alley was still deserted, but they shouldn't linger.

"Wait a second." Michael pried the cap off the opening at the top of the barrel he'd been leaning against and dipped a hand into it. Light-brown grains cascaded over his hands. "This thing is full of rice! We should take it with us."

"Are you crazy? We don't have time," Kim hissed.

"We're not going to last much longer on the food we have," Michael said. "Help me find something to move this. A cart or—"

"Michael," Judith said urgently. "We need to keep moving."

"It won't take long, and there's no one around," Michael said.

He began digging through the piles of rubbish in the alley. Judith pinched her lips together tightly, but she helped him. He was limping and would need more time to get back to the lifeboat. They had to keep walking.

"That probably belongs to someone, you know," Quentin said.

"You think we should leave it?"

"Oh no! They just might be a little upset." Quentin tapped the barrel and looked up and down the alleyway again. Still empty.

"Finders, keepers?" Michael said. "I guess the rules don't count at the end of the world." Sweat had broken out on his forehead, and he was standing on one foot.

"Just hurry, please," Judith said.

"Here! This'll work," Kim called. She dragged a furniture dolly toward them. The tires were flat and the handle rusty, but it would do.

Kim and Judith eased the dolly beneath the barrel. It rocked back and forth and then settled in place. It took both of them to keep it stable while they pushed forward. Michael slung an arm over Quentin's shoulder and they hobbled along behind the women.

They had to be getting closer to the water. The *Catalina* would be waiting. They were almost home.

Suddenly there was an angry shout in the alley behind them. They didn't understand the words, but the tone was clear enough. Then a gun cracked, the shot echoing through the alley like a breaking wave.

"Run!" Judith screamed.

21. Retreat

SIMON

SIMON RAN DOWN THE service stairwell. Manny kept pace beside him.

"Simon, sir, Judith will take care of Esther," he said.

"We have to get them out of the city. Their boat could be discovered any second."

Panic clutched at Simon's chest as he ran. He shouldn't have stayed behind. How had Esther gotten past him?

"Maybe it has already been found," Manny said. "They are saying they'd—"

"No." Simon would not accept that their lifeboat had been discovered, their people taken. He had to get his daughter safely back on the ship.

"How will you be getting by the army boat?" Manny asked.

Simon slowed. He had almost forgotten the PLA speedboat waiting between the *Catalina* and the city. Between the *Catalina* and Esther.

"We need a distraction," he said. "I'll take Michael's speedboat. It's faster than the lifeboats."

The landing party had originally decided not to take the speedboat Michael had "borrowed" from the navy because its motor was so much louder than the ones on the smaller lifeboats. They wanted to avoid being noticed. It was too late for that.

Simon had fetched Captain Martinelli from his cabin and left him in charge. He hoped that wouldn't prove to be a fatal mistake. The man would be able to get them out of the harbor at least. He had done it before. And with Simon's daughter in danger, the captain might actually make a more rational leader than he would. The captain could protect the people on the *Catalina* for once. All Simon cared about was getting to Esther.

JUDITH

Gunshots rang through the alley far behind them. The group broke into as much of a run as they could manage with one damaged foot and one dolly with a barrel. They turned left at the end of the building and ran back toward the main street.

They were in the open, but it didn't matter anymore. They had to get back to the lifeboat. Now. Shouts and shots pursued them.

Judith's lungs burned as she chased rather than pushed the rice barrel toward the waterline. She looked back. Michael must have swallowed his pain, because he was picking up his pace too, Quentin supporting him all the way. Kim, who was at least twenty years older than the other two Catalinans, gasped with the effort of running flat out.

They couldn't see the shooters. They were getting further away. They had to make it.

Judith was almost to the lifeboat. It still bobbed in the shallow water beside the street sign. But a tiny figure perched on its edge beside Pieter.

Esther.

SIMON

Reggie met Simon at the lifeboat deck where they'd stowed Michael's speedboat.

"Good news, Simon," Reggie said. "We got the propeller clear. Only one blade is broken. The rest were tangled on a shitload of wire beneath the surface."

"We need to sail out of the harbor as soon as possible," Simon said.

"The guys'll take care of it," Reggie said. "Now let's get our people out of there."

"Is our distraction ready?" Simon asked.

"Wong is on standby on the foredeck. He'll do it as soon as we clear the port side."

Simon knew Reggie wanted to get Esther, Michael, and the others out of the city as much as he did. The distraction had been his idea, and he had volunteered to drive Simon to the city in the speedboat to bring their people home.

"Good," Simon said. "Manny, make sure all the decks are clear. Keep people out of firing range in case this gets ugly."

"It's going to get ugly all right," Reggie muttered.

They climbed into the speedboat and lowered it toward the water. They were on the opposite side of the *Catalina* from the city, hidden from the PLA boat. Only the open sea and the wrecked harbor mouth were visible from here. They hit the water with a splash. Simon climbed to the bow, while Reggie operated the outboard motor. They sailed forward, the *Catalina* looming beside them like a tower.

As they came abreast of the bow, Reggie raised a hand to signal. A flaming object catapulted through the air from the deck of the *Catalina*. It hit the water and sank with barely a hiss. Reggie cursed softly.

Another flaming object followed the first, this time further to the left. It too sunk without a trace. Reggie cut the motor to the speedboat.

"We can't sail out there while they're keeping watch. They'll blow us out of the water."

"We have to keep trying," Simon said.

A third burning object flew through the air, trailing a wisp of smoke behind it. When it landed, the sea ignited. The patch of oil floating viscous on the sea between them and the PLA boat began to burn. Reggie whooped and fired up the engine. They sped toward the spot where they'd last seen their lifeboat. The blaze slicked along the top of the water toward the PLA boat.

JUDITH

"Esther! What are you doing here?" Judith demanded when she reached the lifeboat. She nearly knocked the rice barrel into the sea.

"I want to see the city, but Pieter won't let me go for a walk," Esther said, pouting.

"I found her hiding in the emergency hold. She locked herself in there and finally shouted for help," Pieter said. "You're being chased?"

"I think we lost them."

Michael stumbled into Judith from behind, winded more from pain than exertion. Quentin leaned down with his hands on his knees, gasping.

"We need to get the barrel into the boat," Michael said.

"There's no time," Judith said. "Leave it."

Kim caught up with them. "Let's just go, please," she gasped.

Michael's jaw set. "Not after we dragged it all this way."

Judith looked back at the city to see if their pursuers had caught up. The street was empty. Michael was already flipping the dolly around to try to leverage the barrel up and over the edge of the boat.

"On second thought," Quentin wheezed, "I don't think I'm cut out for this. I'm staying here."

"You can't!" Michael said. "You'll be killed. Pieter, would you take over here?"

Michael caught Quentin by the arm as he started to walk away. Pieter moved around to help Judith with the barrel.

"It needs to be lower in the water," Pieter said. "Get in the boat."

Judith and Kim scrambled over the gunwale, while Pieter pushed upwards on the barrel. Judith planted her feet and tugged on it. It was almost over the side. Kim huddled back beneath the awning, pulling Esther down with her.

Quentin and Michael were struggling on the sidewalk. "Don't give up, man! If you get caught—"

Soldiers rounded the corner of the building. The barrel seesawed over the gunwale. Pieter scrambled after it and joined Kim and Esther by the motor.

But Michael still wouldn't abandon Quentin.

"We have to go!" Judith screamed. "Leave him!"

"It's too late to go back," Michael shouted at Quentin. "Get in the boat! Let us help you!"

Gunfire shattered the empty street.

"Michael!" Judith shouted.

She stayed by the mooring, trying to loosen the knot keeping them tethered to the shore. Bullets pinged against the street sign, much too close to them. Kim shrieked.

"Please get in the boat!" Judith said. "Michael, we have to go!"

She managed to untie the rope. They were free. The boat lurched as Pieter fired up the motor.

Then several things happened at once.

The heavy barrel teetered sideways.

Judith lost her balance.

Quentin broke away from Michael to run toward the city.

And a look of surprise appeared on Michael's face as a row of holes opened in his chest.

SIMON

They sped through the water. Every second they couldn't see the lifeboat was agony. Simon held on to the bench of the speedboat so hard that cuts must be scoring his hands. Behind him the sea blazed.

The flames forced the PLA boat further away from them. Tongues of fire danced across the water. Black smoke billowed in bigger and bigger clouds, nearly obscuring the *Catalina* from view.

"They ain't seen us yet," Reggie hollered above the rush of the water and the growl of the engine.

Water drenched Simon's face. He leaned forward, searching the broken waterline for the familiar shape.

"There it is!" Simon shouted. "I see the lifeboat."

But instead of speeding up, Reggie cut the engine.

"Why are you stopping? Keep going!"

"Can't. They're sitting right in a patch of oil. And the flames are coming our way."

JUDITH

Judith toppled backwards in the lifeboat. The barrel rolled on top of her, pinning her legs to the deck. The pain was excruciating, but it was nothing compared to the black hole ripping its way through her heart. She realized she was screaming.

Someone was shouting at Pieter to go. The engine kicked to life.

"Wait!" Judith shrieked. "Michael!"

"He's dead. Pieter, go!"

She didn't register who was speaking, but she knew she hated all of them. Michael most of all. He couldn't be dead. Not like that. Not so fast. She pounded her fists against the barrel. If they'd left it behind . . . left Quentin behind . . . Damn Michael for wasting time trying to do the right thing. But the barrel didn't budge. She was stuck.

Water sprayed over the lifeboat. They were moving, sailing away from the shore, away from Michael. An acrid smell choked the air, and something roared in Judith's ears.

"The sea is on fire!"

"There's something out there."

"The fire's headed this way. We're not going to make it!"

Pieter leaned on the motor as if willing it to be stronger, faster than it was. But they were moving too slowly.

Suddenly, Esther shouted, "Look! It's our speedboat."

"Simon's coming for us!" Kim screamed.

"Daddy!"

Nearly delirious, Judith pulled herself up as far as she could with the barrel pinning her legs and looked toward the sea. It *was* Simon, riding toward them in the bow of the speedboat, looking for all the world like a hero from a story. Coming to save them.

SIMON

"We don't have time." Reggie's words barely made sense to Simon. They had to keep moving. "There's a full fuel tank next to that lifeboat motor. It's going to blow any second."

"We have to get Esther," Simon said.

"There's no time."

"Do it!"

Reggie swore and gunned the engine, jetting into the oil slick.

Simon saw his daughter in the lifeboat, her tiny hands, blue T-shirt, drenched pigtails. Beside her he could see Judith's face and her arm waving desperately.

"Help us!" she shouted.

She seemed to be trapped under something. She wasn't climbing any further forward in the boat.

"Get ready to jump!" Simon shouted.

"I'm stuck!" Judith shrieked. "Help me!"

The two boats bumped together. Pieter and Kim leapt across the gap.

"Come on, button," Simon coaxed.

Esther hesitated. "I'm scared."

The flames crept closer. Reggie threw the speedboat motor into reverse.

"It's going to blow! We have to move."

Simon looked back and forth between Esther, crouching petrified on the lifeboat seat, and Judith, trapped beneath a barrel, for one terrible instant. He couldn't reach both. Already the gap between the boats was widening again.

JUDITH

Simon launched forward and snatched Esther out of the lifeboat. He didn't shout for Reggie to stop as it sailed away again. Simon's eyes met Judith's. The distance between them grew larger. As Simon clasped Esther in his arms, his mouth formed words that might have been *I'm sorry.*

Then the lifeboat blew to pieces around her.

22. Burnt Sea

SOUND.

Heat.

Pain.

Fury.

The explosion freed Judith's legs and hurled her into the sea. She dove.

Judith swam deep beneath the water until her lungs felt like they would rip through her chest. She had no sensation of up or down. She only knew she had to get far away from the burning oil slick as fast as she could.

All was blackness around her.

Her head broke the surface. She gulped in the acrid smoke that was sweeping across the water from the blaze. Still close enough to feel the heat. She saw a flash of angel white that she prayed was the Catalina and dove beneath the water again.

The next time she emerged, Judith felt oil on her face. She scrubbed at it but couldn't remove the slick from her skin. Flames raced across the top of the water toward her.

She dove.

The third time Judith rose to fill her lungs, she was in a patch of clean water. The speedboat had reached the Catalina. It rose slowly toward the deck. Simon would be helping Esther aboard now. Judith felt a twist of something in her stomach worse than the pain in her lungs. She swam along the surface. She felt like she was pulling the Catalina closer to her, drinking in the distance with each gasp.

Then the Catalina started to move.

23. Seabound

SIMON

ESTHER STRUGGLED AND SQUIRMED in Simon's arms, trying to see what was happening behind them, but he held her close. If he could open up his chest and put her inside, he would have. He'd lost Nina. He'd lost Naomi. He would never lose Esther.

The sea burned. Smoke from the flaming oil nearly obscured the skyscrapers. Simon could no longer see the PLA boat. He couldn't see Judith either. And what about Michael? Simon didn't think he'd been in the boat. He could only save Esther. He didn't have a choice.

He said it to himself over and over again. He didn't have a choice.

The *Catalina* loomed above them. Pieter helped Reggie attach the speedboat to the winch. They lifted into the air. Forty feet up, hands reached across to pull them aboard.

"Daddy, put me down," Esther said.

She struggled, but he kept her in his arms.

"Esther, you're in big trouble," he said. "You will go straight to the cabin and wait for me."

"Where's Judy?" Esther said, crying now. "And who shot Michael? Is he going to be okay? Why did they do that?"

Simon looked to Kim for confirmation, his lungs squeezing a little tighter. She was trembling, barely coherent, but she nodded.

"I don't know why," Simon said to his daughter.

"Can we go back and get Judy?"

"It's too dangerous with the fire."

"We have to!" Esther shouted, pounding her small fists against Simon's shoulder. "You can't leave her behind like you left Mommy and Namie."

Simon set her down quickly and stared into her eyes.

"Is that what you think? There's no way we could save them. We didn't have a choice."

"We got a choice to save Judy, don't we?" Esther said, glaring defiantly at him.

Without answering, Simon pushed Esther into the waiting arms of Penelope, who'd come to meet them. He ordered the men to lower the speedboat again.

"We're already moving," Reggie said. "Captain must have decided we waited long enough."

"It doesn't matter," Simon said. "We'll catch up."

Esther was right. They did have a choice.

JUDITH

Judith lost all sense of time as she swam. Logically, she should be saving her strength, turning around, swimming for shore. But the *Catalina* was where she belonged. She would get back to it if it took everything she had left.

She was clear of the burning oil now. She wiped the salt water out of her eyes and checked her progress. The speedboat was coming toward her. For one wild moment she was sure it was Michael coming to save her. That was the boat that had brought him to her. Then it was pulling up alongside her, and Simon was reaching out a hand.

She stared at him for a moment, the sour taste of betrayal in her mouth. He'd left her. He'd chosen Esther. She wasn't his daughter.

Simon must have taken her hesitation as an indication of shock. He leaned over and pulled her into the boat. She came to her senses and helped, just managing to scramble over the gunwale. She landed hard on the seat. Cuts from the explosion covered her body. Bruises were already forming, ugly and dark, on her legs.

Simon was talking, saying something along the lines of *you'll be okay thought you were dead so glad to see you're all right sorry about Michael.*

Judith remained silent as they returned to the *Catalina* and were hoisted back on board. Maybe she *was* in shock. People came to help, wrapped them in blankets, summoned food and water. Judith looked around at the familiar faces, the deck, the lifeboat bays. She was exhausted. Manny knelt beside her, placed something soft under her head.

She let the world around her fade to black.

SIMON

Simon lost track of Judith as people came to help her away. He wanted to speak to her, to explain. There was something in the way she had looked at him when he found her swimming toward the ship. Something cold, a little dead even. She must be in shock after what she'd just endured.

Simon returned to the bridge, where he found Kim sitting on the floor. Ren handed her a drink of water, and she explained what they'd learned about China's response to the disaster and impending famine. They wouldn't find a haven here.

The land had rejected them again.

Captain Martinelli had the helm. He didn't look at Simon and the others. He sailed them away from the burning harbor, humming slightly.

"How much fuel do we have left?" Simon asked.

"Not much," Ren said.

"Be specific."

"We can get far enough away from the coast that a storm surge won't throw us back on land. That's about it."

"Let's do it," Simon said.

"Excuse me, Simon," Captain Martinelli began. "I'm the one giving ord— "

"Not anymore. Get us away from the coast, then cut the engines."

The captain shrugged and obeyed.

"Get everyone together," Simon said. "The whole community. It's time we made a decision."

24. Later

SIMON SAT AT THE bar in the Mermaid Lounge. He liked working here. The wide windows provided a decent view of the sea, but it tended to be less crowded than the Atlantis Dining Hall. The sky outside swirled dark and purple.

Simon was writing in a blank notebook he'd taken from the bookshop. The sea was still for once, and a light wind coming through a broken window ruffled the paper as he scribbled page after page. He'd assign someone to fix the window soon, but in the meantime he enjoyed the sea breeze.

He was putting the finishing touches on an extensive plan allotting duties on a rotating basis. It included rationed break time, meal shifts, deck time to make sure everyone got enough Vitamin D, and even who would be on call if a storm came up. It also officially set up a council to make decisions for the ship. Every adult would participate on a rotating basis. The plan was far more detailed than the one they had developed on the journey from Guam, but it followed the same principles. Crucially, it completed the blurring of the divisions between former crew, passengers, and runners. They were all equal now.

After their disastrous attempt to seek refuge in China, they had decided to stay on the *Catalina* for a while. They would drift. They would wait out the troubles. They'd salvaged a fair amount of food as they drifted along somewhere in the Pacific Ocean. They were learning to mine the sea for sustenance: fishing, skimming seaweed, dredging up shellfish whenever they drifted into shallow waters. They would be nearly self-sustaining, at least until the world calmed down.

It might be for a few months or even a few years, but they'd learn to take care of themselves. Until the skies cleared and they were able to communicate with people on land, they couldn't keep wasting fuel by sailing where they wouldn't be allowed to stay.

Frank found Simon in the Mermaid Lounge. He wound his way through the tables and the bits of salvage stored in piles around the room.

"Simon, do you have a minute?" he asked.

"Sure, Frank," Simon said, putting down his pen. "How are you?"

"As good as can be expected." Frank scratched a finger through his walrus mustache.

"Weren't you on salvage duty this morning?" Simon asked.

They had come across a current of flotsam, and they'd been working all morning to pull up anything they might be able to use somewhere on the ship. They had begun stockpiling any raw materials that might be valuable. Who knew what the world's economy would be like next time they connected with other survivors?

"That's what I want to talk to you about," Frank said. "I picked up a few things that might be useful. I might try building a reverse-osmosis system . . . for desalinating water."

"Doesn't the ship already have a water system?" Simon asked.

"It does, but it's an evaporation system. It uses the energy from the engines to evaporate the salt out of the water while we're moving. The ship uses up water reserves whenever we're not actually sailing anywhere."

"So we're using up our water supply now that we're not running the engines?"

"At the moment, yes," Frank said. "Since we don't know how long we're going to be here, I figured I'd start working on a new system."

"You don't need my permission, Frank," Simon said. "It sounds like a great idea."

"To be honest, I was hoping you'd tell me not to, because you have a plan to get us back to land soonish," Frank said.

"I wish I did. Anything you can do to make our lives here more sustainable would be great. We need to wait this out."

Simon believed the situation on land would only get worse. As the famines set in, more people would die. They would fight each other for the remaining scraps of food. They would despair. At least on the ship they were safe. They had a small number of people who could take care of each other, and they had the entire sea at their disposal.

"Roger that," Frank said. "I'll get to work then!"

There was a light in Frank's eye as he turned to go. Everyone needed something to do, something that gave them purpose. If they were going to stay on the ship for a while, they'd have to stay busy to survive.

And one day the land would welcome them back.

JUDITH

Judith and Manny sorted through salvage. They were on suitcase duty on the lido deck. It was amazing how well suitcases floated. They were usually full of strange and useful things that could be cleaned and dispersed among the people of the *Catalina*.

"That's the last of it," Judith said, tossing a pair of children's T-shirts onto a pile. "Would you mind taking these down to Constance in the plaza? I'm going to keep working on the socks."

There were always spare socks. They matched them up as well as they could, relying on size even when the colors didn't go together. The other clothes would go down to Constance Gordon, who was a seamstress by trade. She had set up a shop in the plaza, where she could mend and sort clothes while baby Cally gurgled away on a pile of fabric beside her.

"No problem," Manny said. He wrapped his arms around the T-shirt pile and lifted it, his face disappearing behind the folds.

Judith spotted a familiar blue shade in the stack.

"Hang on a sec." She reached forward, not wanting to stand as her legs were still healing, and pulled the T-shirt from the middle of the pile. It was damp, but the screen print of Thomas the Tank Engine was still intact. "Okay, go ahead."

"I will come back for more soon," Manny said. "And then maybe we go for some dinner. I can help you walk."

"Sure, thanks," Judith mumbled, staring at the Thomas T-shirt in her hands.

Manny turned and tottered toward the door, the clothes piled higher than his dark curly hair. Where most people on the ship deferred to Simon, Manny took his cues from Judith. She had become his lodestar. For her part, she liked having an ally.

She tried hard to think of Manny as her supporter, not her friend. She had lost too many friends. Nora. Michael. She had made the mistake of becoming too attached. They had bonded through the brief, intense trauma of the disaster, but their deaths hurt her far too much. She would guard her heart in the future. She had already set up a barrier between herself and Ren by refusing to talk about Nora.

Judith had been betrayed. By the land. By the navy. By all the people who had refused to help them. By all the people she had put her faith in.

And by Simon.

Things would never be the same between Judith and Simon. She wouldn't let on how she felt, of course. Simon was very popular right now. But she would be a little colder, a little more distant. She'd begin gathering people who resented how much power Simon had accumulated, how much control he now had over what happened on the ship. She'd build up her own supporters, and she'd use Simon's precious rotating council system to do it. She had plenty of time.

Judith crumpled the Thomas T-shirt in her thin hands.

Eventually, she'd make her move.

Find out what happens to Judith, Simon, Esther, and the *Catalina*, in the action-packed post-apocalyptic trilogy *The Seabound Chronicles*. The adventure continues in . . .

Seabound
By Jordan Rivet

When an apocalyptic catastrophe decimates the land, a lucky few escape to sea. 1,003 survivors make their home on a souped-up cruise ship called the Catalina. After sixteen years, the strain begins to show in a floating world of distrust and shifting allegiances.

A young mechanic named Esther wants to prove herself, but she tends to bash things up in the name of progress. When disaster strikes the water system on Esther's watch, she'll risk everything to fix her mistake.

But is Esther ready for the dangers she'll face on the post-apocalyptic ocean? Can she save her friends about the Catalina before it's too late?

Acknowledgments

I WANT TO THANK everyone who has been so supportive during this writing adventure. I couldn't do this without the encouragement and enthusiasm of my writing and reading friends.

The hours I've spent working on this book—even the sad parts—have been more fun in the company of the terrific Hong Kong writing community. Thanks especially to Willow, Laura, Amanda, and Betsy.

My critique groups have helped me with their attention to detail, their honesty, and their wisdom. Thank you for being excited about the *Catalina*'s journey and for gasping at all the right places.

I'd like to thank the early readers of this book for their insights: Willow Hewitt, Rachel Marsh, MaryAnna Donaldson, Ayden and Julie Young, Brooke Richter, Sarah Merrill Mowat, Rachel Andrews, Laura Cook, Betsy Cheung, and Sebastian Brown.

Thank you to the AC crowd for inspiring me to set bigger goals and bring my author game to the next level. Thanks, also, for the laughs.

James at GoOnWrite.com has done it again with an awesome cover. Marcus Trower continues to be my favorite editor. I'm grateful to both of them for helping me put together a professional product.

Thank you, husband, for keeping me honest, giving me space to write, and listening to me when I think out loud.

And I especially want to thank the readers of *The Seabound Chronicles* for your warm response to my books. I'll do my best to keep you guys entertained.

Thanks for reading!

Jordan Rivet
Hong Kong, 2015

ABOUT THE AUTHOR

Jordan Rivet is an American author from Arizona. She lives in Hong Kong with her husband. Prone to seasickness, she likes to watch the ships in Victoria Harbour while standing on solid ground.

Also by Jordan Rivet:

Seabound
Seaswept
Seafled

Made in the USA
San Bernardino, CA
02 January 2016